Beneath
a
Buried House

By Bob Avey

Detective Elliot Mysteries

Twisted Perception *
Beneath a Buried House *

* Published by Deadly Niche Press

Beneath
a
Buried House

A Detective Elliot Novel

Bob Avey

For Art
Happy Reading
Bob Avey

Deadly Niche Press
Denton Texas

Deadly Niche Press
An Imprint of AWOC.COM Publishing
P.O. Box 2819
Denton, TX 76202

Manufactured in the United States of America

ISBN: 978-0-937660-81-2

Visit Bob Avey's website www.bobavey.com

For my wonderful mom, Ruby

Acknowledgements

I would like to thank the following people for making this book possible: Author John Foxjohn for answering my police related questions; Author David Ciambrone for sharing his knowledge of toxins; Susan Lohrer, my editor; and Dan Case, with AWOC Books, for his expertise in publishing, and his patience in dealing with a nervous author.

Chapter One

People go missing. Llewellyn knew that as well as anyone but when a whole family fell victim to such a fate, that tended to get his attention. It had the interest of someone else as well. Threats had been made. But the way he saw it, with Millie gone, he didn't have all that much to lose anyway.

Llewellyn watched his step as he moved from the sidewalk to the street, for it was dark, the sun skimming the bottom of the sky in a thin, red line, the color of embers clinging to life in a dying campfire. A disturbing thought—a deep suspicion that had grown to such proportion that he feared it might twist his reasoning—snaked through him. He'd previously abandoned the project with good reason.

At times like this, he would think back to when he was a boy, visiting his mother. Her house sat on a small hill and behind it was a pond with huge willow trees growing from its banks. It always struck him as odd that the surface of the water remained calm and never rippled, as if it were not real at all, but a painting, an artificial backdrop put there for the effect.

Llewellyn had resolved that he too would be like the waters of the pond, unmovable, unflappable, and later, during his adult life, he would call on that image, not every time the going got tough, but when life got particularly hard.

He stared at the dilapidated building with a sign hanging from it; a cheap plastic job with florescent lights inside that backlit the bar's name: CYMRY'S.

He shook his head and pushed open the door, a heavy wooden model that looked out of place, as if it had been ripped from the hinges of an old house and brought there against its will.

Just inside the door, Llewellyn paused, and when his eyes adjusted to the darkness he took a seat in the second booth by the window, like the man who called himself Jerry Sinclair had told him to do. Llewellyn was five minutes late, and he hoped that wouldn't matter, though he saw no one fitting Sinclair's description. At least the darkness was explained. It was the décor, which included the walls and the ceilings, and even the floors. Everything was black with the exception of a large piece of red artwork that radiated from the center of the floor in a rather unprofessional manner, as if it were a bad afterthought, the awkward brushstrokes obvious even from a distance.

7

Llewellyn waited but no one showed. He checked his watch. Thirty minutes had passed. He slid out of his seat and went to the bar. The man had his back turned but a mirrored wall showed his face. He must've known Llewellyn was there though he did not acknowledge him. Llewellyn laid a five on the counter. "I'd like a beer, please."

The man gave no visible indication he had heard the request.

"I'll just cut to the chase then," Llewellyn said. "What I really need is some information."

Turning around, the man drew a pint of lager, then set it down and snatched up the five. "What kind of information?"

Llewellyn slid his hand around the cool, damp handle, then brought the mug to his lips, relishing the bitter yet soothing brew. After a few sips, he said, "Does the name Jerry Sinclair mean anything to you?"

"Doesn't jump out at me."

"He said he would be wearing blue jeans and a tan corduroy jacket. Have you seen anyone like that?"

"Not since the eighties."

"Right, some people are habitually late. Perhaps Mr. Sinclair is one of those." After a pause, unable to control his inquisitiveness, Llewellyn asked, "What's up with the artwork on the floor?"

The bartender leaned forward, placing his beefy hands on the railing. "Don't know. It's always been there."

Llewellyn had dealt with his kind before; smug, confident with his size, and, as with any animal, the less challenging you could make yourself the better your odds were. He slouched a little. "Do you know what it is?"

"Maybe."

The bartender said this with a crooked grin, as if he and he alone were privy to the mysteries of the universe, which undoubtedly meant he knew nothing.

"If I had to guess," Llewellyn said, "I'd say it has something to do with the occult. But what do I know?"

Llewellyn retrieved one of his business cards and held it out. "I'm a reporter, on assignment."

Taking the card, the bartender examined it. "Florida? Long way from home, aren't you?"

"I go where the story takes me."

"Is that right?"

"So you haven't seen him, the guy I asked about?"

"Who?"

"Jerry Sinclair."

The bartender squinted. "Are you sure you're in the right place?"
"I'm sure."

"What kind of assignment are you on?"

Llewellyn sipped his beer, then set it down. "I look for the unusual. A few years back, I was working some leads, concerning a small town near here. You know, bizarre circumstances and all of that. Good Stuff. I decided to revive it, made a few phone calls, sent some e-mails, ran an ad in the paper. Then I get this reply from Sinclair. He claimed to have some information. It's not unusual. I get lucky like that sometimes."

Llewellyn heard the door and realized someone else had finally come into the place. The bartender had noticed as well, and Llewellyn took the opportunity to return to his booth by the window.

Three people had come in, and unlike Llewellyn they did not look out of place inside Cymry's, which meant they were not wearing dress pants and button-down shirts. Nor were any of them wearing blue jeans and a corduroy jacket.

One of them, a tall, slender girl wearing tight leather pants, strolled across the floor, stopping in front of the jukebox. Llewellyn couldn't imagine what kind of music might be popular in such a place, but it wasn't the anticipation of the music that held his attention. Even dressed as she was, the girl captivated him and he could not stop looking at her, which was a mistake. That indefinable female sense that alerts a woman to a man's attention seemed present in full force; she turned her head toward him.

Llewellyn looked away. He was asking for trouble. He thought of Millie. Not once during their thirty years together had he cheated on her, and he wasn't about to start now. He heard someone walk across the floor toward him, and he prayed that it would be Sinclair, that he had come through the door while Llewellyn wasn't looking and was even now preparing to slide into the other side of the booth across the table from him.

As a thick, musky smell of perfume crossed Llewellyn's senses, desperation shot through him. He turned his head, looking at the smooth patch of skin between the bottom of her shirt and the beginning of her leather pants. A tattoo of Saint Brighid's cross moved sensuously with the muscles of her stomach.

She said nothing. Llewellyn could feel her staring down at him, and when he finally raised his head, allowing for the first time their eyes to meet, he felt like the victim in an old vampire movie: frightened by the nature of his captor but hopeful that she would find him desirable and as he looked into her face, the thought occurred to him that if the eyes are truly the windows to the soul then hers was surely dark.

A color somewhere between purple and black graced her lips, as it did her fingernails. Her hair, which jabbed at the air in choreographed insolence, was as dark as either of these.

Llewellyn slid deeper into the booth, exposing an unused section of the vinyl cushion. She sat down. Llewellyn began to wonder, and not for the first time, what sort of person she really was and why was he, a slightly over-the-hill freelancer, entertaining romantic thoughts about a distant cousin of Vlad the Impaler? She was no teenager, but still half his age, twenty-four or twenty-five he suspected, and about as far away from his type as you could get. The pressure of her leg against his made none of that seem to matter.

She grinned. "You look a little out of place. Are you lost?"

"I'm here on business."

She lit a cigarette, and in response to Llewellyn's answer, she blew the smoke out a little harder than she needed to, the exhaust propelled into the air by something that could only be described as a prelude to a laugh. "What kind of business?"

Llewellyn checked his watch. Nearly forty-five minutes had passed and still his contact had not shown. In his opinion, that was late, even for the very lax. "I'm meeting someone, or at least I was supposed to."

"Sounds to me," she said, playing with the lapel of his jacket, "like maybe you just did."

Llewellyn nodded. He tried to concentrate, but his thoughts were all over the place.

"Maybe your girlfriend changed her mind."

"Come again?"

"Your little trick."

Llewellyn shook his head. "There's no trick."

She leaned closer, bringing her shoulders forward in an unspoken offer.

Llewellyn glanced up to see the bartender hovering over the booth. He wasn't sure how he'd gotten there without his hearing him or seeing his approach. "This guy bothering you?" the bartender asked.

The girl smiled and touched his arm, old friends apparently. "Nothing I can't handle, Snub." She reached over and took Llewellyn's hand. "Just a little business."

"You know this guy?"

She winked. "I do now."

The bartender turned and stalked away. He acted protective, like an older brother, siblings from the dark side looking out for one another. It amazed Llewellyn that no matter how low you sank in life, you could still find evidence of a sense of community.

Llewellyn wondered what it might be like to be with this strange woman. Then, she leaned close, and with a kiss that teased with a slip of her tongue she said that she wanted him as well, or at least she intended to give him that impression.

He pushed away slightly. "Look, I'm not sure this is a good idea."

"Yes you are. You're just afraid to give in to it."

"You read me pretty well."

"I usually do."

Llewellyn felt insecure, trapped. "I really am meeting someone."

"So where are they?"

"I don't know. I'm starting to have my doubts."

She let go of Llewellyn's hand and lit another cigarette. "Okay, I'll lay it out straight. Sinclair sent me."

"Is that right? Why would he do that?"

"I don't know. But he said to tell you that he has the whole story, everything that you're looking for."

She took a long draw on her cigarette. Llewellyn usually felt a mixture of sorrow and disdain when he saw someone do that, but she impressed him as someone who could handle just about anything, and anyone. His sense of good judgment, what he had left of it anyway, was telling him to excuse himself from this odd encounter, yet he resisted that urge. He hadn't told her Sinclair's name, and yet she knew it. He certainly hadn't said anything about a story. He'd always been drawn to the unusual, the unexplained, that which frightens most people—and here it all was, epitomized in this intimidating yet fascinating person. "So what happens next?"

"I'm supposed to take you somewhere. A private place where you can talk."

"Thanks," Llewellyn said, indicating with a nudge that he was ready to leave. "But I really should be going."

He half expected her to move closer and refuse to let him out, but instead she slid from the booth. Llewellyn did the same and started for the door, and then it occurred to him that he had no car and there would be no cabs waiting on the street in this part of town. He signaled the bartender. "Could you call a cab?"

The strange girl put her arm through Llewellyn's, and he realized that not only had they not exchanged names but he had anticipated her actions and welcomed her touch. She evaluated him with her gaze. "Save the call, Snub. I've got a car."

The look on the bartender's face said he was confused, and it seemed that in some strange way he might even be concerned for Llewellyn. "Whatever you think," he said.

"It's nice of you to offer," Llewellyn said to the girl, "but I hate to impose."

His resistance, though, was superficial at best. Still holding his arm, she shook her head and guided him through the door. Once they were outside, she pulled him close and they kissed again. He was in deep, and he knew it, but he kept going along with it. In the parking lot, they stopped beside a red Monte Carlo, and she did something that surprised Llewellyn. She tossed him the keys. "You drive."

Llewellyn stuck the key into the slot and opened the door, and after getting inside he reached over and unlocked the passenger side. She gave him directions and Llewellyn followed them, driving farther from his place with every block. A little later she said, "Turn here. We'll park in the back."

When they got out of the car, Llewellyn glanced around the area, seeing a few spent wine bottles. "No offense," he said, but I'm starting to have second thoughts about this. Maybe I should go."

"All right, but come in for a quick drink. I won't keep you. I promise." She ran a long nail along his jaw, making it an almost predatory gesture and an enticing one.

As they approached the building, it occurred to Llewellyn that her place didn't look much better than the bar.

She turned to look at him and caught him surveying the lines of the building. "Neat old place, huh? I like it here, love the vibes, if you know what I mean."

"It does have character," Llewellyn said.

She unlocked the door and they stepped into a small landing. The place was grim, and populated, Llewellyn suspected, by various strata of socioeconomic defeat, and as they walked the red, carpeted hallway, a red that reminded Llewellyn of blood, he thought of Dante's *Inferno*, for as they walked deeper into the building each successive apartment appeared more steeped in despair.

The girl's place was no exception, and once inside, Llewellyn could not imagine anyone actually living there. From a chip-edged kitchen table, she grabbed a bottle of bourbon and poured some into a glass, mixed in a little soda, and handed it to him.

He swirled the amber mixture, unable to meet her eyes. His heart pounded. Leave. Just gulp it down and leave.

Before he could consider other options, she took the untouched drink and placed it on the table. Then she took Llewellyn's hand and placed it on her stomach, where she began to guide it upward, beneath her shirt, until it came to rest upon the warm, soft flesh of her breast.

Chapter Two

Detective Kenny Elliot stared at the old rock building on North Main Street. The Cain's Ballroom had come into existence in 1924 as a garage for Tate Brady, the same Brady that Brady Street, the Brady District, and the Brady Theater were named after. Within a few years, the garage was transformed into a nightspot where those so inclined could buy a dance for a dime. Madison W. Cain bought the place in 1930 and christened it Cain's Dance Academy. Through the years, the place had seen a lot of action. From western swing to punk to cutting-edge rock, it was said the Cain's could handle anything.

This morning, however, with no one around and the wind blowing last night's paper litter along the sidewalk, it resembled just another building in a city that had been deserted; a ghost building in a ghost town.

If the morning unrolled smoothly, they would find the lead singer in a rock band called Hell's Gate inside—Larry Benson, aka Enrique Savage. They would question him about the death of his girlfriend, Susan Lancaster, an insurance investigator who had been pulled from the Arkansas River a couple of days ago. She hadn't drowned. With five stab wounds to the torso, she'd been dead when she hit the water. If all went well, they'd bring Savage in before someone else got hurt.

Typically Elliot had none of that diffidence to which some rookies prove susceptible these days. He had a job to do, and that was important to him. Today, however, he was distracted, his thoughts jerky and random, moving about like a leaf caught in the wind. He had started the day with a feeling that something, or someone, had just set in motion a chain of events that would bring disaster to his world. Seeing Savage's rap sheet in the Lancaster file hadn't helped.

Elliot glanced at his partner, Dombrowski. "I don't trust Savage. I think he killed Susan Lancaster."

Dombrowski didn't seem concerned. "Take it easy, Elliot. We're just here to question the guy."

"He's not what you think. I've met him." At a club that catered to insomniacs. Enrique had been on the stage, and his dark following of leather-clad, punked-out fans had filled the club to a standing-room-only status.

Dombrowski scowled then turned his collar up against the frigid wind. "Good, you can catch up on old times, then."

The night Elliot met Savage, he had pushed his way inside the club perhaps from a fear of being alone, or maybe it was fate, but he'd taken only one drink when Enrique began spouting Latin phrases in between the lyrics of a song, and the crowd went crazy. At the apex of the frenzy, Enrique had turned his pasty face toward Elliot and grinned acknowledgment of his presence.

Dombrowski pushed open the black doors leading into the building.

As soon as they stepped into the room, Enrique Savage leaped to the front of the stage, brandishing the microphone stand with both hands. The rocker snapped his gaze at Elliot and Dombrowski. He snaked one hand down the microphone stand.

Elliot drew his weapon. As he did this, a ridiculous notion went through him that the gun wouldn't do any good, and that he might've had better luck had he loaded it with silver bullets and brought along a rosary to hold in front of him like a shield.

Dombrowski sighed. "Lower your weapon, Elliot."

Elliot held fast, keeping the Glock trained on the suspect. Black leather contrasted against white skin, the pasty skin of an albino. Enrique Savage stood about six foot seven. With all of that going for him, Savage looked as much like the harbinger of death as anyone Elliot had ever seen.

"Stand down, Elliot. I'm not going to tell you again."

The grin that spread across Enrique's face was even more unnerving than the coldness of his stare. He didn't loosen his grip on the mike stand.

"He made a move I didn't like," Elliot said. "Might have been going for a weapon. Have him raise both his hands."

Elliot knew Dombrowski had questioned Enrique earlier and searched his apartment. He hadn't found anything, and he didn't expect to now. Elliot had convinced him to re-question the suspect based on a gut feeling, and Dombrowski, who'd seemed tentatively persuaded at the office, was clearly now having second thoughts. With a disgusted glare, he said, "Sorry about this, Mr. Benson, but would you please raise your hands and show my nervous friend here that you're not armed?"

Elliot shifted his weight. Dombrowski had warned him about making such quick assessments, sizing people up, categorizing them before he knew the facts, but it was a habit he couldn't seem to break. Enrique was no good—maybe not Charlie Manson, but certainly worthy of close observation.

Dombrowski started to speak again, but fell silent, his mouth gaping.

Elliot thought he'd kept his eyes on Savage the whole time, perhaps relaxing his gaze a bit to glance briefly at Dombrowski now and then, but the suspect had not only moved his hands but had raised them above his head, where he now held what appeared to be a gleaming sword.

Then Savage unleashed the weapon, heaving the honed steel like a spear.

Metal clattered across the floor, not a sword but the microphone stand. Then he was gone. Elliot had never before seen anyone move that fast, especially someone the size of Enrique, but as soon as the microphone spear hit the floor, the rock star was off the stage and out of the building, or at least out of sight.

Elliot glanced at Dombrowski then followed his lead and ran for the back door. The rear entrance opened onto an outside area that was a combination of grass, dirt, and asphalt, and as Elliot ran across the small lawn, littered with beer cans and spent wine bottles, he caught sight of the suspect. Enrique had scaled a black wrought-iron gate, and was dropping onto a deteriorated asphalt driveway on the other side. A different type of fence, which was lower, ran across the other side of the back building. Elliot considered the route but changed his mind. He holstered his weapon and climbed the gate, and as soon as he dropped to the other side, he again slid his hand around the handle of the Glock and pulled it free.

He scanned the area but didn't see the suspect. As soon as Dombrowski caught up, Elliot pointed toward the most likely escape route, and together they made their way north on Boston Avenue, heading beneath the Interstate 244 overpass. Ordinarily there would have been blankets and sleeping bags tucked into the cracks and crevices where the steel girders met the concrete, but the bottom of the highway was a good distance from the street below it, and the concrete that skirted the edges ran perpendicular to the ground instead of sloping, as was the usual design.

Beads of sweat broke out on Elliot's forehead, the feeling of being watched pressing in on him.

"Do you see anything?" Dombrowski asked.

Elliot started to reply that he had not when a movement caught the corner of his vision. "There," he said. A man had ducked around a corner of the bridge.

Elliot and Dombrowsi scrambled after him, catching him on the north side of the overpass. The man, small and bearded, held his hands in front of him, palms open and facing outward, and he shook his head, indicating that he was not the one they were looking for. He slowly moved one finger, trying to alert his captors by pointing to the other side of the bridge without drawing attention to himself.

Elliot interpreted the gesture and swung around to spot Enrique traveling north on Boston Avenue. He was moving fast.

Dombrowski stumbled, caught himself then sprinted after his quarry.

Enrique kept running.

Elliot tore across the street in pursuit, barely aware that Dombrowski was behind him. He assessed the suspect's escape route. At one time, there had been houses in the area, but they had been torn down, leaving the streets and sidewalks to meander aimlessly around empty lots, with stairways and driveways that led to nothing. There was nowhere to hide.

When the suspect reached Fairview Street, he turned west.

Elliot followed. From behind him, he heard Dombrowski shout, "Give it up, Enrique. You're not getting away."

Elliot wasn't so sure. Enrique seemed to possess the speed and agility of an elk. He was at least half a block ahead of them and increasing the distance with each stride. Elliot holstered his weapon and dug in for all he was worth. Seconds later his lungs began to burn, and he could feel his strength fading, but he was gaining on the suspect.

They ran past Main Street, then Boulder Avenue.

A couple of heartbeats later, Elliot made his move. He dove for Enrique's legs, catching one of them.

Enrique stumbled, but before Elliot could get a grip, the suspect kicked loose and again he was running.

Elliot scrambled to his feet, but Enrique had regained his distance. He turned north again, heading into the Brady Heights District by way of an alley just this side of Denver Avenue.

Again, Elliot closed the gap, and he caught sight of the suspect just as he crossed the backyard of a house on Golden Street. After that, Enrique opened the back door and entered the residence. He had proven Elliot wrong. Someone who could run that fast, and sustain the speed for long enough, could find a place to hide.

Elliot waited for his partner, who had already called for backup. The look on Dombrowski's face told Elliot they were thinking the same thing; Did Enrique Savage know the people in the house he'd entered or was he looking for a hostage?

Gesturing his intentions, Dombrowski took the front door, crossing the side yard and disappearing around the front corner of the old clapboard house.

Elliot waited a few seconds, then made his way across the alley and heaved himself over a chain-link fence that surrounded the backyard. He heard a rustling noise, saw movement, and seconds later he was staring at a hungry-looking pit bull. Elliot took a step back, and the dog did him one better. He edged within inches of Elliot's position, his eyes seeming to scan him, size him up. Elliot didn't have time for this. Enrique could come out at any second, and of the two animals, Elliot figured Enrique was the one to fear. He held the Glock in front of him. "I don't have time for this, pooch. I don't want to hurt you, but I will if I have to."

The dog sniffed the air, then turned and walked back to his hiding place in a corner of the yard. As the dog flopped to the ground, and Elliot exhaled, the door smacked open against the clapboards and Enrique busted out, forcing his hostage in front of him—a dark-haired Hispanic woman, her eyes pleading for help. Homemade tattoos stained her arms with crude blue markings. Enrique held a knife to her throat.

Elliot took aim. "Come on, Enrique, this isn't going to help your cause. Why don't you let her go, and we'll talk about it?"

"Not a chance."

Enrique's voice resonated through the yard, deep and full of bass. It reminded Elliot of a demon in a horror flick. "Are you saying you did kill Susan Lancaster?"

"Shut up. I didn't say anything like that."

"Same thing in my book, buddy."

"Yeah, well maybe I'm just scared, couple of cops busting in and chasing me like that."

Behind the suspect, Elliot could see Dombrowski in the house, just inside the doorway. He was waiting for a chance to make a move.

"We didn't break in, pardner. The door was open. Why did you run?"

The suspect shifted his weight from one foot to the other. "Scared, like I said."

From the corner of his eye, Elliot saw the pit bull. "I can understand that, but it's not too late to work this out. Just let the lady go."

The dog didn't bark and didn't growl. The only sound was that of his paws pounding the earth, a sound that Enrique didn't seem to hear.

Suddenly the dog was on him, clamping his jaws around Enrique's leg. The rocker let out a demented yell.

The hostage took the opportunity offered by her captor's lack of concentration and tore free. She bolted back into the house.

Elliot saw what was going to happen, and he closed the distance between himself and the suspect in an instant. Enrique had already stabbed the dog twice and was going for a third when Elliot intercepted his arm and put the barrel of the Glock to his head. "Drop it while you still can."

The suspect relaxed and the knife slid from his hand, hitting the ground with a dull thud. Dombrowski was there. He pulled the suspect's hands behind his back and cuffed him. The dog lay on the ground, whining.

Elliot heard the sound of a car and turned to see the backup Dombrowski had called coming to a stop in the alley behind him. He and Dombrowski walked the suspect through a gate where the fence met the back of the house, then through the yard and into the alley. Dombrowski jerked open the door of the patrol car and shoved the suspect into the backseat.

Chapter Three

Joey Anderson lived with his mother in Broken Arrow, Oklahoma. His father wasn't there but he had one. His mother said so. He thought, maybe he lived somewhere else, another state maybe.

Joey heard the front door opening, which meant his mother was through trimming the rose bushes in the front yard. He turned down the sound on the television then jumped down from the bed. *Law and Order* was on, his favorite program. His mom let him watch it, but he didn't think she liked it. She always shook her head when she came into his room and saw him watching it, as she did now.

"How's my big guy?"

"Hi, Mom. I'm okay."

She smiled. "Let me get cleaned up, then we'll fix something to eat. Maybe later we can go see a movie or something."

"Okay," Joey said. He liked his mom. She was nice but sometimes she forgot he wasn't a little kid anymore.

Joey waited until his mom closed the bathroom door. When he heard the water running, he left his bedroom and walked to the front door. His mom liked to soak in the tub after working in the yard. She would be there for a while. He hesitated, then unlocked the front door and stepped outside. His mom didn't want him to go outside by himself anymore. Sometimes he did, though. Someone had moved into Don and Judy Carter's old house. His friend Sandi had told him. Sandi watched him on Tuesdays so his mom could go to Doctor Colby's office. He wasn't sure why she went. Sandi said she didn't know either.

Joey turned right on the sidewalk outside his house. He walked beside the fence that used to look bad. It didn't look bad now. Someone had fixed it. He suspected the new neighbor had done this. When he reached the end of the fence, he would turn right again. He remembered things like that so he wouldn't get lost. Sometimes his mother would get lost while driving the car, and he would help her get back home.

Joey paused for a moment when he saw Linda Wallace, one of the next-door neighbors. She was outside, sitting in her blue porch swing with her head down, reading a book. She was always reading books, and Joey didn't think she saw him as he walked past.

When he reached the end of the fence, near the street with all the cars on it, he turned right again, but he'd taken only a few steps when

20

Billy Williams came, riding up on his bicycle. Billy lived around the corner, but back the other way. When he saw Joey, he stopped, but he didn't get off. Sometimes Billy was mean, but not always. He never hit Joey or anything, but sometimes he said bad things. Joey thought the other kids made him do it. He was by himself today.

"What are you doing out here, Joey?"

"Going for a walk."

Billy looked up and down the street. "Does your mom know you're out here?"

Joey glanced back to see if Linda Wallace was still there. He could call to her for help, if he had to. But Linda wasn't there anymore. "My mom don't care. She said I could walk."

Billy looked suspicious. "I haven't seen you out by yourself in a while. You sure it's all right?"

"It's okay."

Billy waited a little while, then started riding again. "See you around," he said. "And stay out of the street, buddy."

Joey continued to walk. He was almost there. He could see the man in the driveway. The garage was open, and the man was carrying something heavy into it. Sandi said he might be a policeman. Joey didn't think he looked like one, though. He wasn't wearing a uniform, and he didn't have a black shiny belt or a gun. The cops on television were tough. They had guns.

Joey left the sidewalk and walked onto the driveway where the man was. "Hi. I'm Joey."

Chapter Four

Elliot heard a somewhat unusual voice coming from behind him. He'd just gotten home a few minutes earlier after helping Dombrowski with the paperwork concerning the arrest of Enrique Savage. It'd been a long day and he was ready to go inside and unwind. He turned around and saw a man dressed in khaki shorts and a striped shirt, clothes designed for someone much younger. The shy grin on his face contrasted with his five o'clock shadow. "Hello, Joey."

Elliot scanned the driveway and the immediate area. "Do you live around here?"

"I live up that way," Joey said, "on that street." He pointed first north then east. "What's your name?"

Elliot extended his hand. "My name's . . ." He paused. He'd started to say Elliot but changed his mind. "Kenny."

Joey shook Elliot's hand. His grip was loose, tentative. "You a policeman?"

"A police detective," Elliot said, surprised his new friend would know that.

Joey scratched his head. "Is that like almost a real policeman?"

"Some people seem to think so," Elliot said, holding back a laugh. Again he glanced around the area but saw no one else around. "Do you know your way home from here, Joey?"

"Don and Judy used to live here."

"Yes," Elliot said. It was the couple he'd bought the house from. "Were you looking for them?"

Joey shook his head. "Mr. Carter used to fix my bicycle."

"Where is your bicycle now, Joey?"

"In the shed. My mom locked it up."

"I see. Does your mom know you're here?"

"It's okay, Mr. Kenny. You have a dog?"

"No, just a dog door that belonged to the dogs that used to live here. How about you, do you have one?"

"I used to. He's gone now. Do you have a gun?"

Joey had just spoken when a lady turned from the sidewalk and marched up the drive, stopping outside the garage, a look on her face that was somewhere between worry and anger. "Joey Anderson, what are you doing out here?"

Joey's eyes saddened but they also reflected a hint of defiance. "I went for a walk."

"Didn't we just talk about this?"

"Yes."

She stood silent for a moment, her hands on her hips, clearly at a loss for words. Finally she settled for "Joey."

She said this while shaking her head, a reflection of her frustration. Elliot took the opportunity to introduce himself. "Hi. Name's Kenny Elliot. I guess I'm your new neighbor."

She gave Elliot a strange look, as if she and Joey had been alone, and Elliot had just dropped out of the sky and now stood before her for the first time. Soon a teenage girl joined them on the driveway. She took the lady's hand in hers and looked into her face with understanding eyes.

"Sandi," the lady said, "you're such a doll. Could you please take Joey home? I'll be right there."

"Sure, I can do that."

The girl, Sandi, walked over and took Joey's hand. "Come on. I've got something cool to show you."

Joey and Sandi started down the drive, and before they turned the corner, Joey looked back. "See you later, Mr. Kenny."

The lady waited until her son and the girl had walked away, then she turned to Elliot. "I'm sorry if he bothered you, Mr. Elliot."

Elliot shook his head. "No bother, Ms. . . ."

"Kelly," she said, "Kelly Anderson."

Kelly Anderson wasn't unattractive, but her face reflected the emotional weariness of a life that hadn't been easy, and she showed this not with remorse, but with an attitude that said: I'm not afraid of you because you can't throw anything at me that hasn't already been thrown. She was suspicious of Elliot, but he wasn't offended by it. He suspected she was just weary of a world where mistrust was bred by the very nature of her relationship with it. She was a mother, and she was concerned for her child—in Kelly Anderson's case, a thirty-something-year-old child.

"Would you like to come in for a cup of coffee?" Elliot asked.

Kelly glanced at the sidewalk, then up the street, then back at Elliot. "I don't like Joey being out by himself," she said. "If you see him again . . . I'm in the phonebook. If you see him again, give me a call, okay?"

"Sure," Elliot said, "no problem."

She turned and walked away, and Elliot closed the garage and went into the house. It had been an interesting day. He wondered if tomorrow would be the same. He didn't think so.

For reasons he didn't quite understand, he thought it would be worse. Enrique Savage was just the beginning.

Chapter Five

When Elliot got to the office the next morning, Dombrowski was waiting for him. Dombrowski wanted him present while he questioned Larry Benson, aka Enrique Savage, about the death of Susan Lancaster. It promised to be a grim task—Elliot couldn't get the image of Enrique slaughtering the dog out of his mind.

He sat at one end of the table while Dombrowski and the suspect sat across from each other on the other end. Dombrowski had been hammering him with questions for about thirty minutes when something unexpected came out.

"You were the last one seen with Susan Lancaster," Dombrowski said. "If you can just tell us what happened, then we can clear this thing up, you could be out of here in time for dinner."

Dombrowski was no longer holding on to the idea of Enrique being innocent. He was toying with him now, trying to get information.

"Where was she going? What was she planning to do? She must have said something."

Enrique jerked a thumb toward Elliot. "You get him out of here, and maybe I'll talk."

"No deal," Dombrowski said.

Enrique ran a hand across his pale face. His eye makeup was smeared, his hair more out of place than usual. He'd had a rough night. Dombrowski had allowed him a cigarette, and he took a long drag on it then blew the smoke into the air. "I've already told you what I know. Besides, we both know that's not why I'm here. So why don't we drop the pretenses?"

The sound of Enrique's base-filled voice grated on Elliot's nerves.

Dombrowski shifted in his chair. "I'm not in the habit of pretending, son. And I'm getting tired of the runaround. I think I know why you lied to me about it, but I can't understand why you would kill someone like Susan Lancaster in the first place."

Enrique looked confused. "Hey, no way, man. I didn't kill Susan. She was the best thing to ever happen to me."

"You have an unusual way of showing your love," Elliot said. "I saw you take out the dog. You're pretty good with a knife. Do you suppose Susan felt any pain?"

Enrique took a final draw on the cigarette then smashed it out in an ashtray, all the while keeping his eerie eyes on Elliot. "Night before last, I was at a club. Someone comes up and slaps something into my

24

hand, says it's a present. Few minutes later, cops come busting in." He paused and shook his head. "I thought you brought me down here to ask me about the heroine. And I'm telling you right now, I had nothing to do with it."

Elliot and Dombrowski shot simultaneous glances at each other then turned their attention back to the suspect.

The look that crawled across Enrique's face said he'd just made a mistake, and he knew it.

Just as Elliot and Dombrowski came out of the interrogation room, while Enrique was being escorted back to his cell, Captain Lundsford walked over. "Good work nabbing the suspect, Elliot." He pulled Dombrowski aside.

Elliot figured something was up. The captain's forehead was sweating. That usually meant trouble. A few seconds later, Dombrowski returned. "Let's take a ride to midtown," he said. "Someone found a DB in an apartment over on 15th.

A man with dirty blond hair pushed through the doorway of the Windhall Apartment building, stood on the sidewalk where he steadied himself, preparing for the ice-covered walk ahead of him, and when he once again began to walk his face held a look of uncertainty, its expression worked from emotion. He didn't seem to notice Elliot and Dombrowski coming up the sidewalk.

"What's up," Dombrowski asked Elliot. "The thought of a little real police work getting to you?" After a pause, he added, "From what the officers are saying it looks like a drug overdose, not pleasant but straightforward. It shouldn't take long. You need to get your feet wet, too. Why don't you take the lead on this one."

Elliot nodded, but a feeling of uncertainty cascaded through him, growing in intensity as he closed in on the doorway of the old brick apartment building, and as he forced himself to continue, putting one foot in front of the other, he watched the man that had come from the building striding up the sidewalk. Suddenly, as if he'd become aware of Elliot's attention, he stopped and turned back, pausing briefly, the wind whipping his greasy hair across his face, then he turned and walked away.

Elliot glanced at Dombrowski. If he had noticed anything unusual about the man, he gave no indication. Elliot suspected he had other things on his mind. Then again, Dombrowski always walked with his head down, like he was searching the ground for lost coins.

The Windhall Apartment building rose up from the Tulsa soil just off the exit ramp from the Broken Arrow expressway, a precarious

location, the front door not more than five or six steps from the edge of
15th Street. Not a good place to be. It was a busy street.

Salt had been scattered in front of the building. A front had moved
in during the night and coated the city with a thick layer of snow and
ice. Some of it was still coming down. "Let's go," Elliot said. He and
Dombrowski made their way across the short walk. As they pushed
through the door, a delivery truck crawled out of the alley.

Elliot glanced around. No one guarded the entrance. Not many
doormen made their living on this side of town. They stepped into a
small lobby, which was nothing more than a wide place at the foot of a
set of stairs. Some of the residents crowded around the uniformed
officers there. Beyond that was a hallway with numbered doors,
marking the first-floor apartments. The place smelled of rotting food
and mildewed carpets.

Dombrowski pushed through the crowd, but Elliot stayed behind,
watching the entrance door closing behind him, the journey back to its
original position slowed to a crawl by a somewhat noisy hydraulic
assist. Someone could gain entrance that way without a key if he were
attentive to such things.

"Anything on that delivery truck that came out of the alley?"
Dombrowski asked.

Sergeant Conley stepped forward. "Just a couple of computer techs
working on a problem up the street."

Elliot took off his hat then slid out of his overcoat and hung it over
his arm. "Is the front door usually locked?"

A short, stout man with a two- or three-day growth of beard came
forward, a cell phone stuck to his ear. "Yeah, it's locked. I had it
undone 'cause I knew you guys would be coming in and out."

"And you are?" Elliot asked.

He continued talking into the phone, as if what was happening here
wasn't near as important. "Bob Davis. I manage the place."

Elliot walked to apartment 3 and ducked under the yellow police
tape stretched across the doorway. Dombrowski and the apartment
manager followed.

Elliot managed to hold his expression in check when the stench hit
him. In the middle of the tiny living room, stretched out in a recliner,
the victim appeared to be watching his favorite television program.
Perhaps he had been.

"What time did you find the body?" Dombrowski asked.

Bob Davis rubbed his chin. "It was around eight, I think. Stella
Martin was complaining about the television noise. I knocked on the
door a couple times then used my key."

"Everything here just like you found it?"

"Yes sir, except for the television. It was pretty loud. I took the liberty of turning it down a bit. I hope that's all right?"

Dombrowski gestured toward the body. Elliot immediately understood what he wanted him to do. Reluctantly he searched the victim's clothing, finding a wallet with two hundred-dollar bills inside, but nothing else; no identification.

"Any idea who he is?" Dombrowski asked.

Bob Davis shook his head, cell phone still to his ear.

"So who rents the apartment?"

Another shake of the head, still talking into the phone.

"Sir," Elliot said. "We're trying to conduct an investigation."

The man nodded, but kept talking. Without another word, Elliot reached over and took the phone from the manager, folded it, and stuck it in his pocket. "We need your attention," he said.

Dombrowski frowned. Again he asked, "Who rents the apartment?"

The manager shrugged. "It's been rented for months."

"Let me get this straight," Dombrowski said. "You let somebody move in here but you didn't get his name?"

"Hey, he had cash. Paid more than the room was worth. Most of my clients ain't the kind you'd want to do background checks on anyway. Besides, this ain't him."

"You're telling me this isn't the same person who rented the room?"

"Yeah, that's it, that's what I'm saying."

Dombrowski shook his head. "Would you recognize who did if you saw him again?"

"What, you got a lineup or something?"

"I was thinking more along the lines of photos at this point. Maybe you could come down and take a look, see if anything jogs your memory."

"I don't know. I guess I could do that. I'm kinda busy, though. Anyway, what good would it do?"

"There's a good chance that whoever rented the place is involved somehow," Dombrowski said. "At the very least, maybe they know something about what happened here." He turned to Elliot. "What do you think, kid?"

There were no bloodstains on the victim's clothing, no visible wounds had been inflicted. His left hand rested in his lap, while his right arm hung limply over the chair arm, the hand nearly touching the floor. The sleeve of his dress shirt was rolled up past his elbow.

Beneath it on the carpet was a syringe. Elliot suspected the fruition of his premonition of bad things to come was upon him. This wasn't exactly what it appeared to be, plain and simple so they could wrap things up and go home and forget about it. It wouldn't go down that way. He knew that that just as surely as he knew Detective Dombrowski was standing beside him. Elliot hadn't been a detective for long, and many of his daily experiences were new to him, but there was nothing unfamiliar about the sinking sensation in his gut. He'd had this feeling before, this unequivocal sense of *not-right*. "I don't know," he said. "Why are there no other needle marks on him?"

Dombrowski shrugged. "Maybe it was his first time."

"Maybe," Elliot said, "but he doesn't have that look about him, like he would do something like this."

Dombrowski gestured for Elliot to follow him across the apartment to the kitchen table, where an empty carton of milk and a box of cereal rested. Some sort of symbol had been carved into the wood of the tabletop. "What does the room tell you?" he asked.

It seemed as if Dombrowski had caught on to his apprehension about the case and was pressing him for answers. He wanted to say it looked straightforward, short and sweet, to the point, but what he said was; "It looks a little too generic to me."

"What do you mean?"

"Like a stage play, all set up for the audience to suspend their disbelief."

Dombrowski shook his head. "Sometimes you worry me, kid. Have a look around, see what else you can find."

Elliot nodded, but there wasn't much to see. It was a one-room apartment, not counting the bathroom. He walked to the only window, which was along the outer wall, and ran his fingers across the pane, a thick piece of frosted glass reinforced with chicken wire. The lock was engaged, and several coats of undisturbed paint showed that the window hadn't been opened in a while. He found nothing in the closet, and the bathroom yielded only an old razor and a pack of blades.

Elliot went back to the kitchen table to have a better look at the curious design that had been carved into the wood. He brushed aside the spilled cereal, revealing what looked like the head of a goat carved into a star with a couple circles around it. "What about this?"

Dombrowski shrugged. "What's your assessment?"

Elliot took a final look around the room. The forensic team had arrived and they were busy going about the place. Bob Davis had pulled out one of the kitchen chairs and was watching whatever program was on the television. "No signs of forced entry," Elliot said. "And it doesn't appear as though any kind of a struggle took place."

"There might be hope for you after all," Dombrowski said. "We can rule out robbery, too. Nothing seems to be missing."

"Except for the man's identification," Elliot said.

Dombrowski gave Elliot a curious look then said, "Mr. Davis?"

Bob Davis got out of his chair. "What is it now?"

"You mentioned that a Ms. Stella Martin might have overheard something. Could we have a word with her, please?"

"That won't be a problem. If there's anything Stella likes to do, it's to talk."

Elliot and Dombrowski followed Bob Davis out of the room and into the hallway where the manager began to knock on the door of apartment 4. When it opened, Dombrowski stepped forward. "Thanks for your help, Mr. Davis." He motioned to Elliot. "Give him his cell phone back." After Elliot had complied Dombrowski said, "We'll let you know if there's anything else we need."

The apartment manager shrugged. He looked a little put out. "Suit yourself. I've got other things to do anyway."

Stella Martin kept her little piece of Windhall clean, and she'd tried to make a home of it, draping doilies over the chair arms and throwing rugs across the floor. "Can I get you anything?" she asked. "Some coffee, perhaps?" She moved gracefully for her size, and her demeanor reflected a tough kind of friendliness. Elliot found himself wondering if she had children.

Dombrowski shook his head. "This shouldn't take long. Just tell us exactly what you saw and heard last night."

Stella Martin dropped into a chair and folded her hands across her lap. "I didn't see anything last night, but the night before, that'd be Friday, I saw a few things. There's something strange goes on in that place. I've told Davis about it, but he don't pay me no mind."

"Why did you wait until this morning to report it?" Dombrowski asked.

"Like I said, nobody ever pays me no mind. People are in and out of that apartment all hours of the night, and strange voices come through the walls. It's a damn zoo around here. It was different that night though. The voices were more like conversation, and the TV was blaring. Don't usually hear the TV."

"Do you remember about what time all of this started?"

"It was early in the evening, around seven I'd say. That TV went on all night and it's been going ever since."

Dombrowski paused, and Elliot took the opportunity to ask a question. "You mentioned people coming and going. Could you tell us a little more about that?"

"Honey, I know that hallway and the sounds it makes. Nobody goes up and down those old boards without my knowing about it."

Ms. Martin sounded confident, leaving Elliot not only inclined to believe her, but also wondering just how well her eavesdropping skills were honed, and if she might in fact be able to speculate on the size and weight, even the gender of her hallway trespassers. "Do you suppose they were residents of the building?"

She shook her head. "Ain't nobody lives there." She pointed to the wall, meaning apartment 3, where the body was found. "But Friday was different. There was this man, but he didn't look like anybody I'd ever seen around here. He had a hooker with him, too."

"How do you know she was a hooker?" Elliot asked.

"Cause she looked like one."

"And how is that?"

"Jesus, Detective. Do I have to draw you a picture? You a cop, or a Baptist minister, don't know what a hooker looks like."

Dombrowski didn't even try to hide the smirk on his face.

"Could you be a little more specific?" Elliot asked.

"She had on high heels, tight leather pants, and one of those shirts that shows your belly button."

"Was she tall?"

"Hell yes."

"Was she thin or heavyset?"

"She was thin all right, and her skin had no color to it. Probably a drug user." She paused, then continued, "She had bushy black hair and a tattoo, some kind of funny-looking symbol sticking out of her pants, just below her navel."

Elliot nodded. "You mentioned that the visitors were different this time. What kind of people usually go in and out of the apartment?"

"Oh, they're a weird bunch, mostly skinny white guys with long hair, like bikers or hippies or something like that. Maybe twenty-five to thirty years old. Sometimes they play music, but never the television. They're usually pretty quiet, except for tramping up and down the hallway. Guy last night, he'd seen fifty some time ago, and he was dressed like a businessman." She paused and leaned forward, as if she were telling Elliot a secret. "I think the place is rented just to buy and sell drugs."

Elliot glanced at Dombrowski, and the expression on his face said he wasn't paying much attention to any of this because he was heading to the same conclusion he'd been heading to since their arrival at Windhall Apartments: He thought the victim was a transient who'd simply had too much of his style of pain relief. Dombrowski turned and headed for the door. "Thank you, Ms. Martin. You've been most helpful."

Elliot followed Dombrowski out of Stella Martin's apartment and into the hallway, where several reporters had gathered. Dombrowski smiled. "I'll question the other residents. You take care of this."

Knowing he had no other choice, Elliot turned toward the reporters. There were only three of them. The media must have shared Dombrowski's conviction; there wasn't much to this. One of them, a nicely dressed man accompanied by a cameraman, stepped forward, identifying himself into the microphone as Gary Myers. "Could you tell us what happed here, Mister . . . ?"

"Elliot. Detective Elliot. A body was found inside one of the apartments. We haven't identified the victim, a white male, probably in his late fifties."

"You used the word victim. That usually indicates foul play. Will a murder investigation follow?"

"A slip of the tongue," Elliot said. "I meant to say deceased. It appears he died of a drug overdose, heroine, we suspect."

The reporter's face grew serious. "There are rumors of a drug war in Tulsa. Could this be related?"

"No," Elliot said, "Nothing like that. The victim's history—" He paused. There was that word again. "The deceased's history might reveal something other than what we think we see here, perhaps a hard-luck story of some kind."

Elliot stopped, realizing he'd said too much. He glanced around but didn't see Dombrowski. He was thankful for that. Then again, Dombrowski would see it on the broadcast. Elliot wondered if he might convince Mr. Myers to edit that part out, then figured it wouldn't be worth the try. "There will be a thorough investigation," Elliot said, "but we don't expect to find much."

A few questions later, the reporters gave up. Elliot caught up with Dombrowski.

They questioned the other residents but didn't get much information. The crime scene investigators had already gotten what they needed, so Elliot and Dombrowski talked with the uniformed officers until all of the team members were out of the building, then they gathered their overcoats and left as well, stepping out into the snow.

Neither of them spoke during their trek back to the car, and once there it felt good to climb into the cab and get out of the wind. Dombrowski started the engine and pulled onto the street. "What do you say we get a bite to eat?"

Elliot didn't feel much like eating. He couldn't stop thinking about the strange symbol carved into the kitchen table in apartment 3. The coloring of the wood said it was recent. He suspected it was connected with the death of the John Doe in some way.

Chapter Six

Back at the office, Elliot found an old case file that was remotely similar to what he and Dombrowski had encountered at Windhall Apartments, and he brought it back to his desk, where he began to flip through it. He hoped to gain some insight in reviewing how the case was solved. Captain Lundsford, Detective Lundsford then, had worked it. The victim, in this case, wasn't exactly a John Doe—the information his fingerprints brought up hadn't match the identification he carried—but it would have to do.

Elliot was about halfway through the file when he heard a noise and looked up to see Detective Michael Cunningham knocking on the wall of his cube. He and Elliot had gone through the academy together, got to know each other, and now, whenever Cunningham went to the firing range or to the gym, he'd usually drag Elliot along with him. Elliot guessed Cunningham and Sergeant Conley were the closest things to friends he had around the department. He wasn't unsociable. He just kept to himself most of the time.

Cunningham was a good guy, and a good cop, though occasionally he liked to stay out into the early hours of the morning, making the club scene. He didn't drink that much, but alcohol wasn't what he was after when he went clubbing. Cunningham was a bit of a ladies' man. That afternoon, he had a big grin on his face, like he'd just been on a date with a fashion model.

"What's up?" Elliot asked.

"Some of us are stopping by Torchy's after work, knock down a few beers, thought you might want to join us."

Elliot started to say no, he might have even gotten as far as shaking his head, but then he remembered wanting to talk to Sergeant Conley, and he began to entertain the idea. "What's the occasion?"

A curious look crossed Cunningham's face, as if Elliot had said something he wasn't expecting. After a moment, he laughed and said, "Nobody but you would say that. There's no agenda." He slapped Elliot on the shoulder. "You need to lighten up, buddy."

"Yeah," Elliot said, "I know. By the way, how's your dad?"

Cunningham shoved some papers aside and sat on the desk. "Mean as ever. He asked about you. Just a 'where's your seedy friend' type of thing, but at least it was something. Sometimes he's easy to get along with and sometimes he isn't." He paused for a moment, then continued.

"I don't think he even knows who I am most of the time, just somebody who comes to visit."

"That's not true," Elliot said. "On some level he does. I'm sure of it."

Cunningham slid off the desk and shook his head. "I don't know why that should make me feel better, but it does. Glad we had this little heart-to-heart." As he was leaving he said, "You coming tonight or not?"

"Yeah," Elliot said, "I'll be there."

He figured he would, too. Cunningham was right. He needed to get out more.

A few hours later, Elliot walked into Torchy's. The old case file hadn't been much help, so he'd decided to make a short night of it. He didn't see Cunningham or anyone else he recognized, but then he heard Sergeant Conley say, "Hey, Elliot. What'd you do, get lost and stumble in here?"

Elliot walked over and pulled out a chair next to Conley, the sound of the wooden legs scraping across the concrete floor echoing loudly through the bar, and he made a mental note to raise the chair from the floor, if he decided to move it again.

"About time you decided to be a little more sociable," Conley said. "I was starting to worry about you." He paused and gestured around the room. "I guess you already know everybody?"

Elliot nodded. They were all uniformed officers, with the exception of Mendez, a new detective who'd moved to Tulsa from San Antonio. Mendez was leaning back, his chair balancing on two legs.

"Cunningham asked me to stop by," Elliot said. "It'd be just like him to not show up, after talking me into it."

Mendez laughed. "I guess we know who not to call if we need backup."

"Hey," Conley said, "don't talk like that." He took the tone of a stern but understanding parent. "Cunningham's a good man."

Sergeant David Conley lacked the formal education to move up in the department, but that didn't seem to bother him. He was happy where he was and, Elliot suspected, about as close to the quintessential cop as you were likely to get.

He tapped Conley on the back. "Take it easy. Mendez didn't mean it like that."

Conley made some sarcastic remark, and Mendez winked and leaned even farther back in his chair. After a bit more small talk around the table, the conversation began to split up, the cops drifting into smaller groups of two or three.

Elliot had the John Doe case on his mind but it was Conley who brought it up. "Do you suppose that poor sap back at Windhall had a soul?"

Conley said this with a smirk, feigning sarcasm, but Elliot knew he was referring to the strange symbol he and Dombrowski had seen scratched onto the surface of the table in apartment 3. Turned out it was something called a Baphomet. Conley's question would stick with Elliot, working heavy on his mind throughout the night. He had no answer to it, and it disturbed him that he did not. "At least you noticed it," Elliot said. "Dombrowski didn't give it a second thought."

Conley rubbed his chin. "Don't be so sure about that. Let me tell you something about Bill Dombrowski. He's a smart man, and not a bad guy to know. You would do well to get on his good side. Don't let that I-don't-know-much, Colombo act of his fool you. You think he didn't notice something, ask him about it. He doesn't miss much."

Dombrowski's apparent lack of interest in the case concerned Elliot, but he trusted Conley, and he valued his judgment. "What's your take on it?"

Conley shook his head. "What's an old street cop like me know? You weren't taking anything at face value, though. I could see that and I'm proud of you for it. Don't worry. Dombrowski'll nail it. He has a way of doing that. Might help if the preliminary theories didn't make it on the news, though." He gave Elliot a measured look then lifted his glass.

Elliot took it as the guidance it was meant to be. "Yes sir."

The conversation stopped for a moment. Elliot looked up to see Detective Cunningham coming into the bar. But something beyond that had changed in the room, as if the barometric pressure had taken a nosedive, leaving in its wake a vacuum, a miniature black hole, which drew in all that was around it, leaving the inside of the bar, for a brief moment, completely silent and void of movement.

Cunningham was not alone but was escorted by a woman, the like of which Elliot had not often seen. She and Cunningham made their way toward the group of cops, slowing occasionally to exchange a word or two with acquaintances, but keeping a steady course toward Conley and Elliot. Elliot saw in the expression of Cunningham's date a look of apprehension, as if she recognized him, not as an old friend, but rather as someone she hadn't expected to see.

Moments later, the couple arrived, stopping only a few feet away. Elliot forced himself to look at Cunningham and no one else, but still he imagined the heat of Cunningham's jealousy upon him.

"Hey, Elliot. Glad you could make it."

Elliot silently prayed that the pair in front of him would simply turn and walk away, but instead Cunningham said, "Cyndi, this is Kenny Elliot, one of the guys I work with."

Cunningham introduced the lady as Cyndi Bannister, whereupon she extended her hand, smiling as she ran her fingers through her blonde hair. Elliot knew that touching her would be a mistake, but he ignored his instincts and did so anyway, feeling her warmth course through him, as he'd feared it would. He knew only, too well of such things as this; instant attraction, natural chemistry. He just never expected it to happen to him twice in one lifetime.

When the two of them finally took a seat, luckily a few chairs away, the conversation continued but Elliot could tell by the look on Cunningham's face that he wasn't happy. The thought crossed his mind that this girl must be someone special. Cunningham had many lady friends, and he wouldn't ordinarily get his feathers ruffled over someone giving a little too much attention to his date. Still, Elliot couldn't stop himself from stealing glances in her direction.

Elliot looked away, staring at his hands folded on the table. He knew her from somewhere, must have met her before, though he could not recall where and when. If not, could he be so completely attracted to a total stranger, feeling the pangs of love for nothing more than eyes, and hair, and sensual movement? Yet in their earlier meetings, his feelings had not made themselves known; she must have made a different impression, must have appeared, if not ordinary then certainly not extraordinary. This evening, however, she did not look ordinary but quite seductive, her eyes full of mystery, as is the evening upon the setting of the sun.

To make matters worse, Elliot caught her looking back, her big eyes darting quickly away in an attempt to avoid direct confrontation. He suspected she didn't do this out of fear. She just wasn't sure she wanted to act on the attraction. He understood that feeling as well. He felt pressure on his arm and realized it was Sergeant Conley.

"Pull your tongue back in, Elliot. You're embarrassing me."

Elliot glanced around the table. "Is it that obvious?"

"Hell yes and then some. I got to admit she's a real eye-catcher. Every one of us was looking, but you were *looking*. She's with Cunningham. Show a little respect."

Conley was right and his words were not lost on Elliot. He felt bad about it, though his eyes still wandered in her direction. "Thanks," he said. "Glad you were here to pull me back down to reality."

He had to get out of there. It was the only way to avoid trouble. He made an excuse, said his good-byes, and walked away.

Outside he stood for a moment, his breath vaporizing in the cold air. He had plenty of things to think about, but only one had his attention, pushing aside even the deeply disturbing baphomet symbol. No matter how he tried to redirect his thoughts, they ended up in the same place. Scenarios of his being with Cyndi kept sprouting in his imagination where they would grow wildly out of control. He wasn't sure whether to embrace those feelings, which might well lead to their becoming real, or consider their disconcerting aura as a warning and do his best to abate them.

It was Carmen Garcia all over again.

Chapter Seven

The next morning Elliot sat in Detective Dombrowski's office, though his thoughts were more on Cyndi. Her eyes haunted him, and he could not decide on their color, whether they were blue, or if they were gray. They seemed to be both and yet neither. He finally decided they were the color of the sky, not the deep blue of spring, but rather like that of a summer afternoon, when the blaze of the sun has all but drained the color from it.

Elliot leaned forward. "I'd like to talk to you about the John Doe case," he said.

"What's on your mind?"

"I don't think we should just write it off. Something tells me it's not as straightforward as it looks. There's more to it."

After what seemed an unbearable amount of time, Dombrowski said, "What makes you think we're going to write it off?"

Elliot considered his answer. He hadn't expected the question to be turned around on him. "You seemed distracted at the scene, your thoughts elsewhere. I got the impression you'd already decided everything was just as it appeared to be, even before we left the apartment building."

Dombrowski's face remained flat, expressionless, as if his emotions had been drained from him. He raised the file he'd been holding and held it out, in front of Elliot. "Well, I guess it's your lucky day. John Doe is your problem now. I'm turning it over to you."

Elliot felt his face flush. Conley had tried to warn him. "Turning it over to me? Why?"

"Captain Lundsford's been asking me about it. I've been watching you. You pay attention to detail. I like that. The Captain and I both agree it's time you started handling your own cases." He paused to grin. "This'll be a good one for you to start on. It's different, a little offbeat."

"So you think I'm offbeat?"

"I didn't say that. But being a little unorthodox might not be such a bad thing, in small doses."

Dombrowski paused to sip his coffee then continued. "Let me give you some solid advice. Good detectives solve crimes by using scientific methods, gathering hard evidence."

He paused and lit a cigar, blowing the smoke into the air. "Start with Conley. Find out what he knows about the computer techs that

38

were in the area. Maybe they saw something. After that, see if you can find anything on the long-haired man that came out of the apartment building just as we arrived. And"—he flicked ash from the cigar into an ashtray on his desk—"if it's not too much trouble, try to keep it off the news."

Elliot walked out of Dombrowski's office with a newfound respect for the man. He decided to set aside his suspicions about the strange symbol for the time being and follow the more experienced man's advice. On the way back to his desk, Elliot stopped by the break room. Detective Cunningham was there, stirring something in a cup, some kind of instant cereal. Elliot stopped beside him. "Morning, Cunningham."

"Hey."

Elliot got a Styrofoam cup, filled it with ice, then added water. "I'm sorry about last night. I was acting like a jerk."

"Don't worry about it."

Cunningham's nonchalance was unconvincing. He was more upset than he was letting on. Elliot pretended to examine the cup he was holding. "I feel bad about it."

"Well, you really don't get out much, do you? Probably not used to seeing lovely ladies?"

Elliot frowned. "That'd be funny if it wasn't so true."

That got a laugh out of Cunningham. He left the break room and started toward his office. Elliot followed. Once there, Cunningham sat in his chair then took a bite of the cereal. "I'll tell you this," he said. "If it'd been a little more one-sided, I wouldn't have gotten so miffed." He paused then shook his head. "She was checking you out, too. Do you know each other?"

Elliot recalled that same thought going through his mind earlier. "No. Not that I'm aware of." He immediately realized no man in his right mind would forget someone like Cyndi. "Well, anyway, I'm sorry." He turned to leave. "I'll see you around, okay?"

"Not if I see you first."

Elliot walked away, wondering about Cunningham's last statement. It was a common enough thing to say, but he'd never heard Cunningham say it. When he reached his office, Elliot called Sergeant Conley and asked him to meet him for coffee so they could talk about possible witnesses at Windhall.

Less than an hour later, Elliot talked with Stella Martin, his only witness at the apartment building where the incident occurred.

The trip hadn't been wasted. Stella described the woman who had been with the John Doe in such detail that a sketch artist could easily work up a drawing.

Elliot's luck didn't stop there. When he pulled onto the roadway, leaving the parking lot, he saw the man with the dirty blond hair, the same one that'd come out of the apartment building when he and Dombrowski were there, investigating. Patches of ice dotted the sidewalk, but the man maneuvered past the other pedestrians, weaving around them with a practiced skill, his eyes seemingly trained on a distant focal point. Elliot wondered where he might be going.

He decided to find out. He waved traffic past, then crept onto 15th Street, staying behind the suspect, out of his field of vision.

The leisurely drive didn't last. Impatient drivers blew their horns and swerved around. Not wanting to draw attention, Elliot drove past the suspect and pulled into the parking lot of an insurance agency, just west of Lewis Avenue. Seconds later, the man stepped from the sidewalk and crossed the street. Elliot grabbed some papers from the seat of the car and pretended to examine them. When the suspect drew near, he slowed his pace then altered his course and continued to the other side. He was now heading east.

When he reached what was once an old church, he climbed the steps then pulled the door, pausing briefly to glance in Elliot's direction before he turned and entered the building. Elliot considered going after him, but decided against it. Instead, he drove west a few more blocks, then pulled into another lot and parked again. He didn't think the church was the man's destination, and he hoped that after a moment or two, thinking Elliot was gone, he would resume his original journey.

Elliot's guess proved right. About ten minutes later, he caught sight of the suspect, again strolling west along the sidewalk. Elliot climbed out of his car and followed on foot, keeping his distance, trying to blend in with the crowd whenever he could. When the wind picked up, he pulled his coat together and buttoned it. He felt conspicuous, a lone gunman chasing his prey, but as far as he could determine the man hadn't noticed he was once again being followed.

By the time they reached the area of restaurants and antique shops where 15th becomes Cherry Street, the cold air had begun to blur Elliot's vision, but he managed to keep the suspect in visual range. Turning north on St. Louis, he followed him past empty houses and uncut bushes. Just off Cherry Street, the north end of St. Louis Avenue was a step back in time to an era of Tulsa when oil was king and Ford, parked proudly in the narrow drives of cute bungalows, the automobile of choice. The bungalows were still there, but like an old photograph that had lost its sheen, they, too, had faded, mere shadows of the symbols of wealth they had once been, their wildcatters and drillers having moved on taking their shiny Fords and leaving behind poverty and Japanese imports.

Elliot kept his distance, following the man as he walked toward a small apartment building nestled among oaks and evergreens. When the suspect stopped and dug his keys from his pocket, Elliot came forward and showed his badge. The look in the man's eyes said he wanted to run, but he held his ground. "I need to talk to you," Elliot said.

The man swallowed, licked his lips. "What about? I haven't done anything."

"I didn't say you had. But I have to tell you, your nervousness concerns me."

The man unlocked the door and started to go inside, acting as if Elliot was nothing more than a nosey neighbor that he didn't have time for.

Elliot reached in front of the man and stopped him by holding the doorknob.

"What are you doing?"

"We need to talk."

"Do you have a warrant or something?"

Elliot smiled, trying to look apologetic, friendly, and yet retain an edge of command. "Why would I need anything like that? You're not under arrest. I just need to talk to you. In fact, there's no need to go inside at all. We can conduct our business right here."

The man paused then shook his head. "You can come in. You just scared me, that's all, coming up behind me like that, popping out of nowhere. You can't be too careful these days."

When Elliot stepped inside, the impression that no one actually lived there struck him. The apartment was so devoid of furnishings that the sound of the door closing echoed from the corners.

The man sat in the only chair, a recliner with pockets on the sides for TV guides, and remote controls. If there were any of those things in that chair's pockets, they were flat and well hidden. Like the apartment, the chair looked brand new.

A tall bar separated the living room from the kitchen, but there were no bar stools. Elliot placed his elbow on the countertop and leaned against it. "I'll get right to the point," he said. "I want to know who you are and what you know about the body we found in apartment 3 at Windhall and before you say you don't have any idea of what I'm talking about, let me remind you that I saw you coming out of the front door when I arrived there yesterday. You saw me as well."

A look of fear shot across the man's face. "I haven't done anything wrong."

"Let's start with your name."

"Douglass Wistrom. And I was just walking past the place, that's all."

"Go on."

"It was cold, and I'd left without a coat. I have a friend, someone I hadn't seen in a while, who lives there. I decided to stop in and say hello, warm up a bit. But when I saw all the commotion, with the police and all, I just turned around and walked away."

Elliot pulled out his pad and made a note. The man looked and dressed like a transient, but he certainly didn't speak like one. "Does your friend still live there?"

"I don't know. I didn't go in. I just walked away."

"You didn't call your friend later to see what was going on, see if he was okay?"

Wistrom shook his head. "It's been a while since I've seen him. He may not even remember me."

"I'll need your friend's name for my report."

"Report? I thought you said this was unofficial."

"I never said that. I said you weren't under arrest. This is an investigation, Mr. Wistrom, and it is official."

Wistrom was silent for a moment, as if he was trying to drag something out of his memory. "His name is Morris, Morris Reed."

Elliot straightened from his position and walked around the room. "Do you know anything about the body we found in apartment 3?"

Wistrom shook his head. "I figured something was going on, but I didn't know what, until last night. I was flipping channels when I saw you. Like you were saying, I'd seen you earlier that day, and I recognized you, so I watched the interview. I have to tell you, I nearly got sick, a real burning in my stomach when I saw what had happened. And to think I was there, not more than fifty feet away from a murder victim."

"Interesting you should put it that way, being as we haven't determined whether or not it is a homicide."

Wistrom didn't reply.

"Do you suppose your friend, Morris Reed, might know anything?"

"He might. If he's still there."

"When was the last time you saw him?"

Wistrom wrinkled his forehead. "I think it was about six months ago."

"That's a long time, not to speak to a friend."

"We weren't that close, just casual acquaintances."

Elliot looked around the sparsely furnished room. "How long have you lived here, Mr. Wistrom?"

"Several years," he said. After a pause he added, "I'm a simple person, Detective, with simple needs. Life tends to get complicated, even messy. I can't control the world, but I can keep my place clean and uncluttered."

Wistrom came across as guarded, evasive, and yet Elliot got the impression he was telling the truth, about the John Doe anyway. "What do you do for a living, Mr. Wistrom?"

Wistrom's face went blank, as if he'd been asked a question he hadn't studied for. Finally he said, "I work with computer applications."

It sounded like he had read his answer from a cheat sheet hidden in the palm of his hand. "With what company?"

"Business Solutions."

"Why are you home today? Did you take the day off?"

Again his answer was slow in coming, his actions mechanical. "Yes, that's exactly what I did."

Elliot stepped closer to the suspect. His pale eyes darted back and forth, and he licked his lips. Elliot suspected he made the man nervous, but that wasn't unusual. He made a lot of people nervous. "That makes twice that I've seen you at Windhall. What exactly were you doing there?"

"There's a curio shop near there, that Oz place. I must have passed it a thousand times without going in. I wanted to see what was in there. They were closed yesterday, so I went back today."

"That's quite a walk, especially in the cold, just to satisfy a mild curiosity. There must be some other reason you were in the area."

"No," he said. "There isn't. I enjoy walking. It relaxes me, helps me let go of things. You should try it sometime."

"Maybe I'll do that, Mr. Wistrom. I'll be leaving now, but I suspect we'll be meeting again. You have a good day, now."

Chapter Eight

Douglass Wistrom's story about Morris Reed panned out. Reed had lived at Windhall, though he no longer did. He knew Wistrom, admitting to a failed relationship, a rather one-sided affair that he'd broken off upon realizing it was fantasy, and all his doing—resulting in his moving out.

Elliot was about to cross Wistrom off his list despite the look that had gone through his eyes, leaving Elliot curious and undecided about its relevance. He'd asked Wistrom if he'd seen anyone in the area that day fitting the description of the person Stella Martin had seen with the John Doe. He'd said no, but there was a reaction. It was slight, like a lie that was so white it was barely detectible, but the more Elliot thought about it, the more it bothered him, especially now, being that he was standing in the empty parking lot of an empty building, Wistrom's alleged place of employment.

Elliot had driven by it before, not giving it much thought, other than what a waste it seemed for such a place to be unoccupied. Sitting on the north side of 61st Street, just east of Aspen Avenue in Broken Arrow, a suburb of Tulsa, it resembled others of its kind, abandoned monasteries of business, their inhabitants and trade having moved on, victims of an unfavorable economy.

In the quasi quiet, the only sounds coming from traffic rushing along the expressway, which ran behind the building, the eeriness intensified Elliot's belief that Wistrom was guilty of something. He looked across the street, studying the thick groupings of oaks, and he wondered why Wistrom would lie to him about where he worked. He must have known Elliot would check it out.

He turned his attention back to the building, a rambling one-story structure constructed of rock, with large windows, which were greenish in color and reflective, though as he drew closer he could see through them. Most of the individual offices, which were block-like in design, contained no furniture, no desks, no filing cabinets, and most notably, no people. The grounds, however, were well taken care of, the bushes and shrubs that lined the walkways and defined the entrances neatly trimmed, the lawn freshly cut. Elliot suspected the owner or the leasing company kept it this way, though he saw no signs advertising the building's availability.

He walked to the back of the building. Oak trees grew there as well, though the expressway was visible through gaps in the foliage. When he reached the east end, he found a loading dock.

When Elliot returned to the front of the ghost building, the whisper of an opening door sounded behind him. He turned to see someone approaching, a middle-aged lady in a gray business suit, who smiled and extended her hand as if none of this was the least bit out of the ordinary.

"You must be Mr. Elliot," she said.

Detective Elliot was too intrigued to correct her. "That's right. And who might you be?"

Her handshake was brief, wraith-like. "The name's Patricia Orwell," she said. "Douglass said you might be coming."

Elliot showed his badge. "Do you always hang out in empty buildings?"

She smiled and gestured toward the door from which she'd come. "Perhaps I should show you around."

Chapter Nine

Brighid McAlister turned another page and smoothed it, pressing it flat against her legs, trying to acquire the dream-like state that often overtook her when she examined the shrubs and flowers depicted there. She wished she could dematerialize and reappear inside the magazine, become a part of that world where she could sit on the beautiful garden bench and feel its slats against her legs as it suspended her above the fertile soil.

Still unfortunately grounded in her own reality, Brighid put the magazine aside. She couldn't get the phone call she'd received earlier off her mind. It had been Becket, claiming to have seen her at Cymry's Friday night, flirting with some man, a man she had left with. She had no memory of this, only vague images of meeting someone in the parking lot, and waking up in her car the next morning. The thought of it sent a current of anxiety running through her. Sure she experimented now and then, but never with anything serious and she wasn't habitual, not even close. Had never blacked out before. All she'd had last night was a shot of scotch, maybe two. She knew she'd been drugged.

Brighid picked up her coffee, wrapping her fingers around the cup, feeling the warmth of its contents as it radiated through the stoneware, and she brought it to her lips and drank, holding the cup with both hands. When she put the cup down, she caught a glimpse of her reflection in the toaster, a distorted image caused by the imperfect surface, which she thought quite appropriate. She wasn't quite sure if what people got with her, was not what they saw or if what they saw was not what they got, but it didn't matter really because it all boiled down to the same thing. There was a part of her that no one ever touched because it was so peculiar that even she could not grasp it, not entirely. She once believed she could make it go away, if she wished it hard enough. She no longer harbored that illusion. Her grandmother had tried to explain. "You're different," she would say. "You have a gift."

Had someone at the bar given her something, slipped it into her drink? Yes, she thought they had but that wasn't all. Her purse had been emptied as well. She was five days late on the rent, she had no money, and she hadn't pulled a trick in . . . three days that she knew of. She was afraid to; afraid it might happen again. A thought she'd been trying to avoid snaked through her. Perhaps it had not been drugs at all but magick that had been used against her. Someone had attacked her in a way that was all too personal. She brought her hand across her stomach, touching the tattoo that ran along the left side and prayed for the gods to give her strength.

Brighid pushed away from the table and went to the sink where she washed her coffee cup, performing the act more out of rote memory than anything else, and she began to cry. Why had she allowed herself to get in such a state? The drugs and the partying had caused her to forget her ways, and the gods had done this to gain her attention. She thought about Douglass, the quiet man she'd met at the Full Moon. His interest in her had been genuine, so much so that it had frightened her, and she'd feigned a lack of interest to discourage him. It had worked, though not immediately, and it had been as much for his sake as it had for hers. The bashful gentleman with a verifiable lack of self-interest deserved no place in her world. Then again, such an unconditional act of kindness on her part could be construed as evidence of her evolution, her growth toward a way of life that wasn't so self-centered.

She pushed her hair back. Perhaps she could change, crawl out of her universe and slip into his. The more she toyed with the idea, the more attractive it became. It could be as simple as knocking on his door; her way out of this.

She went into the bathroom and smeared cold cream on her face, letting it set for a spell, then removed it, wiping away the makeup and dark eyeliner encircling her eyes. With a through washing, she was ready. She rummaged through her closet, finding a Bob Dylan T-shirt and a pair of jeans, the most conservative clothes she had, and put them on.

She studied herself in the mirror. A little too plain. She dug through her drawer and found the right touch, some silver jewelry. She put it on and left her house and walked the short distance to the area, where Douglass lived.

As soon as she turned onto St. Louis Avenue, however, she saw someone in the parking lot behind the Full Moon who caused her to pause. The face looked familiar, though it didn't quite fit the distorted image in her mind, like seeing someone through the peephole in her front door, an old customer perhaps. And then it came to her. This was the person she'd been with in the parking lot at Cymry's. She had to do something. Such a meeting would have been too much to believe had she not realized it for what it was: a gift from the gods. She had no choice but to take the advantage and confront what had been laid in front of her. She strode forward, her coat billowing behind her like the cape of a countess, and when she came within a few feet she spoke, demanding to know why such a thing had been done to her.

When Brighid saw the eyes of the stranger, she paused, her
courage draining from her, for they were not the eyes of a mortal, but
those of the dark god, the never-ending veil of darkness who could take
many forms and had done so in this guise of deception. It was then that
Brighid heard the dark god's voice, which was painful to her ears, and
felt the deadly embrace, which was hot in her stomach, for the touch of
the dark god is final.

Chapter Ten

Patricia Orwell opened the door to the building and held it, her right arm trembling slightly under the pressure. Elliot stepped inside. It was cold and shadowy, the only light coming through the tinted windows, and as Elliot watched the door ease shut, a feeling of insecurity crawled along his nerves.

No cars were driving past, no other visitors strolling the grounds. She started forward, walking deeper into the glass tomb, her conservative, low-heeled shoes crackling against the dirty concrete, the sound echoing in the expanse of unused space.

"I just need some information," Elliot said, "about Douglass Wistrom, his connection to this place, and what you know about him."

"We'll get to that," Ms. Orwell said. "I have a few issues with Mr. Wistrom myself, his giving out this address for one."

Elliot ran his finger across a filing cabinet as he walked past, pushing a pile of dust to the floor. "Yeah," he said, "that thought crossed my mind as well."

Near a partial enclosure created by the intersection of two interior walls, Ms. Orwell stopped and turned to Elliot. "I suppose you want to know about Douglass?"

"That's the general idea. Does he work for you?"

"He's employed by Business Solutions."

"Let me guess," Elliot said. "That's his office in the corner."

She looked as if she wanted to find the comment humorous, but too much else was going on. "No, nothing like that."

"What is this place, Ms. Orwell?"

She sighed. "It's exactly what it appears to be."

"Then why are we here?"

"Some pharmaceutical company out of Dallas wants to open an office in the area. They wanted to look at the place. I'm here to show it." After a moment she added, "We specialize in commercial properties."

Elliot noticed a partially open lateral file drawer. He walked over and glanced inside. Empty. "How does Mr. Wistrom fit in with all of this?"

"He's a handyman. He cuts lawns, trims bushes, does minor repairs."

"He told me he worked with computers. Why would he do that? And why would he give me a phony address?"

49

A slight blush came to Ms. Orwell's face. She was embarrassed for Wistrom. Elliot couldn't help but wonder why.

"I don't know," she said. "The grass is freshly cut. Maybe it was the last property he worked at." She paused briefly, seeming to search for the right words. "Douglass might seem a little off-color at first," she continued, "but he's very dependable and always does an excellent job. He loves computers. That's probably why he told you that. It's what he wishes he did. He's actually quite intelligent, when it comes to that sort of thing."

Ms. Orwell rummaged through a leather bag slung over her shoulder. "He's even published some articles," she said, pulling two magazines from the bag and holding them out. "Here. I brought these for you."

Elliot doubted a high-tech computer magazine and a backwoods survival publication could possibly relate to his investigation, but he took them anyway. At the very least, he might gain some insight into Wistrom. "Thanks."

She nodded, her face taking on a serious tone. "Is Douglass in some kind of trouble?"

Elliot thought about that for a moment then said, "He was seen in the vicinity of a crime scene. We're questioning everyone whom we suspect might have been there or seen something. Have you ever known him to become violent or enraged?"

She shook her head. "Quite the opposite. He's quiet, always does what we ask of him, never complains. You couldn't ask for a better employee. In fact, this is the first time he's ever missed a day of work."

Elliot gazed through the windows for a moment then turned back. "How well do you know Douglass Wistrom, Ms. Orwell, and what's the nature of your relationship?"

The same flash of color Elliot had seen earlier returned to Ms. Orwell's face, her hand darting upward to fuss with her hair.

"There is no relationship. I can't even say we're friends and keep a straight face. I mean I'd be bordering on a lie, wouldn't I. But he talks to me. He doesn't do that with just anyone. Hardly anyone would be more accurate."

Ms. Orwell glanced at the floor and straightened the leather bag she'd slung back over her shoulder. "I hope I'm not talking out of turn here, trying to do your job for you, but there's a lot more to that man than he lets on."

Douglass Wistrom had given Elliot the same impression, on the surface a cougar posing as a house cat. But Wistrom wasn't Little Red Riding Hood's nemesis, someone pretending to be what he was not. He was more like an actor who dresses as a man on one side and a woman on the other; though his act wasn't one of gender, but one of character, Don Knotts on one side and Carey Grant on the other, and the line didn't run down the middle, but swirled like the red and white of a peppermint stick.

Elliot's phone rang, and he slapped it to his ear. It was Captain Harry Lundsford. Someone had been shot on St. Louis Avenue, just a few hundred feet from Douglass Wistrom's apartment.

A young woman among the crowd briefly caught Elliot's attention, moving around the edges of his vision. When he turned for a better look, she was gone, and a brief dizziness threatened his balance, leaving him unsettled and lightheaded. He walked clumsily past the police officers and knelt beside the body, an unnerving sensation sweeping through him, a sort of kinship, even an attraction to this fragile and complex female, as if her spirit had not grasped its fate and still hovered close by, and in its reaching out had touched Elliot in some ethereal and intimate way.

Several of the officers were leaning close together, talking about what they saw, and one of them remarked, "What a waste."

This angered Elliot more than it should have, and almost before he realized his actions, he rose to his feet and clamped his hand tightly around the officer's wrist.

Sergeant Conley appeared. He put his hand on Elliot's shoulder and shook his head. "Take it easy, Elliot."

Elliot released his grip and stepped away, returning his attention to the body sprawled across the parking lot behind the Full Moon restaurant, just off St. Louis Avenue. He knew who she was: the slender build, the hair, but mostly it was the tattoo on her stomach. He'd sketched a likeness of it as Stella Martin described it to him. When he'd shown it to Stella, she'd nodded vigorously. "That's it," she'd said.

Elliot flipped through the notepad until he found the drawing—a square with lines coming from each corner, forming a sort of cross— and when he compared the rough sketch to harsh reality, he unbuttoned his coat, a hot sickness running through him in defiance of the cold outside. This was the woman Stella Martin had seen that night, the last person to have been with their John Doe.

He watched a dog walk past the east side of the lot, keeping away, sensing the trouble and wanting no part of it. "Any witnesses?" Elliot asked.

Sergeant Conley answered, his voice, even though he stood next to
Elliot, seeming to come from a distance. "A few people heard the
shots, but nobody saw anything."

"Have you heard from Wistrom yet?" Elliot asked.

As soon as Elliot had gotten the call, he'd expressed his concern
over the suspect, noting his unusual behavior, and his proximity to both
murders. But Wistrom hadn't answered his door, and when the
manager opened the apartment, he and Conley had found it empty.

Conley shook his head.

The victim wore black denim jeans, which, with the button having
come undone during the commotion, were lower on her hips than they
should have been. Curls of reddish pubic hair peeked over the edges.
She'd been shot once in the torso on the left side, and again in the
head, just above the right eye. Ornate silver earrings adorned her ears,
and a large Florentine chain, also of silver, hung around her neck, from
which dangled a set of keys, the brass collection laying over the name
Bob Dylan, which was emblazoned across her T-shirt.

The smell of hamburgers sizzling on the nearby restaurant's grill
turned Elliot's stomach as he stared at the corpse.

The suspect had slipped away. Douglass Wistrom was nowhere to
be found but that wouldn't last if Elliot could help it.

Elliot glanced at Conley. "Any ID?"

"Her name's Brighid McAlister," Conley said. "She lived a few
blocks from here over on Trenton."

Chapter Eleven

Elliot walked along the sidewalk, taking caution so as not to trip over those places where the roots of trees had cracked it, and he paused momentarily to study the bare branches of the massive sycamores. Come spring the foliage would form a canopy over the area, blocking the sun while lending the neighborhood a sleepy and restful ambiance. The leaves were gone now, and those that remained were few and had shriveled into husks, which, even in their best performance, could not hide the dismal gray of the sky that loomed overhead.

After talking with the crime scene crew, Elliot had come to Trenton Avenue to have a look around and talk with the neighbors. He hadn't had much luck. The residents hardly knew Brighid McAlister, except that she was quiet and never caused any trouble. However, there were several houses to the south that Elliot had yet to try, and it was at one of these, a red brick that reminded him of gingerbread, where he now walked into the yard, approaching a lady who worked at cleaning out a goblet-shaped planter beside the front door.

She saw him coming and stood, brushing the dirt from her knees. About five feet tall, she had to tilt her head back to look him in the eye. "Is there something I can do for you?"

Elliot reached into his coat and pulled his badge, holding it out where the lady could see it. After identifying himself, he said, "I'd like to ask you some questions about one of your neighbors, Brighid McAlister."

The lady, who called herself Deborah Thompson, seemed suspicious. She studied Elliot's badge for several seconds before asking, "Is Brighid in some sort of trouble?"

"You could say that."

Deborah Thompson sighed, her breath a puff of fog in the cold air. "I wish I could say that surprises me, but it doesn't."

Elliot watched her face, looking for a reaction. "Why do you say that?"

Ms. Thompson took off her red stocking cap, which nearly matched the color of her cheeks. "Well, her line of work, of course."

"Could you be a little more specific?"

She smiled uncertainly and chafed her hands. "Would you like to come inside? It's a bit nippy out here."

Elliot followed Ms. Thompson inside where they sat in wicker chairs in what had apparently been the front bedroom. It had been

brightly painted and converted into a sunroom. After bringing Elliot a
cup of hot tea, Ms. Thompson said, "Haven't done your homework,
have you? I really hate to say this, though I suppose the truth is what
you're after. Brighid sells herself for money, Detective. She's a
prostitute."

"I know about that. Is there anything else you could tell me?"

Ms. Thompson set her teacup on a table beside her chair.
"Brighid's a nice person, really, perhaps a bit lacking in the area of
judgment, but as sweet as you'll ever meet. What has she gotten herself
into, Detective? Maybe I could help."

Elliot studied the lady then set his cup down as well. He hated this
part of his job. "Brighid's dead, Ms. Thompson. She was shot."

Deborah Thompson's hand came up, covering her mouth. After a
moment, she lowered it to her lap. "Dear God."

"Do you know of anyone who might have wanted to harm her?"

She shook her head. "She never brought her customers home, at
least that's what she told me. And I've never seen anyone hanging
around."

Ms. Thompson paused briefly, then adding, "There is something
else you need to know, something rather odd."

Elliot turned to a fresh page in his notepad. "Go on."

"Brighid was a bit delusional. Believed she was the descendant of
a Celtic goddess, her namesake, I suppose."

Elliot thought of the strange symbol carved into the table where the
John Doe had been found. "Was she a member of a religious group?"

"Not that I know of."

"Anything else?"

"I'm afraid that's all I know. I'm sorry I can't be of more help."

Elliot added this to his notes, then folding his notepad, stood, and
put on his coat. "Thanks for you help, Ms. Thompson."

He handed her a card. "If you come up with anything, give me a
call."

After being let out, Elliot walked the short distance to the victim's
address.

The house appeared as steeped in mystery as its owner was.
Overgrown shrubs and bushes crowded the small lot, and vines
covered the serpentine picket fence that surrounded the yard. The
forensic team had arrived. Elliot stood on the porch for a moment,
observing empty flowerpots and wooden planters, then pulled on a pair
of latex gloves and went inside the 1920s bungalow on Trenton
Avenue. He hoped to find something that might give him an idea as to

the victim's connection with the unidentified body at Windhall. Raymond Clark was there, dusting for prints.

"How you doing, Elliot?"

"Long day," Elliot said. He felt strange, lightheaded. "I could sleep for a week."

"Hope you're not coming down with something," he said. He went back to his work.

The first bedroom, which was on the south side of the house, just off the living area, had been outfitted for sleeping, but the closet and the dresser were empty and nothing sat atop the furniture but a lamp: a guest room. Elliot took a quick look around the adjoining bath, then went back to the living area.

He picked up a small box sitting on the fireplace mantle and looked inside. It was filled with potpourri. Brighid kept a neat house; the antique furnishings, purposely selected to fit the bungalow's era, polished and free of dust; the oak floors, covered in places with lush rugs, clean and shiny. He found the same care had been taken in the kitchen. Everything was in its place except for a coffee mug in the sink. A gardening magazine, its open pages displaying pictures of spring flowers, rested on the small table, beneath a window.

Elliot backtracked to the dining area, where the fragrance of cinnamon and apples lingered, which preceded a sensation of presence, that of the young lady who'd lived there, and it tiptoed through Elliot's imagination as he came to a door along the south wall of the dining room. He opened the door and stepped inside.

Candles dotted the floor around the bed, and posters of curious, mythological creatures hung from the walls: depictions of a beast, half man and half animal, with a rack of horns growing from its head, and a lady who appeared to be facing in three different directions. But it was the bold design painted onto the wall that grabbed Elliot's attention: a five-pointed star with a circle around it.

Elliot called Robert Arnold in vice to see what he knew about Brighid McAlister. He said he'd look into it, and asked Elliot to meet him for lunch at Goldie's across from Utica Square. Elliot didn't have much of an appetite, but a cup of coffee sounded good. He saw Arnold sitting in a booth at the front of the restaurant, near a large window that overlooked 21st Street.

A middle-aged waitress with her hair tied up grabbed a menu as she walked by. "Be with you in a moment, sweetie."

"I'll be joining the gentleman in the corner. Could you bring some coffee, please?"

She stuck a pencil in her hair, just above her ear. "Sure thing."

Elliot walked over and slid into the booth, then looked across the table at Arnold. He'd already started on a hamburger. He put it down and wiped his mouth with a napkin. "Glad you could make it."

The waitress brought Elliot's coffee and set it in front of him, and he was just getting settled in when he looked through the window and saw Cyndi Bannister. It took a moment for the recognition to register, and it seemed bilateral, this feeling of surprise. Once again he found himself staring, mesmerized by the face of Michael Cunningham's girlfriend. Her path indicated she had intended to come inside but had changed her mind upon seeing Elliot.

She turned and walked away, her pace quickening as she headed east. She triggered the light at the corner, then crossed the street, disappearing behind the trees and shrubs that lined that part of Yorktown Avenue.

Arnold turned to see what Elliot was looking at, but Cyndi was already gone. "So what are you doing, working vice now?"

Elliot took a moment to clear his head, get back to the work at hand. "Not exactly. This one's dead. Turned her last trick today."

"Disgusting business we're in, ain't it?" Arnold's throaty voice slid under the murmur of conversation coming from the other booths.

"Yeah. What have you got?"

Arnold wiped his mouth again, then shook his head. "I couldn't find anything on her. If she was working, she was doing it independently. Probably had a select clientele."

"How select?"

"You know, a high-priced piece, only worked conventions or something."

Elliot slumped. "It's hard to keep track of girls like that."

Arnold took another bite of burger. "It is if they're careful, don't get busted, especially if they ain't connected, don't have a pimp."

Elliot thought about his own nightmares and suddenly it was difficult for him to imagine Arnold with a family, being able to turn it off at the end of the day, and almost before he realized what he was saying, the question came out: "How's Karen?"

Arnold set his half-eaten burger on the plate and took a drink of soda. "She's good. Started back to school, sociology classes, something she's been thinking about for years." He paused and nodded. "It's good to see her happy again. And, hey, Jeremy made the team this year, even got a little playing time. Went to his head, though. You know, big time Union football player. He's all right, though. He's a good kid."

This time Arnold changed the direction, shifted it back. "I did get something for you. It's the tattoo. Hamilton remembered seeing a girl like that. Couldn't remember exactly where, but he thought it was downtown somewhere. Said he figured her for a hooker, the way she was dressed and all, but she didn't seem to be hustling, so he left her alone." He shook his head. "It's weak but it's all I got."

Elliot pulled a twenty and laid it on the table. "I appreciate it, Robert. Let me get the tab. I have another question. Have you ever run across a john named Douglass Wistrom?"

"Wistrom," he said, more to himself than anyone else. He stared through the window for a moment, then turned back. "Maybe. I'll check it out and get back with you."

Chapter Twelve

Elliot left Robert Arnold at the restaurant and went to the office. Once there, he called Patricia Orwell with Business Solutions.

"Detective Elliot. Have you heard from Wistrom?"

She hesitated, then said, "He called right after you left, saying he wouldn't be in for a few days."

"Do you know where he is?"

"At home, I expect. He didn't really say."

Elliot hung up the phone. He'd figured Wistrom for a lowlife, albeit one intelligent enough to be a good freelance writer, but the role of murderer still didn't fit, though his running had definitely tipped the scales in that direction.

Elliot heard someone tapping on the filing cabinet near the entrance to his cube and turned to see Detective Dombrowski.

"Got a few minutes?"

Elliot sat forward. "Sure. What's up?"

It took Dombrowski a while to answer, his eyes studying Elliot during the silence. "Looks like you were right about Enrique Savage. We found the murder weapon from the Susan Lancaster case, just like you thought we would, down by the river, in the bushes close to the jogging trail. A hunting knife. Had his fingerprints all over it." He paused and shook his head. "How did you know?"

"I didn't. Like I said, there's just something about Savage that bothers me."

"What about the weapon?"

"A lucky guess, based on where the body was found."

"You're a regular Sherlock Holmes," Dombrowski said. Then he laughed. "Just kidding."

As Dombrowski was leaving, an idea occurred to Elliot. "Do you think Savage would be willing to talk with me?"

Dombrowski raised his eyebrows. "Why?"

"I want to ask him about Brighid McAlister."

"What, you think he had something to do with it?"

"No. But he has occult connections. I thought he might be able to give me some information regarding some things I saw in her apartment."

"What kind of things?"

Elliot showed Dombrowski the photos he'd taken in Brighid's bedroom.

He looked them over. "I don't know. I doubt he'd do it willingly. You saw how he was earlier."

"You're right. It's a bad idea. He'd probably just lie to me anyway."

Dombrowski nodded. "You'll get to the bottom of it. A little advice, though." He handed the photos back to Elliot. "Be careful you don't read too much into things like that. It'll bog you down."

After Dombrowski was gone, Elliot studied Enrique Savage's case file, looking for a connection or a similarity, anything. After an hour or so without any luck, he closed the file and left the office.

In the parking garage, Sergeant Conley came over. "Hey, Elliot, how's the McAlister case going?"

"Could be better."

"Anything I can do?"

"That depends. Do you know anything about religious symbolism?"

Conley shook his head. "I can't help you there, kid."

Elliot was climbing into his car when Conley added, "But I know someone who could."

He fished a card from his wallet and handed it to Elliot. It read: DR. THOMAS MEADOWS, SENIOR MINISTER, BROOKWOOD UNITED METHODIST CHURCH. "He's a very intelligent man, Dr. Meadows. I can call him if you want, let him know you're coming."

Elliot stuffed the card into his pocket. "That'd be great. And thanks."

He wound his way out of the garage and left the downtown area. A few minutes later, he pulled into his driveway, where he again saw his neighbor, Joey Anderson, standing in the front yard.

Chapter Thirteen

Elliot brought the car to a stop and climbed out, noting as he drew near that Joey wasn't wearing a coat.

"Hello, Mr. Elliot."

Elliot visually scanned the area but saw no one else. It wasn't dark, but it was getting there. "Hey there, buddy. What are you doing out here?"

"I go for walk."

Figuring Joey was tired of hearing it, Elliot hesitated, but then asked the question anyway. "Where's your mom?"

"It's okay."

"You may be right, but I don't think your mom sees it that way."

"She doesn't want me to go out by myself. I'm okay."

"She worries about you because she loves you, Joey. She's not trying to make things hard, just trying to protect you. Come on. I'll walk you home."

Elliot put his arm on Joey's shoulder both to guide him and to show him he wouldn't take no for an answer, but they'd only taken a few steps when an angry Kelly Anderson came around the corner of the fence line and stalked up the small incline of the yard.

She stopped and crossed her arms. To Joey she said, "I might have known I'd find you here." She then turned her attention to Elliot. "And just what do you think you're doing?"

Elliot removed his arm from Joey's shoulder. "I was about to take him home."

"How long has he been here?"

"I don't know. I just got here myself."

Kelly Anderson sighed. "I'm sorry. I don't mean to be so confrontational. But I've made it clear that . . ." She shook her head then said, "Come on Joey. We need to go now."

"Wait," Elliot said. "We're probably going to be neighbors for a while. Perhaps we should try and be neighborly. Why don't you come in? I'll make some coffee. And I'll bet Joseph here would like some hot chocolate."

Joey seemed to like that. "He called me Joseph."

Kelly studied Elliot for a moment, then glanced at Joey. "All right. But just for a moment. I've got a lot to do tonight."

As they neared the entrance, the outside light flickered on, then went off again. Elliot shook his head. "I've been meaning to have that fixed. There's some kind of sensor built in so the light will only come on when it's dark. That's the idea, anyway. It doesn't work very well."

Once inside, Elliot showed his guests to the living room. "Sit anywhere you like," he said. "I'll just be a minute."

He went into the kitchen to start the hot chocolate for Joey and coffee for himself and Joey's mother, but a few seconds later the conversation had already started.

"How long have you been a . . . police officer?"

It was Kelly Anderson, still in the living room, her voice carrying between the rooms.

Elliot thought about correcting her. He was a detective, not a police officer, but he dropped it and said, "I've been with the department about four years."

When he turned to get the milk from the refrigerator, he saw that Kelly had come into the kitchen.

She looked at the floor then glanced at the countertops. "It's certainly not what I expected."

Elliot thought for a moment, then realized she must be referring to the floor plan, specifically the inadequate size of the kitchen. "Interesting layout, isn't it. I've thought about moving the counter back, taking some of the breakfast nook. That'd give me more room. I really don't use that space anyway."

She ran her hand across the top of the stove. "That's not what I meant. It's . . . well, clean, everything in its place. Most men don't do that. I guess you have a housekeeper."

Elliot poured some milk into a small pan and placed it on the burner. "No. I just like to stay organized."

She stared at Elliot for a moment, her face blank, unreadable. "Joey's certainly impressed. You're all he talks about."

"I'm the new kid on the block, that's all."

"It's more than that. He admires you, looks up to you. It's my job to make sure his trust isn't misplaced."

Elliot poured a cup of coffee and handed it to Kelly. "You're a good mother."

"I try. But it's difficult with Joey. It seems to be getting worse."

"He's just trying to stretch his wings," Elliot said. And then, as he often did, he said what should have been left as a thought. "I suspect it isn't easy to let go of a child, and, in Joey's case, you can never do that, not completely. You might want to consider loosening the reins a bit, though. He just wants to be treated like an adult, an individual."

She bristled visibly, and Elliot immediately wished he had put that a little more tactfully.

"Did Joey tell you that?"

"No. It's intuition."

"Is that right?"

"It's what all children want, eventually."

Her face was no longer blank. It was angry. "What all children want? And what makes you such an expert on the subject? Do you have children, Mr. Elliot?"

"No. I don't."

"Then I guess you don't really know what you're talking about, do you?"

Elliot put some chocolate into a cup, then poured the hot milk into it. "About being a parent, probably not. But that's only part of the equation. The other half is children, being a kid. And I do know a little bit about that."

"I see. And how, exactly, did you come by this knowledge? Do you like to hang around kids, Mr. Elliot?"

"No, but I used to be one, Ms. Anderson, something I remember quite well. Perhaps you could, too, if you tried." Elliot opened the bag of marshmallows he'd pulled from the pantry and put a few into the chocolate.

The action seemed to diffuse the situation momentarily. Kelly Anderson watched him do this, and her face softened a bit. She sipped her coffee. "Perhaps you're right. Maybe I should lighten up. Joey gets by. He always has. It amazes me at times. I mean, life is hard enough, isn't it. But I think others realize his weakness and leave him alone. It seems even the worst sort of people won't cross that line, like it's taboo of the deepest level, a code of humanity that even they aren't willing to break. There's just something about complete honesty when it's wrapped up with defenselessness. I guess I should be thankful for that."

Elliot had neither the heart nor the desire to tell Kelly Anderson that there were people out there who would do Joey harm, if they thought they'd gain by it, or simply get away with it. Thankfully those types, the ones who'd smile and tell you how sorry they were for dirtying up your clothes while they stuck a knife in your gut, were few and far between but they were out there. Elliot knew because he'd met a few of them. What's more, he suspected the John Doe's killer was one of these.

He had no more than completed that thought when both he and Kelly turned toward the sound of footsteps coming into the kitchen. It was Joey, arms outstretched in front of him, holding something with both hands. It was a .38 Smith and Wesson, the one Elliot kept in the top drawer of the nightstand beside his bed.

At that moment, as if a membrane had been torn, a barrier between realities penetrated, Elliot caught a glimpse of a Joey who was not so encumbered; one who knew enough to deduce the situation and conclude, in his way of thinking, that his unfortunate double might find salvation in the instrument of his death, the weapon he now held in his hands, for it was at Joey that the threat was aimed.

Kelly Anderson was caught in the limbo of a parent paralyzed into doing nothing by fear of what the opposite might bring.

Elliot stepped between Joey and his mother, holding out his hand in a gesture he prayed would work. "Give me the gun, Joey."

Joey answered, though Elliot had the distinct impression that it was the alternate, the one who could see things for what they were, that was pulling the strings. "Look what I got, Mr. Elliot."

"Yes. I see it. Could I have it, please?"

"I found it."

"I know. But it's mine. And I need it back."

Joey shook his head, the movement sending chills along Elliot's spine. "It's not nice to take people's stuff."

"That's right," Elliot said, wiggling the fingers of his open hand.

A struggle played across Joey's features. The real Joey wanted to comply, but the alternate would not relent. He ran his finger across the trigger. "It loud?"

"Very loud. It'll hurt your ears."

Elliot knew Joey wasn't going to give him the weapon. He would have to take it. He edged forward. "You're scaring your mother, Joey. You don't have to give the gun to me. Just put it down. Lay it on the floor."

Joey dropped his head and nodded, surely aware on some level of the stress he was causing. It was the moment Elliot was waiting for, he took one large but careful step towards Joey; then slid his hand around the .38 and pulled it free. "Thank you, Joey."

For several seconds, Kelly Anderson looked as though she might faint, but then she came to life, legs pumping like pistons as she propelled herself out of the kitchen, her son in tow via a stern hand clamped around his wrist. She didn't look back and she said nothing as she crossed the living room and exited the house through the front door, slamming it shut behind her hard enough to jar a picture from the wall.

Elliot poured himself a cup of coffee, then slumped down in a chair in the living room.

Three hours later, when he could no longer take the silence, he went downtown. He wanted to be alone, listen to some music, and get his thoughts together, and he'd chosen the Hive, a place packed with people in which to do that. It usually worked quite well. But not this time. He'd taken only a few sips of cold beer when he felt someone watching him. He looked across the room and saw the guilty party gliding toward him out of the smoky haze.

She stopped a few feet away and, with a playful gesture, raised a portion of the gold chain she wore around her neck and slid it seductively into her mouth, where she held it momentarily, clinched between her teeth, before letting it slip away allowing it to fall across her neckline, drawing Elliot's attention to her slightly low-cut blouse.

If the action was meant to rattle Elliot, it had done its job. "Oh," he said, "it's you."

"Yeah. . . . It's me."

Her words came out softly sarcastic, mocking him.

"We keep running into to each other," she continued. "Are you following me, Detective?"

"I'm sure it looks that way."

She raised her eyebrows, but remained silent.

"When you saw me at the restaurant earlier, I was having lunch with another cop, discussing business. It's the only reason I was there."

Cyndi Bannister pulled out a chair and sat across the table from Elliot. "What about now? What brought you here?"

The sincere nature of her question brought a fire to her eyes that Elliot found nearly irresistible. "I come for the music. Ask around."

She glanced around. "It's one of your regular haunts, then?"

"I guess you could say that, which brings up an interesting point. I don't recall seeing you around here. Maybe you're following me."

She smiled. "If I decide to do that, you'll never know it. But you're the detective, aren't you? Maybe you should take a few lessons." Her low chuckle entranced him.

Elliot took a sip of beer. A few seconds later, he said, "Are you offering?"

The fire blazed in her eyes again, but before she could respond Elliot said, "I'm sorry. That was inappropriate." He took another drink, a long swallow then set the bottle on the table. "Where's Cunningham?"

She fussed with her purse, then put it aside, as if she wanted to smoke but had changed her mind. "We don't keep tabs on each other. It's not that serious."

"I'm not sure Cunningham feels that way. Is he still miffed at you for the other night?"

She took a while to respond, and when she did it was just a small nod.

Elliot twirled the beer glass around with his fingers but left it on the table. "Look, I'm sorry about the way I acted. I was completely out of line. Cunningham had a right to be angry. He's not a bad guy. You could do a lot worse."

Cyndi reached across the table, her hand brushing against Elliot's as she took the beer from him. She took a long, slow sip then put it back on the table and slid it across to Elliot.

Elliot wanted to run the bottle across his lips as though he could capture some ethereal part of her before it disappeared, but he resisted the urge.

"It's all right," she said, pushing back from the table and standing. "A girl likes to be noticed. You just need to be a little more subtle about it next time."

With that she turned and walked away.

Elliot watched her cross the room and leave the bar, but he figured he hadn't seen the last of her. That thought was solidified when he glanced down to see a folded scrap of paper on the table. He opened it to find a phone number, Cyndi's, probably. He wasn't so sure that was a good thing. In fact, he knew that it was not.

Chapter Fourteen

Carrying a folder containing photos of various occult objects, Elliot entered the Brookwood United Methodist Church. A finger of guilt snaked through him, and he tried to rid himself of the lingering thoughts that lay at the root of it: He hadn't slept well, falling in and out of dreams, all of which involved Cyndi Bannister in one way or another. He took the first hallway he came to, as instructed, and stopped at the third door on the left.

The door was open, and Doctor Thomas Meadows rose to his feet when he saw Elliot. His handshake was light but honest, and he was a small man, his demeanor blended and understated, like the natural and muted colors of the church's interior. Elliot felt at ease in his presence.

"David Conley speaks highly of you," Doctor Meadows said. "He's a good man, and I value his opinions. How might I be of service to you?"

Elliot opened the folder and pulled out the photos from both crime scenes plus the shots from Brighid McAlister's bedroom, but before he displayed them he said, "I'm sorry to bring such disturbing matters to a church, but I'm involved in a rather unusual investigation. David said you might be able to help me identify some symbols."

Doctor Meadows lowered himself into his chair. "Thanks for the warning. May I see them, please?"

Elliot spread the photos across the minister's desk, placing them in sequence. He indicated the baphomet. "This was carved into the tabletop where the first victim was found. It had been done recently." He moved down the line. "A similar symbol was painted on the wall of the second victim's bedroom, yet it appears to have been there for a while."

Doctor Meadows studied the material briefly, then took off his glasses and looked up, but before he could speak, a phone call interrupted him. "I understand," he told the caller. "This will only take a moment." He placed the phone in its cradle and leaned forward.

Elliot wondered if he had actually seen a flicker of concern cross Doctor Meadows' face as he studied the first photo. Yes, he thought maybe he had.

"The five-pointed star," the doctor began, "which is commonly referred to as a pentagram, is an old symbol, even being found scrawled onto the walls of caves. Needless to say, its history is complex, nebulous. Some scholars claim the design was inspired by the star-shaped pattern formed by the path of the planet Venus as it moves across the sky. For medieval Christians, it symbolized the five wounds of Christ. However, in pagan terms, the symbol is used to represent what's thought of as the four elements—earth, air, water, and fire—with the fifth point symbolizing spirit."

Someone knocked at the door, then opened it slightly. Doctor Meadows waved his hand, indicating his dismay at being disturbed, and the intruder retreated, closing the door once again.

The doctor traced along the first photo with his finger. "With a circle around it, which represents unity and wholeness, it becomes an entirely new symbol, that being a pentacle."

Elliot leaned forward. "So the pentacle, with a circle around it, like we have here, might indicate that we are dealing with more than one individual, perhaps even a group?"

"Not necessarily. The meaning of unity, as it's used here, has more to do with the search for divine knowledge, unifying body and spirit. That being said, if your suspect is a true pagan, it's highly probable that he would be associated with like-minded individuals, a group as you put it. That's not to say that the group would be responsible for any one individual's actions."

"So what you're telling me is that I shouldn't consider someone dangerous just by the virtue of their association with a pagan religion?"

The doctor was silent for a moment, giving his answer some thought, a rare quality that Elliot had grown to appreciate. When the doctor finally spoke, however, his expression gave Elliot cause for study, for it was one of slight humor, but tempered with an edge of worry, the same concern Elliot had noticed earlier.

"Ambiguous answers are not always my forte," he said. "At times, however, the circumstances leave no room for avoidance. Let me put it like this. Ordinarily, one who joins a pagan religious group does so for the purpose of associating with like-minded individuals, those who seek enlightenment and spiritual development in a similar fashion. Inasmuch, they should not be considered evil, simply misguided. On the other hand, alternative religious groups, by their very nature, have a tendency to attract unstable individuals."

Again, there was a knock at the door, followed by its being opened.

"If there's something else you need to take care of," Elliot said, "we can do this another time."

Doctor Meadows pushed back from his desk and went to the door. "That won't be necessary," he said. "Just give me a moment."

The doctor left the room. Elliot sat quietly and waited. He was quite impressed with Doctor Meadows.

A short time later the doctor returned. He sat at his desk again and continued. "I wish I could give you a better answer."

Elliot tapped the photo of Brighid McAlister, or rather a blown-up portion featuring the tattoo on her stomach. "What can you tell me about this?"

After a moment, the doctor said, "It appears to be a depiction of Saint Brighid's cross."

"Saint Brighid? So this is not a pagan symbol?"

Doctor Meadows drummed his fingers against the desktop. "Here again, the answer to that question depends upon whom you ask."

Elliot felt the look of disappointment crawl across his face, and he was powerless to hide it. He suspected the doctor recognized it for what it was.

The doctor grinned. "Let me tell you the story, such as I know it, then you can decide for yourself. There are those who believe that Saint Brighid, the person, never actually existed but was invented as a guise, a cover for pagan worship. However, there is evidence that around AD 451 a daughter was born to Dubthach, the pagan king of Leinster, and Broicsech, his wife and a Christian woman. The father named his daughter Brighid, after the pagan goddess of fire. If indeed she existed, she would have been raised under the influences of both Druidism and Christianity.

"As the story goes, Brighid became associated with Bishop Mel of Ardagh, who later, around AD 468, consecrated her as a nun. Brighid went on to form a monastery at Cill Dara, which means cell of the oak. The area is now known as Kildare. According to legend, Brighid spent her life converting pagans to Christianity, though not in the typical way through sermons, but rather by example, showing God's love by performing acts of kindness.

"As for Saint Brighid's cross, depicted here in the tattoo, and by the way its similarity to both the pagan solar cross and fire wheel should not be overlooked, the story goes something like this. At some point, Brighid was called to the deathbed of either her father or a pagan chieftain. To comfort him, she gathered some rushes, remnants of marsh plants, which were scattered on dirt floors for warmth, and wove them into a cross. Having done this, she explained the meaning of the cross, and how Jesus died there to pay for the sins of man. Upon hearing this, the man asked for forgiveness and accepted Christ as his savior before dying.

"It's a good story, but whether Saint Brighid was a real person who got mixed up with the mythical pagan goddess or she was merely invented as a cover for the goddess, we will never know for sure."

Doctor Meadows paused and glanced at his watch. "I'll have to cover the rest rather quickly. I have an appointment I need to keep." He touched one of the photos. "This, which appears to be three separate women, each facing in a different direction, is an artist's rendition of Brighid, the pagan goddess of fire, healing, and smithery."

"The same goddess," Elliot asked, "that Saint Brighid is confused with?"

"Exactly, and this interesting fellow, with deer antlers sprouting from his head, is Herne the Hunter. Here again, myth is mixed with reality. Herne, an actual person, employed by King Richard the II as his main huntsman, later becomes a god after he's mortally wounded while protecting the king from a charging deer, only to be brought back to life by a wizard. There's more to the story, but you get the idea."

Doctor Meadows rose from his chair. "I hope I've been of some help to you."

"You have," Elliot said, getting to his feet. "Could I ask you one more question?"

"Of course."

Elliot gathered the photos from the desktop leaving the one of the baphomet from the apartment where the John Doe was found on top. "Forgive me if I'm being presumptuous, but your reaction to this particular photo seemed apprehensive. I'm curious as to why."

Doctor Meadows nodded. "You're very observant. If I had to guess, I'd say you are quite good at what you do."

Elliot shrugged. "All in a day's work."

"Judging from the photograph, this section of the table would face the room and, therefore, would be the point one would approach to make such a carving."

"That's correct," Elliot said. "And based on that, this pentacle is inverted, or upside down when compared to the one found in Brighid McAlister's bedroom."

"Yes, and precisely my point of concern."

"So the positioning or orientation of the symbol is important? What does it mean, being upside down?"

"That depends upon whether the person creating the symbol did it out of understanding or misunderstanding."

"If you ever consider changing your occupation," Elliot said, "I'd recommend politics."

Doctor Meadows smiled. "In pagan terms, the topmost point of the star depicted in an upward fashion represents the triumph of spirit over earthly matters. However, when the symbol is inverted, it could mean several things, the most benign being that the user is on a spiritual journey and has yet to achieve a sufficient level of enlightenment to warrant the symbol's correct position. On a little more serious note, it could also mean that the user or creator of the symbol considers earthly gratification superior to spiritual development. It is most likely due to this darker faction of paganism that the meaning of the symbol became confused as a representation of evil, and later, during the twentieth century, actually associated with Satanism."

A feeling of sickness wafted through Elliot's senses. "So you're saying I might be dealing with Satan worshipers?"

"Not necessarily. But the official symbol of Satanism is the sigil of Baphomet, a double-circled pentacle superimposed with the head of a goat, like you have here. Taken together with the other pagan symbols, I'm not sure what to make of it." Again, he checked his watch. "I do need to be going."

Elliot extended his hand. "Thank you, Doctor Meadows. You've been more than helpful, and I appreciate your time."

In the hallway outside the doctor's office, Elliot rubbed the back of his neck in an attempt to ease the tension that had settled there. He needed to find Wistrom. If the man had pagan connections, that might explain a few things.

Chapter Fifteen

In the parking lot outside the Brookwood Methodist Church, standing next to his car, Elliot placed a phone call to Patricia Orwell, Douglass Wistrom's supervisor, and asked her if she'd heard from Douglass. She had not, but he'd been lucky enough to catch her in her office, and she promised to contact him if she did. He asked her if she wouldn't mind digging up information about Wistrom's parents, then disconnected.

The temperature had warmed over the last couple of days and the snow was starting to melt, but a cold mist rode the wind, leaving a chill in the air. Elliot climbed inside the car and started the engine. A few minutes later, he answered the phone. It was Orwell. As she relayed the information he'd asked for, he jotted it down in his notes. Howard and Maud Wistrom lived in Montana. A phone call would have to do.

A man answered, and Elliot identified himself and indicated what he was after.

"A Tulsa Police Detective? Why are you calling me?"

"As I said, I need to talk to you about your son, Douglass."

"What kind of trouble has he gotten himself into?"

"It may be nothing. We just need to ask him some questions. There was a murder. It happened close to his apartment. We're questioning everyone who lives in the area."

"I still don't see why you're calling me."

"We can't locate Douglass. His apartment's empty. Do you have any idea where we might find him, where he might go if he got scared, perhaps back to Montana?"

"I don't think he'd do that. We didn't move up here until he was already out of the house."

"Are there any brothers or sisters, any other relatives in the area?"

"No. I've got a brother in Texas, and Maud has an aunt in West Virginia, but neither of them knew Doug, never met him. And we never had any children."

"I take it you're not a close family."

"Well, I guess you could say that, but mostly they just didn't agree with our decision."

"You said you never had children. I guess you meant any other children?"

"No. I meant what I said. Doug wasn't ours. He was adopted."

"That sounds a little cold."

71

"We loved Doug, like he was our own. There's no question about that. He just never returned it. He was the cold one. Maybe detached might be a better word."

"How did Douglass end up in Tulsa?"

"That's where the adoption occurred. We lived there until Doug got out of college. He stayed in Tulsa. It's his home, I guess."

Elliot heard a click, followed by a woman's voice. Maud Wistrom, he presumed. "Do you know where our Douglass is, Detective?"

"No, Mrs. Wistrom. That's why I'm calling, hoping to find out."

"Is he all right? Do we need to come and help him?"

"Only if you know where he is. How about his natural parents? Do you know how I can get in touch with them?"

"We can't help you there either." It was Mr. Wistrom again. "We never knew them, never had any contact with them."

Elliot had one more question, one that loomed at the top of the scale in importance. "Do you know if your son was ever involved with any alternative religious groups, perhaps something with a pagan influence?"

"I wouldn't think so," Mr. Wistrom said. "Quite the opposite, I'm afraid. Doug never wanted anything to do with church."

At that moment, the call was dropped. Elliot had the information he needed, so he didn't bother trying to reconnect, and as he sat alone in the parking lot, the only sound coming from the car's engine, a sick feeling formed in his stomach. This case was even more not-right than he'd earlier suspected. He could feel that just as surely as he felt the steering wheel against his hands. He kept going over the question as to why any organized religious group might go out of its way to draw attention to itself, especially in the area of murder. The obvious answer to that question was that they would not.

He slid the car into gear and pressed the accelerator. An image of Brighid McAlister sprawled across the parking lot went through his head, and he wondered if she'd been discarded after she'd served her purpose. Brighid had been involved in the death of the John Doe, of that Elliot was certain, but what kind of role she'd played he wasn't sure. There were a few McAlisters in the phone book, but none of them had claimed any knowledge of Brighid, let alone being related to her.

As Elliot guided the car through the traffic, he noticed he was heading downtown, toward the department. He called Captain Lundsford and told him he needed to search the latest victim's house again. A few minutes later, he walked out of Lundsford's office with the key and drove to the home of Brighid McAlister.

The smell of potpourri greeted Elliot as he entered the house, coupled with a renewed wash of guilt, and it seemed he intruded, entering the house to steal something, to take that which wasn't his and use it to gain knowledge of an all-too-personal nature, the names of those close to the victim. Elliot walked through the living room and the dining area, paying little attention to the antiques and rugs that decorated that part of the house, and entered the only room that seemed out of place: Brighid McAlister's bedroom.

Elliot pulled on a pair of latex gloves, well aware that the team hadn't turned up anything, no address books, no photo albums, nothing that would indicate who the victim's friends and relatives were. He wondered if someone had intentionally removed these things. It was certainly a possibility, though there had been no prints left behind. Then again, those knowing enough to remove evidence of that nature would also know not to leave evidence of their doing so.

The house was too quiet, and as Elliot began his search, he felt like someone was watching him, standing close by and peering over his shoulder. About ten minutes into the venture, when the sensation had grown unbearable, he swung around, half expecting to catch the voyeur in the act. He saw no one.

Unable to shake the feeling, Elliot went into the bathroom. The shower curtain was drawn. He edged near, then yanked it open. Again, nothing. He walked back into the bedroom and checked the closet. Moving the clothes aside, he found only that which should be there. Finally he went back into the main part of the house. The living room was empty and quiet, as were the dining room and the kitchen.

Elliot returned to the bedroom, and in a last-ditch effort he crouched and peered beneath the bed. What he saw there was not a spy or an intruder, though it was equally intriguing. He reached up and pulled an envelope from where it had been pinned to the bottom of the box spring.

Elliot stood and backed away from the bed, wondering what he had found, his curiosity heightened by the knowledge that it had been important to the victim, enough so that she would hide it. He flipped it over a couple of times, then used his small pocketknife to open the envelope.

When Elliot slid the knife back into his pocket, he saw movement from the corner of his eye. He turned and saw someone outside, scurrying away from the window, heading toward the back of the house.

Elliot scrambled from the bedroom and through the kitchen. When he reached the back door, he threw it open and stepped outside, descending the back steps to a small sidewalk. He saw no one. A small dog cowered beside the fence line. Elliot went to the north side where the window was located, but found only an empty driveway. A one-car garage sat at the end of the drive.

The only door to the garage was an overhead, and when he tested it, he found it was locked. He peered through the glass of the door. The garage held no car, only a few boxes, and Elliot could see well enough to determine that no one was inside. He crossed the backyard, stopping at the fence, a four-foot decorative barrier that he easily leaned across to check the alley, which ran behind the property. After that he walked to the south side of the house and on to the front yard. Whoever the voyeur had been, he or she was gone now.

Elliot hesitated briefly, watching his breath condensing in the cold air, then went back inside the house, where he noticed the dog door and a couple of empty bowls sitting on the floor near it. He filled one of the bowls with water, then found a bag of food on the bottom shelf of the pantry and filled the other bowl as well.

With that done, Elliot dumped the contents of the envelope he'd found onto the kitchen table: a brass lockbox key and a folded piece of notebook paper with three names written on it. The last name on the list had a large red X beside it.

Chapter Sixteen

After leaving Brighid McAlister's place, Elliot saw Sergeant Conley's patrol car sitting at a Quick Trip Store, so he pulled in. He and Conley bought a couple of sandwiches and sat in the sergeant's Chevy and ate them.

Elliot informed Conley of what he'd found and explained that he wanted to gain access to the lockbox. Conley told him to ask for Judge Miranda Broussard. Her husband had been a police officer. Judge Broussard turned out to be no pushover, but she seemed to understand Elliot's needs, and the time-sensitive nature of his request.

A few hours later, Elliot walked into the lobby of Arvest Bank. The receptionist smiled. "May I help you, sir?"

Elliot identified himself and showed her the key. "I believe this belongs to one of your lockboxes. I need to look inside it. Could you help me with that?"

The receptionist picked up the phone and spoke into it.

When the assistant manager came out of her office, the flushed look on her face told Elliot he was going to have trouble.

"What is it exactly that you want, Detective?"

Elliot kept his impatience in check and held up the key. "I need to look inside the lockbox that this key goes to. Could you open it, please?"

"But you're not the owner of the box."

He glanced at her name tag. "No, Ms. Davenport. I have a warrant. I don't need to be the owner."

"I see. Well, how did you determine that the key you have is for a box at this bank?"

Elliot held up the envelope he'd found beneath Brighid McAlister's bed, an envelope that had Arvest Bank emblazoned across it.

"Yes, well I don't know if I can do that or not, open the box that is. Can you wait until Susie gets back?"

"Who's Susie? And what does she have to do with this?"

Ms. Davenport tried to look put out, but her embarrassment showed. "Susan Taylor. She's the manager."

"When will she be back?"

Ms. Davenport checked her watch. "Well, you just missed her. It'll be an hour, maybe more."

"I can't wait that long."

Ms. Davenport stood before him, wringing her hands.

"Can you call her?"

"Oh, no, I can't do that. I'm not to bother her during lunch."

Elliot pulled his phone and flipped it open. "What's the number?"

Ms. Davenport put a hand to her forehead. "I'm not sure if I should do that."

Hearing footsteps, Elliot turned to see the receptionist coming toward him. She smiled and handed him a sticky note with a name and phone number written on it. Elliot immediately punched the number into his phone. Behind him he heard the lady say, "For heavens sake, Rhonna. He's a police officer."

When the party answered, Elliot identified himself, then said, "Sorry to bother you, Ms. Taylor, but I'm getting a little low on patience, and I need you to do something for me. There's a lockbox at your bank, and you need to either cut your lunch short and come and open it or instruct one of your employees to do it for you."

As asked, Elliot handed the phone to Ms. Davenport. Glancing at Elliot, she took the phone, then turned away. "I'm sorry. I didn't know what to do."

"I know. But this wasn't covered in our training."

She was silent for a moment, then she nodded. "Yes, Ms. Taylor."

Ms. Davenport turned back and handed Elliot the phone. He flipped it shut and stuck it in his pocket.

"I'm sorry," she said. I've just never had to deal with anything like this before."

"I understand. Could we please proceed?"

"Of course, as soon as I can determine which box your key goes to."

Again the receptionist appeared. Elliot was beginning to believe that the wrong employee had received the promotion. The lady handed Ms. Davenport another key and another sticky note. "I figured you could use a little help. I looked it up for you." She paused then added, "Everything's going to be all right, Rhonna. All you have to do is unlock a box for the detective."

The two women stared at each other briefly, then the receptionist went back to her post.

Ms. Davenport asked Elliot to follow her. About halfway down the east wall, she opened a black gate made of steel, and she and Elliot entered a long, narrow room where small brown metal drawers filled three of the walls. Ms. Davenport searched along the north wall until she found the correct number, then put her key into the slot and turned to Elliot, waiting for him to do the same.

Elliot slid his key into the lock, but before he opened it, and before Ms. Davenport could leave to give him privacy, he said, "I want you to remain in the room as a witness to the contents of the box. You will need to prepare an inventory, which should be signed and notarized. In fact, it would be a good idea if you would ask one of your coworkers to come and act as an additional witness."

As soon as the efficient receptionist came into the room, Elliot turned the key and pulled the lockbox from the wall, then carried it to a table placed there for that purpose. With both bank employees watching, Elliot opened the lid to the box. Inside, arranged neatly as if in a small filing cabinet, were three brown envelopes, which had names and addresses written on them. The names corresponded with the ones on the list Elliot had found along with the key.

Elliot grabbed the envelope labeled "Zachariah Holsted," the only name on the list that had a red X beside it, and carefully unhooked the metal clasp that held it shut. When he removed the contents, three 5x7 photographs, and spread them across the table, Rhonna Davenport gasped.

The photographs, which had been taken from different angles, allowing the faces of the subjects to be in full view and easily identifiable, depicted a couple engaged in bizarre sex acts. The female was Brighid McAlister. Her partner, Elliot suspected, was Zachariah Holsted.

Brighid McAlister was running a blackmailing scheme.

Elliot climbed the slight incline of the drive to the Holsted property, following a hazy blue light that crackled from the open doors of a metal building crammed into the yard behind the house. Entering the shop, he saw a man leaning over a motorcycle frame.

He approached the suspect. No one else was around, and when he drew near, the man turned off the torch and raised the face shield of his welding helmet. He wore a denim jacket and greasy denim jeans.

"Something I can do for you, mister?"

Elliot recognized him as the man in the photo with Brighid. "Are you Zachariah Holsted?"

He took off his gloves and removed the welding helmet, placing them on a workbench. "Who wants to know?"

When Elliot showed his badge, a look of fear flashed across the man's face. "I need to ask you a few questions."

"About what?"

"Do you know Brighid McAlister?"

"Yeah, I know her. So what?" A belligerent tone crept into his voice.

"When was the last time you saw her?"

The man used one of his hands to push his greasy hair away from his face. "I don't know. It's been a while."

Elliot decided to go ahead with the big question, just to see the man's reaction. "If you had to, could you account for your whereabouts on Monday, January sixth from 10:00 a.m. to noon?"

"Hell, I don't know. What's this about?"

"Brighid McAlister is dead, Mr. Holsted. Do you know anything about that?"

"Jesus H. Christ. No. Hell no."

Elliot watched a bead of sweat run down Holsted's face. "Then you need to think about where you were during the time period that I asked you about. It's important."

The suspect shook his head. "I'm not good with stuff like that. I need some time to think."

"Do you own any firearms, Mr. Holsted?" Elliot already had a warrant. As soon as he'd seen the photographs, he'd called Judge Miranda Broussard again, explaining what he'd found and what he needed.

"Well, what do you think?"

"Just answer the question."

"Hell yes, I've got firearms. Who doesn't?"

Elliot pulled the paperwork from his jacket pocket. "I have a warrant to search the premises, Mr. Holsted. Could you show me the guns, please?"

Mr. Holsted dragged his hand through his hair again. "Ah, Jesus. You got the wrong guy, Detective. It doesn't surprise me none that somebody killed her, but it wasn't me. Whatever gave you a crazy idea like that?"

Elliot put the warrant back in his pocket. "Oh, I don't know. Maybe it was the explicit photos of you and Brighid in bed together. I did my homework, Mr. Holsted. Brighid McAlister was blackmailing you, or at least she was trying to. That gives you a pretty good motive to kill her, wouldn't you say?"

The suspect buried his face in his hands for a moment, then pulled them away and tried to regain his composure. "All right, Detective, I'll cooperate. But let me explain something to you. I got me a good thing going here. I got a good wife and a baby daughter. I don't want that messed up."

"Maybe you should have thought of that before you jumped in bed with a prostitute."

"Ah, come on. What are you, some kind of saint or something, ain't never done nothing like that before?"

For a moment, Elliot was lost in thought. Zachariah Holsted's question had taken him back to his high school days, and Marcia Barnes's long blonde hair falling across his chest. It was a moment he would live to regret. Marcia wasn't the one he was supposed to be with that night, and this had hurt someone he cared deeply about. "All right, Mr. Holsted. I'll do what I can. But this is a murder investigation. I can't promise it won't come out."

A hint of a smile crossed Holsted's lips. "Fair enough."

The suspect led Elliot into the house through a door that opened into the kitchen. Unlike the shop area, the house was immaculately clean and uncluttered, everything in its place, the result, no doubt, of Mrs. Holsted's efforts. As soon as they were inside, Holsted called out. "Hey, baby."

Within seconds she appeared, a short and slightly overweight blonde wearing a miniskirt and a T-shirt that were about two sizes too small for her. Her skin was fair, almost translucent. Elliot guessed she was about nineteen, five or six years younger than Holsted. She tried to smile, but her husband squinted his eyes and shook his head. "What's going on, Zach?"

Holsted went to her, putting his arm around her. "Just a little trouble, baby. But don't you worry. I'll get it cleared up. This here's a police detective. He wants to look around a little bit. It'll be all right."

"What do you mean look around? Look around for what?"

Elliot took the opportunity to introduce himself. He stepped forward and extended his hand. She timidly took it, her embrace soft and warm. "Detective Kenny Elliot, ma'am."

Her name was Courtney, and Elliot wanted to ask her how and why she'd hooked up with such a man as Zachariah Holsted, but he remembered Dombrowski's lectures about professionalism and managed to restrain himself. "I apologize for the inconvenience," he said. "But I'm conducting a murder investigation. I just need to look around, maybe ask a few questions."

Courtney Holsted's face lost what little color it had, and she turned to her husband. "Murder? What does this have to do with us?"

"Hopefully nothing," Elliot said. "Does the name Brighid McAlister mean anything to you?"

Zachariah's jaw twitched, and Courtney looked equally nervous. As she stared at her husband, he vigorously shook his head. "No," she said. "Should it?"

"I don't know. But I'm here to find out."

Elliot questioned Zachariah and Courtney for a few minutes, then asked to be shown around. In the living room, he noticed a brochure to some church called Open Arms Unitarian, or something of the sort.

While Courtney looked after the baby, a cute and chubby three-year-old with curly brown hair, Mr. Holsted led Elliot into the master bedroom, where a gun cabinet sat in the northwest corner. He unlocked it, then stepped aside to allow Elliot access.

Inside the cabinet, Elliot saw one rifle and one shotgun, both weapons standing upright in the rack. With a small flashlight he pulled from his coat he leaned forward and searched inside the cabinet, checking the floor and the walls. After that he pulled out a long, narrow drawer located halfway between the glass doors and the base. It contained gun-cleaning equipment. "Do you own any handguns?"

Holsted shrugged. "What would a deer hunter need with a handgun?"

"You tell me."

Holsted frowned. "Ah, Christ. You're going to find out anyway." He went to a nightstand beside the bed and slid out a drawer, from which he pulled an old army-issued .45 caliber. Handing it to Elliot, he said, "It ain't registered, but it's mine. I bought it at a gun show a few years back. Hell, it ain't even loaded. The wife won't let me with the baby around."

Elliot pretended to be interested, performing an inspection of the weapon, then handed it back to the suspect. It wasn't the weapon that killed Brighid McAlister. It was the wrong caliber. "Do you own any others?" Elliot asked.

Holsted shook his head. "That's all I got. Hell, you got the warrant. Look around for yourself. But you ain't going to find nothing."

The search of the house and the shop out back turned out just like Mr. Holsted predicted, no evidence found. Later, with the search completed, Elliot walked over to the workbench where Zachariah Holsted was standing, and it was then that the suspect removed, for the first time since their meeting, the jacket that he wore, exposing his inked-up arms. One symbol in particular, a star with a circle around it, caught Elliot's attention. "Interesting tattoo," he said. "What does it mean?"

Holsted glanced at Elliot, a puzzled look crawling across his face, as if Elliot had asked about something he shouldn't be privy to. "Hell if

I know. I drink a little now and then. Sometimes I get a little carried away, wake up in strange places, or with a new one of these carved into my skin." He shook his head. "It don't mean nothing."

"It's called a pentacle," Elliot said. "And it can mean quite a lot, especially with it being upside down like that. But you already knew that, didn't you?"

Holsted didn't answer the question. Instead he motioned for Elliot to follow him as he went to the east end of the workbench. Grinning, he tapped the page of a calendar that hung on the wall there. "Come to think about it, I do remember where I was yesterday morning, at Cymry's Bar for Drifter John's birthday. I got plastered, if you know what I mean. My missy was there too. Go ask her. She'll tell you."

"Was there anyone else there who could confirm your story?"

Zachariah Holsted smiled and said, "Hell yes, there was people there, lots of them."

"I'll need a list of names."

"Sure thing," Zachariah said. "No problem." Then his face grew serious. "There's something else I need to tell you, Detective. Since you're going to be poking around at Cymry's you'll find out anyway, so you might as well hear it from me."

Elliot nodded. "Go on."

"Brighid McAlister hangs out there, or at least she used to."

Chapter Seventeen

Elliot sat in his car in front of Zachariah Holsted's house, staring at his cell phone. So far, Holsted's alibi was checking out. Then again, he suspected Holsted's friends wouldn't think twice about lying for him. His alibi and the lack of a murder weapon would keep him out of jail for now, but Elliot wasn't through with him.

Elliot had plenty of information to sort through, though the details of the case weren't the only things going through his mind. He thought of Holsted's wife, Courtney, especially the way her eyes tilted when she smiled. The unsettling thoughts caused him to realize their true source. It was Cyndi Bannister. He'd purposely left the note with her number on it at home, though as he thought of her the sequence played through his head, as clearly as if he held the note in his hand. He knew without a doubt that he shouldn't do what he was contemplating, knew it all the way to his bones, yet his fingers crawled across the cell phone, keying in the numbers that would connect him with her.

When Cyndi answered, Elliot's words caught in his throat. What was he thinking? She was Cunningham's girl. Finally, in the discomfort of the silence, she spoke again. "You shouldn't be calling me."

All Elliot could manage was, "You're right."

"What do you want?"

Elliot thought of the sensuous way she'd drunk from his beer and how it might feel to touch her, but what he said was, "How about dinner?"

"Why?"

"Because I'm hungry."

"That's a stupid answer."

Elliot dried his hands on his pant leg. He felt like a teenager who'd conjured up the nerve to call a popular cheerleader. "Actually it was a stupid question."

"I told you to leave me alone."

"Really? I must have missed that part. How does six o'clock sound?"

"Sounds like you're serious about this."

Elliot fought the urge to give in and tell her just how much he wanted her. "I'd like to be."

The phone went silent for a moment, and he almost thought she'd hung up on him. Then she huffed. "You don't even know where I live."

"I'm pretty good at finding out things like that."

"You'd never get past the guard."

Elliot wasn't sure what she meant by that. "Oh, I don't know. I have good credentials."

"I'll meet you."

"Where?" Elliot asked.

"Where are you?"

He told Cyndi his location, and she suggested meeting at a convenience store at 21st and Harvard. He wasn't sure she would show up, but he hoped that she would. Elliot smiled and punched the END button on the phone. He started the car and pulled away from the Holsted house.

A few minutes later, he saw the cab coming up Harvard Avenue and knew even before the cabbie wheeled into the lot and stopped that it was Cyndi. With a slow fluid movement, she stepped from the cab and started toward him. She wore tight blue jeans and a black leather jacket with a wool scarf of red draped around the collar. Elliot climbed out and met her halfway.

He embraced her, brushing her cheek with a kiss, and during their brief touch the scent of her perfume drove his desire, though his guilt over the clandestine meeting worked to keep it in check. When he released her, her eyes shone with the same curiosity that filled him. Once at the car, Elliot opened the door for Cyndi, then went around to his side and climbed in. "What are you in the mood for?" He realized too late that the question might be construed as loaded. He didn't think he intended it that way, though in his present state of confusion he wasn't totally sure.

"How about a sandwich at the Knotty Pine?"

Elliot knew the place, an old barbeque joint on the west side of town. It didn't fit. He'd expected a classy restaurant. Was she mocking him? "You've got to be kidding."

"Not at all. My dad used to take me there. It's been years since I've had one. But if you'd rather not."

He shrugged. "Sounds good."

Elliot turned north on Harvard, and when he reached 3rd Street he headed west. "Where are you from?" he asked.

She shot a quick glance in his direction then looked away, but before she could answer, Elliot's phone rang. Flipping it open, he brought it to his ear. "That you, Elliot?" It was Donald Carter from the medical examiner's office. "Yeah," Elliot said, mouthing *sorry* as he looked at Cyndi. He could hear Donald Carter eating. It seemed he was always eating. "What's up?"

"Maybe you should take up horse racing," Carter said.

"What are you getting at?"

"Looks like you were right. I thought you were wasting your time, chasing after that hooker. I wouldn't have given a nickel for your chances of tying her to the John Doe."

Elliot came to a stop at a traffic light and brought the phone closer to his ear. "What have you got?"

"Oh, not much, just a little old drug that might give you the connection you're looking for. Flunitrazepam, a benzodiazepine, works on the nervous system. Like Valium only a lot stronger. Both the john and the hooker had traces of it in their systems."

When the light turned green, Elliot drove forward. "Could you put that in layman's terms?"

"You probably know it as Rohypnol."

Glancing at Cyndi, Elliot said, "A date rape drug?"

Cyndi shifted in her seat with such force that Elliot realized he'd frightened her. He covered the phone and said, "Sorry. Just a little cop business. It shouldn't take long."

She edged closer to the passenger door.

Turning his attention back to the phone, Elliot heard Carter say, "Yeah, it's just too bizarre not to mean something. I mean what would a hooker, or her john for that matter, need with something like that?"

"Good point. I owe you one."

Elliot started to tuck the phone away but when he saw the fear in Cyndi's eyes, he paused. "This stuff would scare anyone. You shouldn't have to hear it. I'll turn the phone off if you want me to."

"You don't have to do that. If you turn it off, I'll end up sharing your attention with your worry over missed calls."

A smile turned the corners of Elliot's mouth. "Not a chance. And by the way, you look lovely tonight."

She smiled and scooted closer, away from the door. "So do you."

Elliot's smile turned into a laugh, but the cause of his joy went deeper than her calling him lovely, too, for at that moment he knew that the rapport he'd experienced on their first meeting had been genuine. Cyndi had already begun to fill the empty spot inside of him, and her eyes and her body language and her words told Elliot that she felt something as well. He'd waited a long time for someone like this to come along, and now that she had, he hoped she was as attracted to him as he was to her.

As Elliot drove, he saw something that cut through his state of euphoria—a sign that read CYMRY'S. It was the place Zachariah Holsted had told him about, the club Brighid McAlister had frequented.

The one-story building, constructed of rock stacked narrow side out, like brick, stood on the outskirts of town. He glanced at Cyndi, and she gave him a radiant smile. He knew the place would still be there tomorrow. But the detective in him argued he needed to check it out tonight. He slowed the car and pulled in.

Cyndi stared at him, a look of disappointment covering her face. "Why are we stopping here?"

Elliot opened the car door, but paused before stepping out. "I need to follow up on something. It'll only take a moment. I promise."

Cyndi looked dubious. "What kind of place is this?"

Elliot thought of Holsted, and his comments about Brighid. "I'm not sure."

"And you actually mean to go in there?"

"I was planning on it."

"Are you insane?"

Elliot gripped the wheel. It was a bad area. She had a right to be upset. But this was important. He might turn up something that'd help the investigation. "Maybe."

Cyndi shook her head. "I hope you don't expect me to go with you."

"Why, don't you like it?" Elliot asked, winking. But he wouldn't dream of dragging her into such a dive.

"Oh, I don't know," Cyndi said, joining in on the humor. "Maybe it's the car over there with blocks under it instead of wheels, or the collection of broken beer bottles paving the parking lot. Take your pick. Why don't we just forget about this?"

To comfort her, he grinned and joked, "I've been thrown out of worse places."

Cyndi slid across the seat and put her hand on Elliot's arm, her eyes turning the color of gray smoke. "Seriously, Kenny. I don't like this. Why don't we just go?"

"Just give me one minute," Elliot said. "It has to do with the case I'm working on, a solid lead. I need to check it out."

"Then why don't you come back in the daytime, and bring some help with you, another officer."

Elliot opened the door and stepped out. "I always work alone. It's better that way. The keys are in the ignition. Lock the doors after I'm out. If anything happens, honk the horn. It'll be all right."

Cyndi shook her head. "If I can't talk you out of it, then promise you'll make sure the safety's off your gun, and keep it handy."

Elliot stared at Cyndi for a moment, surprised that she would think of such a thing. He was way ahead of her on that move, but he slid his hand inside his coat anyway, and pulled the Glock free, acting as if he'd just now complied with her wishes. "If it'll make you feel better."

"I'll honk the horn all right. But if you're not out here by the end of the second blast, don't be surprised if you find your car missing when you do get here." Her tone said she wasn't kidding anymore.

Elliot winked at her then turned away. Once he was at the entrance, he pushed open the door and stepped inside.

The door closed behind Elliot, and when his eyes adjusted to the dimly lit room, he got a bit of a shock. He'd expected dirty floors and run-down furniture. In contrast to its location and ramshackle building, the bar's interior was clean, the booths that lined the walls and a couple of tables with chairs in the center of the room of high quality.

Elliot made his way to the bar, a polished mahogany antique that ran along the back wall, noticing, in addition to the wide assortment of European and domestic beers, a food menu, limited to Irish stew and corned beef with cabbage. He waited for the heavyset bartender, who had his back to him, to finish whatever task he was involved in and turn around. A few moments later, when Elliot decided the man wasn't going to acknowledge his presence, he said, "Excuse me."

The man didn't answer.

Elliot slapped the counter, a little harder than he should have. "I don't appreciate being ignored, sir."

After a second or two, the bartender turned around, a rag in his hand.

Elliot showed his badge. "Detective Elliot. I need to ask you some questions."

The bartender's gaze darted to a strange painting on the floor. He glared at Elliot. "Charles Miller. They call me Snub. What kind of questions?"

"What do you know about Brighid McAlister?"

"She's dead. Saw it in the paper." He shook his head. "I knew this was going to be trouble, figured you guys'd be coming around before long."

"Looks like I'm in the right place, then. What can you tell me about Brighid?"

"There ain't much I can tell you, except she hung around here now and then."

"Looking for business?"

He gave a noncommittal grunt and wiped at the spotless bar.

Elliot pulled out his notepad and flipped it open. "Was she here the evening of January third?"

"She could have been. She'd show up two or three times a week for a while, then sometimes she wouldn't, kind of sporadic."

Elliot pulled out the photograph of the John Doe's face and placed it on the bar. "How about this guy?"

The bartender leaned over and examined the photo. "Can't say for sure. This is a busy place." He grabbed a couple of empty mugs from the counter, dunked them first in one sink and then another and placed them upside down on a rack. He nodded toward the photo. "Dude looks funny. What's wrong with him?"

Elliot studied the bartender for a moment. He seemed a bit nervous, but not overly so. "He's dead. He was dressed in business clothes when we found him. My guess is he would've been wearing the same thing when he came in, would've looked out of place."

The bartender took another look. "Now that you mention it, there was someone like that." Picking up the photo, he nodded. "Yeah, I think this is the guy." Glancing at Elliot, he shrugged. "The thing about the clothes, it jogged my memory. Yeah, he was here all right. Said he was looking for someone."

"Did he give a name?"

The bartender shrugged. "Just said he was supposed to meet someone here."

"Could it have been Brighid McAlister?"

"No, but now that I think about it she and the dude there hit it off. They had a few drinks. They left together."

Elliot picked up the photo and put it away. Snub's selective memory concerned him. "Did the person he was looking for ever show up?"

"Not that I know of." Pausing, he tapped his fingers against the countertop. "It's coming back to me now. Seems like the dude said he was some kind of journalist, a newspaper reporter or something."

Elliot made a note of that. "What time did he and Brighid leave the bar?"

"It was early. Things hadn't picked up yet. Around seven. Do you think Brighid had something to do with it?"

"Something to do with what?"

"You said the dude was dead."

"It's possible," Elliot said.

The bartender wiped the counter again. "It's hard to believe. I mean, Brighid was a pretty straight-up gal for a hooker. I guess it just goes to show you. You never know about people."

"Yeah," Elliot said. "Which reminds me, were you here all night that evening?"

"That's right. Closed the place up."

"You never left?"

"Nope."

Elliot put his notepad away, and he was about to ask another question when a brutal noise blasted through the bar.

The car horn.

Cyndi.

Elliot pulled the Glock from its holster and sprinted for the door. When he reached it, he yanked it open and flattened himself against it, weapon raised. The parking lot, except for his car, was empty.

He searched the lot as he made his way to the car. If the attacker was fleeing, it was impossible to hear over the strident blaring of the horn. As he drew near the car, he saw Cyndi slumped over the steering wheel, and his heart fell about three inches in his chest.

She was alone in the front seat. Elliot pressed his face against the glass of the rear door. Nothing. He holstered the weapon then tapped on the glass. As Cyndi raised her head, relief flooded Elliot, but it was quickly negated by the fear in her eyes. Regret tore through him. What had he been thinking, leaving her alone in a place like this? Dazed and confused, Cyndi sat motionless for a moment. Again, Elliot tapped on the glass. This time she unlocked the door and slid over to the passenger side.

Elliot climbed in beside her. "What happened?" She fell into his arms, and as he drew her trembling body close, he felt lousy, personally responsible for her pain. "Sorry. I should've known better, leaving you alone like that."

Finally, she raised her head and reached up to his face. "I'm okay."

Slick moisture touched his cheek. "No you're not," Elliot said, taking her right hand into his. One fingernail had been ripped off, and a droplet of blood welled bright red.

Panic once again contorted her face, and she jerked her hand away. "Oh, no."

Elliot gently pulled her hand back and examined it. "It's not as bad as it looks. I'll bandage it for you, and you can tell me what happened."

He leaned over and opened the glove compartment, where he kept a package of adhesive bandages. Removing the paper from one, he wrapped it around the injured finger. "There," he said, "that should do it." She didn't pull her hand away.

"I don't know where he came from," she said. "I looked out the window and there he was, just staring at me, and grinning, as if he'd been there all along. I couldn't move. I couldn't even scream."

"You were frightened. It happens."

She nodded. "He yanked on the doors like some lunatic, but I'd locked them like you said. When that didn't work, he started banging on the windows. I've never been so scared."

Again Elliot told her he was sorry, though he suspected the words fell far short of what he wanted from them. "I shouldn't have brought you here. I guess I've forgotten how to worry about anyone other than myself."

A sad look crossed Cyndi's face, as if Elliot's last words had touched her in a way the ones before them had not. She leaned close and kissed him lightly on the cheek. "Don't say that, Kenny. It's just not true."

Elliot wasn't sure how she would know, but the sincere nature of her words was enough. "What happened after that?"

Cyndi hesitated. "You're not going to like this part. I thought it was over, but he picked up something from the ground, a piece of beer bottle I think." She started to cry again. "He scratched the hood of the car. The sound of it made my skin crawl. I'm surprised you didn't hear it. Anyway, that's when I got the nerve to honk the horn. He ran off after that, and I guess it finally hit me, and I panicked." She gestured to the hood with her bandaged finger.

Elliot looked through the windshield and saw the damage. He scrambled out of the car, and when he saw what had been scratched into the paint, an assortment of emotions ran through him, most of it anger. "Lock the doors again. I won't be long." He stormed back into the bar.

The bartender took one look at him and headed for a back exit. Elliot caught him just before he reached it. Snub acted surprised. "I told you everything I know. What gives?"

"Yeah, well, I thought of something else I wanted to ask you about." Elliot guided the big man outside, stopping in front of the car.

His eyes widened when he saw the symbol. "What's that?"

"You tell me."

"Hey, I had nothing to do with this."

Elliot grabbed him by the collar and shoved him toward the hood of the car. Snub caught himself with both hands, his nose about an inch above the symbol scratched into the paint. "Take a closer look," Elliot said. "It bears an uncanny resemblance to the artwork slopped across the floor of your bar."

"There's such a thing as police brutality, you know."

Elliot tightened his grip. "Is that right? Well someone crossed the line, sport. This is personal now, and I don't care much about anything except for finding out who messed with my car and scared my date. Tell me and I'll go easy. Otherwise, it's going to be a long night."

"I don't know. I swear."

Elliot slammed the guy onto the hood of the car. "I don't believe you."

A hand gripped his arm from behind. Considering his awkward position and the proximity of his attacker, the only thing he could do was let go of the bartender and spin around and face whoever was behind him, but before he could, a soft voice stopped him.

"No, Kenny. This isn't the way."

It was Cyndi.

Snub scrambled to his feet. "Honest man. I don't know anything about this. But I'll put the word out. I don't like this any more than you do. It's bad for business."

"That's funny," Elliot said. "I thought it was your business."

The bartender straightened his clothes. "What's that supposed to mean?"

"I don't know. You're the one who decorates with pagan symbols."

Snub looked shocked for a moment, then he said, "If you understood anything about paganism, you'd know about karma. You know, what goes around comes around." He gestured toward the car. "We don't do this kind of stuff. Besides, the symbol in the bar is a pentacle." He shook his head. "This is some kind of Satanic thing, not pagan at all."

"Maybe not," Elliot said. "But some people preach one thing and do another." He leaned over and ran his hand across the hood of the car, feeling the roughness of the paint where it had been disturbed. "And those that do so lean that way not because of a lack of knowledge, but an accumulation of it." He traced the inverted star with his finger. "You might say their perceptions of the world are out of kilter, upside down if you will."

The bartender's face went blank, and he was silent for a moment. "I don't know who messed up your car, Detective. That's all I'm saying."

Elliot took a step toward him, but again Cyndi stopped him. "Come on, Kenny. Let's just go."

Elliot handed the bartender one of his business cards. "Let me know if you hear anything, about this or the dead guy in the picture."

Cyndi was already in the car. Elliot sank in beside her.

After leaving Cymry's, Elliot offered to take Cyndi home, apologizing and offering to make it up to her, but she said it was okay and reminded him that he still owed her dinner. Perhaps the gesture was as inconsequential as Cyndi trying to salvage the evening, but Elliot hoped it was of more significance than that.

Inside the Knotty Pine, Cyndi walked across the room and chose a table along the wall. Elliot sat across from her. He watched as she ran her fingers through her hair, an act that would have pushed it back had it been long and straight, but in its short and curly state the action just fluffed it. In the smoky atmosphere of the dimly lit barbeque joint, she looked as if she'd just stepped off a movie set, the leading lady in an old Alfred Hitchcock film.

"What are we doing?" Cyndi asked after they'd ordered. "We both know it's a bad idea, being together like this."

"It's completely by design," Elliot said, "motivated by my dark agenda."

"Which is?"

Elliot smiled. "I want to get to know you."

"Why would you want to do that?"

The waitress came over and set their order, a couple of chopped beef sandwiches on the table, along with a jug of beer, and Elliot waited until she'd left. "You stir something inside of me," Elliot said, though after getting the words out he couldn't believe he'd said them. "Old feelings that I haven't felt in a while."

Small barrel-shaped beer mugs sat on the table. Cyndi carefully filled the one closest to her. "In a while? That would suggest there have been others who captured your attention before. How many *befores* have there been?"

Elliot took the pickled banana pepper from his plate and bit into it, grabbing a napkin as the juice squirted out. He wiped his mouth then took a swallow of beer. "There have been a few," he said. "But only one like you."

"So who was she? Or should I ask, who is she?"

Elliot finished off the pepper. "It was a long time ago. High school."

She raised her eyebrows. "What's a guy like you been doing for entertainment all this time?"

Elliot had spent a lot of that time trying to anesthetize the memories he'd just dragged up. The wise thing would've been to forget the whole thing, put it behind him and go on with his life, but he had not been able to do that. He took another drink of beer, wanting the cold liquid to lessen the sting of the pepper's heat, but hoping at the same time that it would not extinguish it entirely. It was, after all, why he indulged in such culinary delights, and why women like Cyndi tantalized him. "The usual things."

A hint of a smile touched her lips. "You climbed out of that one nicely. So who was she?"

With that Elliot let the memories run free. "Her name was Carmen."

Cyndi put down her sandwich. "That sounded rather final. What did you do, get rid of her?"

With Cyndi's question running through him like an accusation, Elliot wiped his mouth again then folded the napkin. The old doubts and wounds still ran close to the surface.

Cyndi reached across the table and stroked his arm. "It's okay if you don't want to talk about it. So I remind you of someone. That's not exactly what a girl wants to hear, but it doesn't bother me that much. Anyway, she must have been pretty special."

Elliot looked at the woman with the smoke-colored eyes who sat across from him, her delicate features, the faint smattering of freckles on her face. "You're nothing like her," he said. "And you don't remind me of her at all."

"Then why did you bring her up?"

Elliot took a sip of beer. He wasn't sure, exactly, who had led the conversation in the direction it had gone, but since the subject was now on the table he decided to address it. "It's the way you make me feel."

Again Elliot could not believe what he'd said, for if fear could be underpinned with seduction, then that was the look that came over Cyndi's face.

She ran her fingers through her hair. "And how do I make you feel?"

Elliot picked up his sandwich. "Hungry."

The non-answer made her smile. "This could be a dangerous relationship. We wouldn't want you to become overweight."

"No," Elliot said. "People from my neck of the woods live a lot longer if they stay in shape. That reminds me. You never answered my question."

"What do you mean?"

"Earlier in the car, I asked you where you're from."

She shrugged. "Right around here. Tulsa, I mean. Listen, I have to go."

Cyndi opened her purse and pulled out her phone.

Elliot could tell by the conversation that she was calling for a taxi. "You don't have to do that. I can take you home."

She shook her head. "Maybe some other time."

"Why do I get the feeling you don't want me to know where you live?"

"Maybe I don't."

A few silent minutes later, a man came into the restaurant, stopping at the door. Cyndi got up from the table. "My ride," she said.

Elliot signaled to the waitress that he'd be back, and he followed Cyndi outside to the parking lot, where a taxi was parked. The cabbie opened the back door, but before Cyndi could get in, Elliot gently wrapped his fingers around her arm, just above the elbow. "Will I see you again?"

"That depends," she said. And she rose up on her toes and kissed him, not a heavy kiss but a touching of their lips that left Elliot near drunk with passion. Then she climbed into the cab and closed the door. Elliot watched until the taxi was out of sight, then he went back inside and settled the bill with the restaurant.

Chapter Eighteen

Elliot had been tired when he'd left the restaurant, and he was halfway home when his sense of duty kicked in, telling him he should go to the office and catch up on the work he had there. He enlisted the help of the tar-like brew that passed for coffee in the department. An image of Cyndi staring at him through the window of the taxi still haunted his thoughts while he clicked on the icon that took him to his e-mail. Among the unread messages, one stood out with the label NO IDENTITY.

Probably spam. He sipped his coffee and opened the e-mail to make sure he wasn't going to delete something important.

Sorry about your paint job, but I had to get your attention. I hope you got the point, otherwise my artistic medium might have to get a little closer to your heart, or should I say your flesh. I could have taken your girlfriend tonight, but that wouldn't have been very sporting of me. Let the John Doe rest in peace, Elliot. Don't make me tell you twice.

Elliot read the message over and over. On his fourth time through, with the disturbing content still filtering through him, he felt the pressure of someone's hand gripping his shoulder. He jumped up from the chair and spun around, only to find himself staring into the face of Michael Cunningham.

Cunningham didn't look happy. In fact, Elliot had never before run into him late at the office—whatever was bothering him had to be serious. "What's up?" Elliot asked.

Cunningham took a while to answer. "I need to have a word with you."

Elliot had once stolen a bicycle, a crime he could've easily gotten away with, but he'd felt so bad about it that not only did he return the bike, he also spent half a day repairing it before taking it back. The feelings that now ran through him were not dissimilar. To make matters worse, the congenial Detective Cunningham, whom everyone liked, had taken an adversarial stance. "What's on your mind?" Elliot asked.

"You know damned well what's on my mind."

Cunningham was right. Elliot knew what was bothering him, and being the one dating the man's girlfriend sent a surge of guilt through him that couldn't be undone by giving her back. Nor could he convince himself, now that he'd started to get to know her, that she would prefer to be with Cunningham. Had Cyndi, feeling as bad as Elliot did about the rendezvous, spoken to Cunningham about it? Perhaps it was nothing more than pure instinct on Cunningham's part. "Why don't you enlighten me?" Elliot asked, feeling worse than ever.

Cunningham's cheeks reddened. "She means a lot to me."

"I can understand that."

Cunningham glanced away, looking at his feet for a moment before bringing his eyes back to Elliot. "Then understand this. She's my girl, Elliot. My girl."

"Isn't it her decision too?"

He nodded. "You've been dating her, haven't you?"

Elliot thought about that for a moment. "We had dinner."

Cunningham squared his stance. "You stay away from her, Elliot. Completely away."

He stabbed a finger into Elliot's chest. Elliot grabbed Cunningham's hand, pulling it away and down to his side. His other hand balled into a fist. Elliot didn't want this to get ugly. Still restraining Cunningham's hand, he brought it back up across his adversary's chest and backed him into the filing cabinet. "You don't want to do this, Cunningham."

Cunningham tried to free himself, but Elliot held firm, increasing the pressure until the cabinet threatened to tip over. "Come on, buddy. Take it easy. We're both adults. We can find a more amiable solution to our problem."

"You're the problem," Cunningham said. "And there's only one solution. You need to back off and stay away from Cyndi."

Elliot relaxed his grip. "I don't know if I can do that."

It wasn't what Cunningham wanted to hear. He jerked his right leg up against the cabinet and lunged toward Elliot. His ploy was only marginally successful, but it was enough for him to wrench himself free from Elliot's grip.

He didn't waste any time. He threw a right cross. Elliot ducked under it, then came back up. He could've had Cunningham clean, but he used his forearm instead of his fist and again shoved him into the cabinet, this time with more authority, wedging his arm against Cunningham's throat, driving him upward.

The look on Cunningham's face said he was furious, but it also showed that he was beginning to understand that his current tactics were not going to work.

"I don't want to fight you, Michael."

"You should have thought of that before you—"

Cunningham's gaze hardened and focused over Elliot's shoulder.

"Is there a problem here, boys?"

It was Captain Harry Lundsford.

Elliot released Cunningham and stepped away. "No, sir. Just a little overzealous horseplay. Sorry if we disturbed you. It won't happen again."

Captain Lundsford looked skeptical, but he nodded and continued down the walkway between the cubicles. As soon as the captain disappeared into his office, Elliot gathered his things and started for the elevator.

Behind him, Cunningham said, "This isn't over, Elliot."

After leaving the department, Elliot stopped at a grocery store and picked up a few cans of dog food, then drove to Brighid McAlister's house. He'd been giving it some thought and he'd decided he didn't want Brighid's dog to end up in the animal shelter, or perhaps suffer an even worse fate on the streets of Tulsa. Those who worked for animal control had good intentions, but it didn't always pan out for the animals. Rather than requesting the key and explaining what he intended to do, he'd simply coax the dog outside.

Elliot parked the car just down from Brighid's house, then got out and made his way to the back of the house. Not wanting to attract attention to himself, he didn't use a flashlight and he stumbled a few times before reaching the back door. However, as soon as he popped the top on one of the cans of food and waved it around a few times beside the pet door, the little fellow came wiggling out. As if he'd been waiting for Elliot to come for him, the dog took the time to frolic around, greeting Elliot by licking his hands before jumping on the food. He was young, less than a year old, Elliot suspected.

He waited for the dog to finish the food, then scooped him up and went back to the car. After placing the puppy on the passenger seat where he could keep an eye on him, he started the car and drove home to Broken Arrow.

Once there, Elliot fashioned a makeshift bed from a cardboard box, throwing some old towels in the bottom for comfort. As soon as he put a bowl of water beside the box, the dog appeared to understand it was his and hopped in. Elliot considered the long-unused dog door for a moment, then unlocked the small flap, pushing it open a few times to show the dog it was there. The dog was familiar with such things, having used one at his old house, and Elliot's backyard was fenced.

The room where he'd put the puppy was the rather large area designed to function as a breakfast nook. A dimmer switch controlled the light, a chandelier that hung low over the table. Elliot set the light to a low setting, then took a shower and went to bed.

The next morning, he sat at the breakfast table, sipping a cup of coffee and marveling over how quickly the dog was adapting—other than demonstrating a slight propensity to bark at odd hours—when the doorbell rang. Elliot put down his coffee and answered the door. He found Joey Anderson and his mother standing on the porch.

Joey held his clenched hands in front of him, and he looked as if he might jump over the threshold. "Can I see him, Mr. Elliot?"

The look on Kelly Anderson's face said it all. "It's the dog. He kept us up half the night."

Elliot glanced at the Glock sticking out of his shoulder holster, then grabbed his sport jacket from the coatrack and put it on. "Sorry. I just picked him up last night." The dog stood between Elliot's legs. "He was sort of homeless."

Kelly Anderson's face softened. "He has quite a bark. What kind of dog is he?"

Elliot picked up the pup and handed him to Joey. It just seemed like the thing to do. Eying the dog's build and coat, he stepped aside. "Mostly beagle, I think. Would you like to come in?"

Kelly shook her head. "We won't keep you. But do try to keep . . . What's his name, anyway?"

Elliot looked at Joey. The dog, his tail wagging a fast circle, licked Joey's face. "I don't know. What do you think, Joey?"

"I call him Colorado."

Kelly Anderson's mouth curved into a smile as she watched Joey and the dog, but her voice was authoritative. "You can't do that. I think Mr. Elliot should choose the name." Turning to Elliot she added, "It was our dog's name. Joey's father called him that." Pausing, she shook her head. "It's a long story. Anyway, about the barking . . ."

"He's just confused right now. I'm sure that's all it is."

She nodded. "Just try to keep him a little quieter, all right? Joey, give Mr. Elliot his dog."

Joey glanced at his mother, then at the dog, and finally at Elliot, his eyes pleading.

"Colorado will need someone to watch after him when I'm not here." Elliot said. "Perhaps Joey could help me out, check on him in the backyard now and then."

"Is he my dog, Mr. Elliot?"

Kelly Anderson gave Elliot a look that said: Don't you dare. But then she reached over and stroked the pup's head. "He is a cute little fellow."

Elliot couldn't stop the smile that was spreading across his face. "As a matter of fact, I had planned on looking for a home for the dog. I'm not here very much, and a pet needs someone to interact with. Maybe Joseph could take him for a few days, on a trial basis."

Joey nodded. "I can take care of him. Please, Mom. I promise I do a good job."

Kelly tried to look upset, but her happiness at seeing Joey bond with the dog showed through. "A few days, Mr. Elliot. And if it doesn't work out, he's coming right back to you."

"Fair enough."

"You probably planned this whole thing, didn't you?"

Elliot thought about that for a moment. "No," he said. "My plans haven't worked out so well."

Kelly Anderson was, though, a mother, a demanding position in its own right, and yet her situation carried an extra dose of responsibility. She gave him a friendly smile that told him she'd picked up on his implicit meaning. "It's easy to feel that way from time to time, Mr. Elliot." Putting her hand on Joey's shoulder, she said, "Ready, sport?"

Joey nodded and started across the lawn. About halfway, he stopped and said. "Thank you, Mr. Elliot."

Elliot waved. "You're welcome. You're going to do just fine."

Kelly Anderson held a dubious expression. "Take an inventory of the good things in your life," she said. "That usually works for me."

Chapter Nineteen

At 8:30 a.m., Elliot walked into the office of Felicia Mullins, a forty-year-old who taught dance at a private school, sponsored by the Open Arms Unitarian Universalist Church. "I'll get right to the point," he said. "I'm investigating the death of Brighid McAlister, and your name showed up on a blackmail list she was keeping. She was holding some potentially damaging photographs, and you were making payments to keep her from going public with them."

Ms. Mullins fumbled for her chair and sat down, both her color and her posture fading in the pale light that filtered through the glass blocks of the north wall. Her hands moved about her desk, straightening papers. "You're telling me that Brighid McAlister is . . ."

"Quite dead, Ms. Mullins." Elliot strolled over to the east wall where photographs of students, girls ranging in age from ten to fifteen, were displayed. "Nice-looking kids," he said.

"So you came out to ask me about my involvement with Brighid, is that what this is all about?"

Elliot turned away from the wall and came back to the desk. "It's about murder, Ms. Mullins. Fear of exposure is a powerful motive."

"Surely you don't think . . . No, I would never do anything like that."

"Then you won't mind telling me where you were between the hours of 10:00 a.m. and noon on January sixth?"

A daily calendar sat precisely centered near the front of her desk, and Ms. Mullins turned a few pages back, paused for a moment, then folded them back into position. "I wasn't here that day. I wasn't feeling well."

"If you weren't here, then where were you?"

"At home, of course."

"Can you verify that?"

As if she were applying some type of lotion, Ms. Mullins rubbed her hands together. "Verify?" she asked. "I'm not sure."

"You might want to give it some thought," Elliot said. "It's important. Did you have any visitors, did the postman come by, or perhaps a delivery person, anyone who might confirm your story?"

She massaged her temples, then shook her head. "There's no one. I was alone."

Elliot flipped the calendar to January 6 to see if anything was written there. The notation simply read: VACATION. He returned the pages. "Do you own any firearms, Ms. Mullins?"

"Firearms? You mean like guns or weapons?"

"That's precisely what I mean."

"Then the answer is no. I abhor violence of any form. I find it repugnant."

"I don't care for it myself," Elliot said, "though I do see quite a lot of it."

"In your occupation, I guess one would."

"That's right. You get to know people pretty well, sensing at times when they're telling the truth . . . or not."

"What are you saying?"

"If I searched your office, would I find anything?"

"I don't know what you would be looking for, but I doubt you would find it here."

"How about your home?"

Ms. Mullins' face lost a little more color. "You would need a warrant for that, wouldn't you? It would take time."

Elliot pulled the warrants to search her home and her office from his coat pocket and placed them on the desk. "I've already taken care of that."

Tears formed in Ms. Mullins' eyes. "I didn't kill Brighid, Mr. Elliot. I swear it."

"But you're holding back. What are you hiding?"

She shook her head. "Nothing. I've told you nothing but the truth."

"My instincts tell me otherwise."

She buried her face in her hands, then brought them away again. "You're going to arrest me, aren't you?"

"Not unless I have to," Elliot said.

She pulled a tissue from a box on her desk and wiped her eyes. "Am I going to need an attorney?"

"That's up to you. I suspect you would know more about that than I would at this point."

She nodded. "Do you want to know what hurts the most about this?"

"Sure, if you feel like telling me."

"It's Brighid, or rather what she was doing to me. She seemed like such a nice girl when we met."

Elliot thought of Cyndi . . . how she'd turned his world upside down. "You just never know, do you?"

"In spite of what you might think, I am sorry about what happened to her."

Elliot began his search of the office. "Perhaps if she'd had someone around to give her some good advice, things might have turned out differently."

Close to an hour later, after having found nothing that would connect the dance instructor with Brighid's murder, Elliot slid the drawers of her filing cabinets closed and turned to Ms. Mullins. "I'll need to search your private residence now. It might be best if you came with me."

The suspect slid out of her chair and put on her coat and hat. The look on her face was that of someone who'd just been to a funeral.

Felicia Mullins owned a large ranch-style home of beige bricks in an established subdivision near 51st Street. She lived alone in the house, which she explained she'd grown up in, her parents having left it to her. She and Elliot waited in the car until another white sedan pulled up and parked in front of them. It'd taken Elliot several hours to search Holsted's place alone. He wanted some help this time.

Elliot got out of the car and shook hands with Detective William Dombrowski. But a second officer had come with him. Michael Cunningham. Elliot said hello, but Cunningham didn't answer, and he didn't offer to shake hands. Elliot could feel his glare even though Dombrowski stood between them.

"Sorry," Dombrowski said. "It wasn't my call."

Elliot shook his head. The news of his falling-out with Cunningham had already spread through the department. "Don't worry about it," he said. He then brought them up to speed on the case. Cunningham looked at the street the whole time.

Elliot got Felicia Mullins from the car and introduced her.

Moments later, she found her keys and unlocked the door. She was nervous, and once they were inside the house she shook visibly. "Please be careful. And try not to break anything."

The formal living area where Elliot and the other detectives now stood wasn't cluttered, and everything was in its place, but it had been that way too long. The vases and figurines looked as if they had grown organically from the shelves and tables that supported them, existing now in a state of petrified stillness, collecting dust since the former owners had passed away.

The thought that this might be an elaborate hoax, with Ms. Mullins owning the house but living elsewhere, crossed Elliot's mind until he glanced through a doorway that led to the room on the other side of the wall, where he saw the red light of a cable television box and the telltale blinking of a telephone answering machine. That a person might actually live here sent cold fingers etching a path up his spine.

"What exactly are we looking for?" Cunningham asked. "Killer dust bunnies?"

Wherever Elliot went, Felicia Mullins followed. It seemed strange, discussing such things in front of her. "Evidence," he said, uncomfortable with how quick he'd been to cut his colleague with a statement of the obvious. "Specifically a .32 caliber handgun or anything else that might tie Ms. Mullins to the murder of Brighid McAlister. I'll start with this room. Dombrowski, if you wouldn't mind taking the kitchen. Cunningham, you got the den."

"Aye, aye, Captain."

Elliot didn't respond, but Dombrowski did. "Knock it off, Cunningham. You too, Elliot. I don't want any crap from you guys. Don't think I won't report the both of you." Without another word, he spun around and left the room. Elliot stared at the floor for a moment, then glanced at Ms. Mullins. He wondered if she could see the shame he felt, for letting his desire affect his professional life.

He pulled on a pair of gloves and began his search, looking behind doors, inside drawers, and anywhere else he thought something might be hidden. He saw a lot of things, but none of them came close to being the evidence he needed. About a half hour later, he left the room and started down the hallway.

At the east end of the house were three doors clustered in an L shape, with one on the end and two along the south wall. The end room was open and looked like any other bedroom. The other two were locked.

Elliot turned to see Ms. Mullins standing about two feet away from him. "You can't go in there," she said. "It's not allowed."

Elliot stared at her for a moment. "Unlock the doors, Ms. Mullins. If you don't, I'll force them open."

Felicia Mullins nodded, but tears ran down her cheeks as she pulled a key from her pocket. Elliot reached for it, but Ms. Mullins seemed to cling to the notion that she might stop him and pulled away. "Please don't do this. It's not what you think, not what you're hoping to find."

Sorrow ran through Elliot, but he suspected those doors weren't locked because the beds were unmade or the furniture wasn't up to par. They were locked because the owner of the house didn't want anyone to know what was on the other side of them. He took the key then slid it into the lock of the first room on the south wall, and opened the door.

Evidently it no longer served as a bedroom, but was now what might best be described as an observation post. Chock-full of photographic equipment, the room overlooked, via a large opening cut into the wall and fitted with a two-way mirror, the remaining bedroom, though it too had been converted. With hardwood floors and handrails bolted to the walls, it looked like a dance studio.

The walls of the observation room were covered with photographs. Elliot wasn't sure if they were enough to be incriminating, just some photos of Ms. Mullins' students, nine- to ten-year-old girls, going through dance routines, but their outfits were skimpy and their poses suggestive. Exposure of her little games might cause her to lose what was, for a sexual predator like her, the perfect job, being able to work and live around that which she coveted. The exposure of her relationship with Brighid McAlister could be equally damaging to her career. The question was; how far would she go, or how far had she gone, to protect it?

Elliot called Dombrowski and Cunningham into the room.

Dombrowski put his hand to his forehead, "For the love of . . ." He shook his head. "It's not enough to connect her for murder. Disgusting, but not enough."

"What'll we do?" Elliot asked.

"Seize the equipment, the photographs."

Elliot turned to the suspect, who had sunk to the floor, her back to the wall of the room. "We'll be in touch, Ms. Mullins."

Elliot caught up with Paul Atwood, the third member of Brighid's dirty little party, at his store, a shop just off Sheridan Road that specialized in used sporting equipment. Several customers milled around the store. Atwood, an average-sized man in good shape, bounced around the showroom, trying to give everyone his fair share of attention. He wore blue jeans and a plain gray sweatshirt.

Elliot stood near the checkout counter and waited, casually at first, but as time dragged on, he began to lose patience. He wondered if the suspect thought he might avoid him this way. "Excuse me," he said.

Glancing at Elliot, Atwood began working his way to the register, but then he detoured and engaged another shopper. Elliot put up with it for another minute or two, but he'd had enough. When Atwood came around again, Elliot flashed his badge. "I need a word with you."

Atwood smiled. "All right. Just let me finish with the customers, and I'll be right with you."

Three people remained in the store and Elliot figured he'd let Atwood deal with them, then he'd have the man's undivided attention.

Until he heard the now-familiar bell ring and turned to see two more coming in. At that point, he pulled his badge and held it over his head. "I'm a police officer. I need to ask everyone to leave the store." He ushered the last one out, then flipped the door sign to CLOSED. Turning to Atwood, he said, "Lock it."

As soon as Atwood complied, Elliot explained to him why he was there. The suspect nodded as if he'd known Elliot was coming and had been waiting for him. "I read about it in the paper," he said. "I wish I could say I was sorry about it, but the truth is I'm relieved. She was putting a lot of pressure on me."

"I can imagine," Elliot said. "Perhaps in the future you'll be more careful of whom you associate with."

"I guess you already know what happened, or you wouldn't be here. I've never done anything like that before, and believe you me, I've learned my lesson, and then some. I'll play it straight from now on. You can count on that." He paused and shook his head. "The whole affair was insane, started at a party. Someone suggested we go bar hopping, and one thing led to another, then . . . well, you get the picture. I barely remember sleeping with her. Scared me to death when she came after me like that."

"Why would she do that, Mr. Atwood?"

The look on Atwood's face said he thought the question was silly. "For the money, I guess." He paused and then decided to elaborate. "Seems to me that someone in her profession might have a drug habit."

"That's not what I meant," Elliot said. "Let me rephrase the question. Why would you go along with it? What did she have on you?"

Atwood looked away for a moment, staring down at the checkout counter where he would later conduct business. "I'm a prominent member of my church, Detective. I have a good wife and two beautiful children who love and respect me. Something like this, well it goes beyond embarrassment. You get the picture."

"Yeah," Elliot said. "I need to ask you something else. Did you kill Brighid McAlister, Mr. Atwood?"

He looked up from the counter, the expression on his face somewhere between appalled and frightened. "No, sir," he said, "I most certainly did not."

Elliot studied Atwood's face. He was inclined to believe him. "Where were you on January sixth, first half of the day?"

Atwood fumbled through his date book. A few minutes later, with wrinkles creasing his forehead, he made a phone call. "Hey, hon.

Could you look on the calendar in my office. Yeah, January sixth. Didn't I go to Jenks, or somewhere?"

Atwood hung up the phone. "I was in Jenks, picking up a load of softball equipment from the high school. Took me most of the morning and part of the afternoon. Check it out. The coach knows me. He'll remember."

Elliot handed him a card. "Contact me if you think of anything that might help solve the case. I'll be in touch."

Elliot walked out of the store and got into his car. He wondered what his next move would be. All of Brighid McAlister's marks had something to lose through their relationships with her, or rather the exposure of the lurid nature of those relationships. Through the car window, Elliot could see traffic starting to snarl along 51st Street. He wondered if Brighid chose her victims at random, taking photos and hoping some of them fit the profile. Somehow that didn't sound right. More than likely, she knew who to pick on. There had to be a connection.

Elliot's phone rang. Captain Lundsford needed him to drop everything and come downtown to attend a scheduling meeting.

When Elliot got to the department, Detective Dombrowski was already in the captain's office. Elliot took a seat next to him, leaving plenty of room on his colleague's other side for whomever else might join them. A few minutes later, he found out that wasn't going to matter. Besides Lundsford, he and Dombrowski were the only two in attendance.

Lundsford had a habit of nodding and squinting when he talked. The more he talked, the more he squinted, until his eyes were nothing more than a couple of slits on his face. Elliot found this distracting and he tried to look elsewhere.

"We're understaffed," the captain said. "You're working on the case where the victim has yet to be identified?"

"Yes, sir."

"I'd like you to put this one to the side for a while."

"Excuse me," Elliot said. From the corner of his eye, he saw Dombrowski grimace. "Could I ask you to reconsider?"

"Reconsider?"

"I'm getting somewhere with this, starting to build a case."

"He died of a drug overdose?"

"Yes, sir."

"What makes you think it was anything other than just that?"

Elliot did a mental inventory of the case. "The victim was seen with a prostitute the night he was killed. The next day, she was found dead, too."

"Same thing, drug overdose?"

"No, sir. She was shot to death."

Captain Lundsford leaned back in his chair and made a few notes. "I appreciate your concern, Detective. But I'm not convinced that you have a case. What makes you think there's a connection between the two?"

"Rohypnol, sir. Both of the victims had traces of it in their systems. Heroine killed our john, but he was so far gone by then that he probably never knew what hit him, which means he didn't administer the drug."

"How does the prostitute figure in?"

"It's a jump, but maybe she needed the money. Someone contacted her for a hit, told her what to do, probably even supplied the heroine. She found the john in a bar, put the rape drug in his drink, then took him to Windhall and shot him up. She never collected the money, though. She took a bullet in the gut instead."

Captain Lundsford opened a stick of chewing gum and stuck it in his mouth. "Why would anyone go to all that trouble?"

"Brighid McAlister was blackmailing her customers. It's no surprise that someone wanted her out of the way. What I can't figure is the john. If I knew who he was, that might help."

"I don't know, son. Don't get me wrong. That's good clear thinking, the kind of thing we need in this department. I'm just not sure it's well spent."

"I disagree, sir."

Dombrowski cleared his throat. "What Detective Elliot means, sir, is that he's put a lot of time into this. It's his first case. You know how that is."

The captain's eyes were open now, but as soon as he started to speak, they again began to narrow. "Do you have any suspects?"

"Yes, sir," Elliot said. "A man named Douglass Wistrom, a drifter, tops the list."

"What's his connection?"

"He was seen in the vicinity where the john was killed, and the prostitute was shot just up the street from his apartment."

"Do we have a motive?"

"I've yet to establish that."

"Then why is the man number one on your list?"

"Because he disappeared right after I questioned him."

Captain Lundsford muttered something under his breath then shook his head. "What else do you have?"

The captain's attitude was beginning to get to Elliot, and for that reason the words he had only intended to think came out. "A drug dealer and a pedophile."

Captain Lundsford leaned back and laughed. "Good lord, son. Maybe you're using the wrong bait."

"No, sir. I'm on the right trail. I can feel it."

The expression that came over the captain's face told Elliot that he was in trouble. Dombrowski shook his head and mouthed *no*.

"Feel it?" the captain said. "Are you telling me you're one of them clairvoyants, or a genie with a crystal ball?"

"No, sir. Nothing like that. It was just a figure of speech."

Elliot paused, then continued. "There's more to it, sir. Last night, when I was questioning the bartender at Cymry's, someone scratched a pagan symbol onto the hood of my car. Later I got an e-mail telling me to drop the case."

Captain Lundsford opened another stick of gum. "That's interesting all right. You make notes?"

"Yes, sir."

"Good. You got three days, Elliot. And this department runs on facts and hard evidence, not some hoodoo crap."

Elliot took the opportunity and got up from his chair. "Yes, sir," he said. As he was leaving, he added, "Thank you, sir."

Chapter Twenty

Elliot walked out of Captain Lundsford's office knowing he needed to find a connection, some common ground between the victims and the remaining suspects, and before he reached his office it came to him. Both Zachariah Holsted and Brighid McAlister had related symbols tattooed onto their skin, Felicia Mullins worked for a church-sponsored school, and Paul Atwood was concerned about what his congregation might think should they learn of his involvement with a prostitute. The answer was religion.

But there was a problem with his theory. Elliot had a gut feeling about one of the players, and it was the only one who didn't appear to fit the motif. He logged on to the computer, then patched into the county records. While he waited for the search results, he placed a phone call to a couple of new acquaintances.

The phone number for Howard and Maud Wistrom had been disconnected, and there was no record of the couple ever having adopted a child in Tulsa County. He did, however, find another type of record.

Elliot printed off the information, then left the office. From there he drove to Memorial Park Cemetery.

Once there, he stopped and got directions, then made his way to the site. Getting out of the car, he stepped onto the soft ground, being careful not to walk across the graves, though with the names running in all directions in this part of the cemetery, it was a difficult task. When Elliot reached his destination, he stopped and stared down at the bronze plate on the ground. The person buried there had been born at Hillcrest Hospital in Tulsa on February 18, 1977, but he'd never lived to tell about it. Douglass Wistrom, the son of Howard and Maud Wistrom, had been stillborn.

A noise broke Elliot's concentration, and when he realized it was his phone he pulled it from his pocket and brought it to his ear. "Elliot."

"We need to talk."

The words that'd come from the phone were not inviting, their tone was anything but that, but the soft voice behind them tugged at Elliot's heart. It was Cyndi. The temperature was dropping, and a brisk wind made him pull his collar up. He waited until the wind died down, watching as it whipped the dead leaves around, concentrating them in the slender ditches alongside the narrow road. "Where are you?"

A long pause followed, and Elliot wondered if he'd lost the call, but then she answered. "In my car."

With Cyndi's clipped answers, and again the tone of her voice, Elliot suspected something was bothering her. "Are you all right?"

"Not really. Could we meet somewhere?"

"Sure."

"How about Woodward Park?"

Elliot gripped the phone. It seemed an odd place to meet on such a cold day. "All right. Where will I find you?"

"The first parking area near the west entrance," she said, and then she disconnected.

Elliot stuck the phone in his pocket. The area Cyndi was talking about was off of Peoria Avenue near 21st Street.

When he arrived, he found Cyndi, leaning against her car, a burgundy-colored Mercedes, one of the newer models with the aerodynamic design. Cyndi wore a black wool coat with a blue scarf, and black pants that hugged the curves of her legs. She looked fabulous.

A stiff wind blew through the park, and, as Elliot climbed out of his car, he couldn't help thinking that it was the same wind that had circulated through the cemetery. The park was surrounded by expensive homes. Cyndi looked as if she belonged there with the old money of Tulsa. Elliot, on the other hand, did not. He walked over and stood next to her. "What's on your mind?"

Cyndi took his arm in hers. "Let's walk."

As they made their way through the park, Elliot began to change his mind about the location, stepping along the narrow blacktop road, then across the brown grass, and even though they didn't speak their touch was natural, and their being together felt as right as Elliot had ever dreamed of right being. It was like that until they reached the rose garden.

It was in the garden where Cyndi stopped and said, "You've turned out to be a bit of a surprise to me, Kenny. I never figured you for the type to kiss and tell."

Elliot tried to make sense of her words, but couldn't. "What are you talking about?"

The wind had turned Cyndi's face a delicate hue of pink so that it contrasted attractively with her blonde hair. "Michael confronted me today. He knew about our dinner date. He was angry. I've never seen him like that."

Neither had Elliot, and he knew he'd been the cause of it. He reached for her hand, but she turned away and looked across the beds of dormant rose bushes. "It has to be over between us."

Elliot shook his head. "Cunningham jumped on me, too, last night at the office, not long after I'd left the restaurant. I don't know how he found out, but it didn't come from me."

"Then who told him?"

A shiver ran through Elliot as he relived the events outside of Cymry's, recalling the e-mail that'd come afterward. "I don't know." Then, because she was involved in this too, he told her about the e-mail.

Cyndi hugged herself. "It could be Michael."

"Cunningham?"

She nodded. "I think he's been following me."

"That doesn't sound like Cunningham."

"I know, but it is. He's possessive. It's why I broke it off the first time." She paused and then added, "I really like the guy. I decided to give it a second chance. I guess I was wrong."

"Don't be so sure," Elliot said, though he had to admit it made sense. How else could he have known so quickly? "It could be someone else."

She shook her head. "It's him. I can feel it. I've suspected it before."

Elliot watched a squirrel run along the wall of the garden. Things had gotten pretty bad when he'd rather suspect a friend of stooping this low than embrace the alternative: the very real possibility that whoever had been following him around was tailing Cyndi as well. "I hate to bring this up, but the guy who frightened you at the bar . . ."

"No," she said, "that wasn't Michael."

"I didn't think so."

A worried expression crossed Cyndi's face. "What are you getting at?"

"Somebody's trying to shake me off a case I'm working. It's possible that you're . . ."

"Wait a minute. What case? And what could it have to do with me?"

"Probably nothing," Elliot said, "but it's possible they're trying to get to me through you."

"Who's trying to get to you?"

"I wish I knew."

Cyndi slowly raised a gloved hand and rubbed her temple. "Jesus, Kenny."

She was still looking away, staring at the rose bushes. Elliot took her arm and turned her toward him. "Look, the smart thing for you to do is to walk away from this, get back in your car and go home, forget you ever knew me." He paused, fumbling for the right words. "I know this is selfish of me, but I hope like hell that you won't do that."

Cyndi gently touched Elliot's face with her hand. "What are you saying?"

"You do something to me, Cyndi. I don't know what it is, but I do know that I like it, and I don't want to lose it."

Cyndi smiled, but then she turned away, burying her face in her hands momentarily before looking up again. "I don't know what to tell you right now. I need time to think."

Elliot felt his face flush, and he wondered why he'd allowed himself to be so foolish. "Sure," he said, "I understand."

She stared at him for a moment. "I don't think you do, not really." After a pause she added, "There's something terribly wrong with me."

Elliot took a moment to gather his courage. The conviction behind her words was unnerving. "What do you mean?"

She turned toward him, her eyes moist and as blue as he'd ever seen them. "There must be," she said, "I keep falling for cops."

A sense of relief waved over Elliot. "That's not so bad."

"I don't know if I'm cut out for it. That's what worries me."

"What do you mean?"

"You're a police detective, Kenny. You saw what happened with Michael because of me. Some people say I'm bad news. I didn't want any of that to happen, but maybe . . . are they right?"

Elliot pulled her close. "I don't believe that for a second," he said, drawing her even closer. And when they came together, their lips touching in a way they had not before, Elliot began to understand that the embrace, and everything from that moment forward was beyond attraction, was in fact beyond his comprehension of passion.

She pulled back. "I have to go."

"Maybe I'll quit being a cop. Would it make a difference?"

"You would do that for me?"

"Maybe," Elliot said. But he knew that he would do anything for her.

Cyndi didn't comment further. She simply turned and walked away.

Chapter Twenty-One

Elliot stepped onto the brick walkway and followed it toward an English Tudor–style house, pausing for a moment at the front entrance, a medieval-looking door with thick, translucent windows on either side of it, giving all that was seen through the glass a rippled effect. His encounter in the park with Cyndi had left him distracted, and he fought to focus his thoughts and reconcile his dual purpose for being there as he rang the bell. It was the home of Reverend Ellery Palmer, senior minister of the Open Arms Unitarian Universalist Church, the church that sponsored Felicia Mullins's dance classes. After making the connection with religion, it had been only a matter of time until Elliot remembered seeing a related brochure in Holsted's living room.

When the door opened, Elliot identified himself and walked in, though his heart wasn't completely in it. He kept toying with the idea of dropping the whole thing, like the e-mail had told him to do. The captain didn't seem that concerned about it. Why should he continue and risk making Cyndi a target, if no one cared?

"Thanks for agreeing to see me," Elliot said.

Palmer let out a sigh. "Make it quick. I don't like getting involved in police matters."

The quiet stuffiness of an old library hung over the foyer, but Palmer led him to a cheerful sitting room with large glass doors that looked over a courtyard made of brick.

Reverend Palmer leaned back in his chair and stroked his beard, a neatly trimmed growth the color of an old nickel. His knee bounced up and down, like he was a kid about to be lectured. "What can I do for you, Detective Elliot?"

Of the three people Brighid McAlister had been blackmailing, Paul Atwood was the only one who had a solid alibi. That left two. "I've run across some information that might pertain to you and your church. But first I'd like to ask you a few questions. It concerns Felicia Mullins and Zachariah Holsted."

The names registered with the reverend. Elliot saw it in his face. They sat across from each other, he in a leather recliner, and Elliot in a wicker chair. The reverend put his fingers together, forming a steeple. "Neither of them are members of my church."

"But you do know them?"

He turned away for a moment, gazing outside at the courtyard, then looked back and said, "I was against the appointment of Ms. Mullins

112

simply because I was in favor of hiring someone from within our organization. I think it's best to go with those who share our spiritual outlook. However, we are strong believers in democracy. We had a meeting and it was decided that, due to her background and experience, she should be employed by the church. She did come highly recommended."

He paused then said, "You mentioned an investigation. Might I ask what it entails?"

"Murder," Elliot said. "And two of my suspects appear to have a connection with your church."

Reverend Palmer sat back in the chair, his eyes narrowing. "I see. Then you do understand that I might be bound, in certain areas, by an oath of confidentiality?"

The reverend seemed defensive, and Elliot found it curious that he'd throw that out even before he knew what Elliot was after. "I thought you said neither of them were members."

He didn't answer.

"What's your connection with Zachariah Holsted?" Elliot asked.

"There is no connection. There was a time when he attended our church, but that time is over."

"That sounds rather final. What happened?"

Reverend Palmer frowned. "Our spiritual philosophies did not coincide."

Elliot made a few notes. "I'm curious as to the significance of the term *Unitarian Universalist*. Could you give me a quick rundown on that?"

"Certainly," the reverend said. "Unitarianism began as a form of Christianity, identified by the belief in God as a singular entity, thereby rejecting the doctrine of the Trinity of the Father, the Son, and the Holy Ghost. The movement was rebuffed by orthodox Christianity as early as AD 325, but rather than fade away it continued to resurface throughout the years.

"Universalism, which also traces back to early Christianity, rejects the notion of eternal damnation and embraces the belief that God will redeem all souls. Both movements evolved from Christian and Jewish roots, but they were also characterized by a more liberal view of spiritual beliefs. It isn't surprising that they eventually came together, which happened in 1961."

The reverend paused then added, "Unitarian Universalism changes and grows as a living tradition, modifying to reflect changes in spiritual beliefs among its members. We gather in community to support individual spiritual journeys, regardless of what religious form that might entail. We value aspects of Christian and Jewish beliefs, but the incorporation of any certain spirituality is a matter of personal choice, in keeping with our creedless, non-dogmatic approach."

Elliot sat back for a moment, thinking about what the reverend had said. "Do your members consider themselves to be Christian?"

Reverend Palmer shrugged. "Some do and some don't. I admit to being old school, thinking of myself as Christian, but in holding to our open-minded approach I realize that not everyone follows the same path. Our varied membership includes humanists, agnostics, pantheists, and even natural theists, such as neo-pagans."

"I see," Elliot said. "And yet, even with this liberal, tolerant approach, you still couldn't find room for Zachariah Holsted. Why is that, Reverend Palmer?"

"Even an association such as ours has its limits."

"That doesn't answer my question."

The reverend frowned. "The belief closest to Mr. Holsted's orientation would be pagan, but Holsted places earthly gratification, or triumph of the individual, over the sanctity of the spirit. While we are tolerant, recognizing there are many paths one can take, we believe the journey should ultimately lead to a spiritual destination. We believe that all life is sacred, all existence interconnected, but justice and compassion should be the foundation of our thoughts and deeds. Each of us has a responsibility to grow spiritually and act in a moral fashion."

"Do you consider Mr. Holsted to be immoral?"

"I didn't say that. It's not for me to decide."

"You're talking in circles, Reverend Palmer."

"I beg your pardon."

"I need to know exactly why Zachariah Holsted was kicked out of your church."

"Who said that he was? Perhaps he left of his own accord."

"Did he?"

"That's all I have to say, Detective Elliot."

"All right. But if I find you've been withholding evidence, I can promise you the consequences won't be pleasant."

Elliot stood. This case went a lot deeper than the captain realized, while each new lead proved more elusive than the last. But the reverend wasn't the only one who knew Zachariah Holsted. "I'll let myself out."

As he walked away he said, "We discovered some disturbing photographs of students from your school in Felicia Mullins's home."

He opened the door and walked out, leaving the reverend to decide whether he should make a moral judgment about it.

After leaving Reverend Palmer's house, Elliot drove to Cymry's to visit with his new friend Charles Miller, aka Snub the bartender. With the focus on Brighid last time, he hadn't had much opportunity to ask him about Zachariah Holsted.

It was early afternoon, and the bar was empty except for Snub. He poured a cup of coffee and set it in front of Elliot. "What a surprise. I was just thinking about calling you."

A slight odor of beer hung in the air. "Is that right? And why would you want to do that?"

Snub opened the register, then came back and laid a business card on the counter. "Something for your investigation."

Elliot picked it up and examined it, reading the words: JIM LLEWELLYN—FREELANCE WRITER AND PHOTOGRAPHER—SAINT GEORGE ISLAND, FLORIDA. He looked up. "And the significance of this is?"

"Last night," the bartender said, "I was counting the receipts, getting a deposit ready, when I found it. Brighid's john gave it to me. I'd forgotten about it until I saw it lying in the bottom of the register."

Elliot took a sip of coffee. If Snub had this right, it was indeed significant. It identified the John Doe. After setting it down, he asked, "The guy I was asking about, the pictures I showed you, this is his card?"

"Yes, sir."

"Is there a reason for this sudden fit of cooperativeness?"

Snub shrugged. "It's the least I could do, after what happened to your car in the parking lot."

Elliot studied the card. "I need to ask you something else."

"All right."

"What can you tell me about Zachariah Holsted?"

The bartender went to the sink and started rinsing glasses, talking while he worked. "Zack's not a bad guy, really. He just takes a little getting used to."

"He was having trouble with Brighid McAlister. Did you know about that?"

"Zack's always got somebody riled. He likes to shoot his mouth off."

"Did you ever observe him and Brighid fighting or arguing?"

The bartender shook his head. "If you're going where I think you're going with this, you're wasting your time."

"Why's that?"

"Zack's no killer." He paused and pointed to the business card. "If anybody did it, it was probably your man there."

"Interesting theory," Elliot said, "considering the john was already dead when it happened."

He shrugged. "She did have a lot of enemies."

"Including you?"

He shook his head. "I never had any problems with her."

Elliot got up from the chair and walked to the middle of the floor. "I just had a little talk with one of Tulsa's religious leaders. He told me Holsted had some unusual religious beliefs." Gesturing toward the symbol painted onto the floor of the bar, Elliot asked, "You wouldn't happen to know anything about that, would you?"

Splotches of color formed on the bartender's face. "Why would I?"

Elliot could tell he wasn't going to get anything more out of Snub. He put on his coat and started for the door. "Thanks for the coffee," he said, "and the card."

Elliot walked out of the bar, wondering whether the bartender was being straight with him or the business card was a ploy.

Chapter Twenty-Two

Elliot sat at his desk, staring at the business card Charles Miller had given him. The only thing that number delivered was an answering machine. He'd left a message, though he didn't see much point in it. He wondered if Jim Llewellyn had been connected with the occult.

What Doctor Meadows had told him about someone valuing earthly gratification over the sanctity of the spirit bothered him. Reverend Palmer had seconded the notion of someone like that being potentially dangerous.

Elliot put down the card and logged onto the Internet, typed *travel writer* into the search box, then clicked on a link for the Society of American Travel Writers. Scrolling down, he found a phone number and called it. He identified himself and explained what he wanted. Soon he was talking to a woman who'd known Llewellyn.

"What would a travel writer from Saint George Island, Florida be doing in Tulsa, Oklahoma?" Elliot asked.

The editor of the magazine laughed. "Tulsa's a beautiful place," she said, "but are you sure it was Mr. Llewellyn? He's retired, has been for a couple years."

"Could you describe him for me?"

"Fiftyish, around five foot eight, maybe one hundred seventy-five pounds, sharp dresser."

Elliot turned Llewellyn's business card over in his hand. The description fit. "I'm pretty sure it's him."

"What's this all about, Detective? Is Jim in some sort of trouble?"

Elliot explained the situation.

After a brief silence, she said, "My God. I just talked with him a few weeks ago, tried to give him an assignment, but he turned it down, said he was enjoying retirement and was thinking about getting back into some of his hobbies."

After a pause, she added, "He was an interesting fellow. Why does it always have to be the good ones?"

Elliot laid the card on his desk. "You wouldn't happen to know what sort of hobbies he was into?"

"Sorry. I can't help you there. In fact, I can't recall him ever mentioning hobbies before."

"Do you know if he had any ties with alternative religious groups?"

"Religion?" she asked. "I don't think so. Come to think about it, though, he did have a fascination with the unusual, the unexplained, tabloid-type stuff. He mentioned writing for them."

"He wrote for the tabloids?"

"Yeah, you know, Satan and his demons seen at the local grocery buying cabbage, that sort of thing."

Elliot thought about Reverend Palmer's reaction to, and Doctor Meadows's explanation of Zachariah Holsted's unusual religious beliefs. "Do know which publications he wrote for?"

"Sorry," she said. "But there aren't that many of them. It shouldn't be too difficult to find out."

"Thanks for you help," Elliot said. But just as he put the phone back in its cradle, Sergeant Conley walked up and knocked on the filing cabinet at the entrance to his cubicle.

Elliot knew something was up. Conley had his hands in his pockets and he stared at his feet. "You got a minute?" he asked.

Elliot had a pretty good idea of what was on Conley's mind. "Take a number," he said, "and get in line."

Conley didn't even crack a smile. "This isn't right and you know it. And it's not like you." Finally making eye contact, he added, "Hey it's me, David Conley, the one who's always telling you to get a life. But not like this. This ain't the way, buddy. Hey, she's a real looker. Ain't nobody saying that's not so. But come on, Kenny, she's Cunningham's girl."

Elliot looked away momentarily in an effort to regroup, noticing that his hands were clenched. Why was he angry with Conley? He'd done nothing. He was only trying to ease the pressure between friends. But then Elliot thought of Cyndi, and how right it felt to be with her. He turned back, meaning to temper his response with reason. But after all, he had feelings too. "Why is everyone so damned concerned about Cunningham?"

Conley didn't answer. He just shook his head and walked away, leaving Elliot to wonder where the bitter words had sprung from.

He sat for a moment, then shook his head to put Conley and Cunningham out of his mind for the moment. He had two days to find the piece of hard evidence that would prove his instincts were right. He logged onto the Internet and gathered some phone numbers. After that, he grabbed the phone and started calling rag magazines.

It turned out to be easier than he'd thought. A few minutes later, he'd contacted the correct tabloid and now had some information to go on. Six days ago, Jim Llewellyn had flown into Tulsa to work on a story. The editor hadn't known the details, but he'd worked with

Llewellyn before and trusted him to deliver. He was shocked to learn of Llewellyn's death. He'd talked with him last Friday. The call had come from the Ambassador Hotel.

The ten-story brown brick building rose up out of the Tulsa soil at 14th and Main. General Patrick Hurley had created the Hotel Ambassador in 1929 to provide temporary upscale housing for oil barons who had brought their families to Tulsa, but had to wait for their mansions to be built. The place had been through some changes since then, but it was still the Hotel Ambassador.

Elliot entered on the south side of the building where a black cloth awning protruded over the sidewalk, offering protection to the patrons. Once inside, he walked to the front desk and showed his badge. "Search your records. I believe you'll find that a gentleman by the name of Jim Llewellyn checked into your hotel on January second. My guess is, he never checked out."

The clerk studied Elliot's badge, then frowned and picked up the phone. "This is Allen. Could you come down for a moment?"

A few minutes later, the hotel manager appeared. Instead of facing Elliot, he walked behind the counter with the clerk. "Is there something I can help you with?"

Elliot explained again.

The manger typed something into his terminal keyboard. He ran his finger alongside his nose, then nodded. "Yes," he said. "Mr. Llewellyn is one of our guests. He isn't in right now. Would you like to leave a message for him?"

Elliot shook his head. "It's too late for that. He won't be coming back to his room. He's been murdered."

A sick look moved across the manager's face, but he said nothing.

"I need to check his room," Elliot said. "I can get a warrant, but I'd hoped that wouldn't be necessary."

The manager frowned, then grabbed a keycard and came around to the lobby side of the room. "Follow me," he said.

They took the elevator up, then walked along the hallway. When they reached the room where Jim Llewellyn had stayed, the manager unlocked it and held the door. Elliot walked in. His thoughts kept wandering back to the look on David Conley's face, and the things the sergeant had said, and he had to remind himself to focus on the job at hand.

Llewellyn's clothes were still there, nice tailored suits, like the one he had been wearing, pressed and hanging in the closet. In contrast to the dirty apartment where he'd spent his last few hours, his room at the

Hotel Ambassador more resembled the type of place where Jim Llewellyn would belong.

The manger shook his head. "I hope this won't take long. I have other appointments."

Elliot checked the closet and the bathroom, then came back into the room. The maids had done their job. The room was clean and Elliot saw nothing that might give him a clue as to why Jim Llewellyn had come to Tulsa. "I'll do my best," he said. He went to an area along the north wall where an arched niche had been cut and outfitted with shelves and a work surface. There were no drawers, and on the marble work surface among the various decorations, Elliot saw only a couple of pens, resting beside a vase of fresh flowers. He pushed the chair to the side and searched around the books and decorations that'd been placed upon the shelves. Finding nothing, he ran his hand under the work surface. Something was there.

Elliot knelt and looked beneath the marble slab, where he saw a piece of cardboard taped to the underside. He peeled away the tape and removed the item, and when he stood, he saw that he held what must have been directions for the construction crew.

"What do you have there?" the manager asked.

Elliot gave the paper to him, then walked to the window and pushed the curtains aside and gazed through the glass. Seconds later, it dawned on him that he should check the bed. He turned around and pulled the comforter and sheets back, then ran his hand between the thick, plush mattress and the box spring. It was as clean as it was luxurious. He thought of Cyndi. She, too, looked like she belonged in such a place.

The manager checked his watch. "Will there be anything else?" he asked.

Again Elliot had to drag his thoughts back to the present. "No," he said. As he walked out of the room and took the elevator down, he wondered if this case was destined to be unsolved.

When he reached the lobby, he started across the floor. Before reaching the exit he noticed someone sitting in one of the lobby chairs who hadn't been there when he'd come in. Elliot paused for a moment. Something about the man's build looked familiar, though he had his face buried behind a newspaper.

An idea occurred to Elliot. He turned back and went to the front desk. "Excuse me," he said. "Are there any messages for Mr. Llewellyn, or did anyone leave anything for him?"

"Just a moment," the clerk said.

He finished with a customer then turned to Elliot. "Now, what were you asking?"

"Jim Llewellyn. Did anyone leave anything for him?"

The clerk glanced at the manger. Again the manager frowned, but nodded his approval. The clerk disappeared for a moment. When he returned, he handed Elliot a yellow writing tablet. Elliot glanced at the clerk then to the manager. "That's it?"

"Yes, sir," the clerk said.

The tablet appeared unused. Elliot leafed through the pages, finding each of them blank, nothing scribbled upon them, until he reached the last one. But as he scanned the words written there, another thought vied for his attention. He wondered who the man in the lobby might be. He lowered the tablet, just in time to see the man push through the exit door.

Glancing at the clerk and the manager, Elliot held the tablet in the air. "Thanks," he said. He turned and walked briskly across the lobby, then opened the door and stepped outside. The stranger was gone. But Elliot knew what was happening. The way the man hid his face, his taking off when Elliot noticed him, all seemed to indicate one thing. He was being followed.

Elliot headed for the parking lot. This thing just kept growing, and he was feeling more helpless all the time. When he reached his car, he reached for his phone. Knowing he shouldn't, but unable to stop himself, he called Cyndi.

She said she'd been about to call him, too. They agreed to meet at Utica Square.

Elliot pulled into the shopping center expecting to see Cyndi waiting in her Mercedes in the parking lot, but instead he saw her standing in front of Margo's, a classy gift shop. When he joined her on the sidewalk, she held her arms out and gave him a hug. Pulling back, she said, "Thanks for coming." Then she slid her arm around his waist. "Let's walk."

When Elliot returned the gesture, putting his arm around her as well, she laid her head against his shoulder. He tried to savor the moment through the churning of his stomach. "After our little chat in the park, I'm not sure where I stand."

"Where do you want to stand?"

"I think you already know the answer to that."

She pulled closer as they crossed the lot, making their way toward 21st Street. "Dinner's on me tonight, at McGill's," she said, "but first I need to ask you something."

Elliot shrugged. "What's on your mind?"

Cyndi stopped walking and tugged at Elliot to do the same. When he complied, she stared at him. "Why do you want to be with me?"

Elliot looked around. They were in front of Pepper's Grill. If the season had been spring, or summer, people would have been sitting at the outside tables, and several of them would've stopped eating long enough to eavesdrop on their conversation. But it was cold and everyone was inside, leaving them alone in the silence. "Because I like you," he said. His answer was simple, but it was the truth.

Cyndi's eyes darted back and forth, searching Elliot's face. "You find me attractive, is that it?"

"There's a little more to it than that."

"If I looked different, would you still be attracted to me?"

He cupped her cheek in his hand for a moment. "There's so much more to you than just your looks. You know I would."

She smiled hesitantly. "All right, but if this is some kind of look-at-me, look-what-I've-got kind of thing, you can forget it."

Elliot wondered why she would feel so uncertain about the depth of emotion she instilled in him. He shook his head. "I take my relationships seriously. I would never treat you like that."

"I feel the same way," she said. "And if I like someone, I play for keeps. Does that scare you?"

Elliot shook his head again. It scared him a lot, but in a thrilling way. He wasn't sure what to say, though on some level he must have known because the words came out. "I want to be with you, Cyndi. And I cannot imagine my ever not wanting that."

Her face softened as she smiled. "I hope I didn't frighten you too much. I knew you'd pass the test."

"The test?" Part of him bristled.

She shrugged. "I've been hurt too many times. Aren't you going to kiss your girl?"

"Are you my girl?" Or was he still under evaluation?

"Isn't that what you want?"

Elliot ran his hand across Cyndi's cheek, then slid it behind her neck and gently pulled her toward him. He couldn't judge her for trying to protect herself from being hurt. "It is," he said. "It most definitely is."

She tiptoed and their lips came together, and even though Elliot had thought their kiss in the park could not be outdone, she proved him wrong. At that moment Elliot lost all anger he'd held for Michael Cunningham, and he felt sorry for him.

The restaurant was a bit of a walk, but Elliot didn't mind. He felt like he could walk a thousand miles with Cyndi by his side.

They stopped at McGills, an upscale steak-and-seafood place about a block from the square. Even before seeing the car Cyndi drove, Elliot had suspected she came from money. In this setting, with the smell of well-prepared food wafting through the air, and the dim light sparkling from her diamonds, there was little doubt in his mind. As soon as the waiter took their order, Cyndi stood. She touched Elliot's shoulder and brushed past him, saying that she would be right back, then headed for the interior of the restaurant.

Elliot used the time to call the department. The captain wasn't in, but Dombrowski was. Elliot brought the phone closer to his ear to overcome the slight buzz of the restaurant. "I want to bounce something off you," he said, "see what you think."

"All right."

"I'm going to need more time on the case."

"You heard what the captain said."

"I know, but there've been some new developments."

Dombrowski was silent for a moment. Finally he said, "You know the captain once he makes up his mind. I wouldn't count on anything."

Elliot put a hand in his jacket pocket and fingered the business card Snub had given him. "I ID'd our John Doe."

"You're kidding?"

"No. His name's Jim Llewellyn, a freelance writer from Florida."

"Are you sure?"

The business card, along with the physical description given by Llewellyn's former editor, went way beyond a gut feeling. "It's him, all right."

"What was he doing in Tulsa?"

Elliot watched a couple walk past his table. "Working on a project for a magazine."

"That should give you some leads."

"Yeah," Elliot said, "you would think, but the editor didn't know what exactly Llewellyn was working on."

"So it's a dead end?"

"Not completely. Llewellyn left some notes at the hotel where he was staying, something he'd labeled the Stone Family Project. It's not much, just a couple of contacts. A Jerry Sinclair, who he was supposed to meet at a bar called Cymry's, except I don't think he ever showed. Llewellyn left with the prostitute instead."

"What about the other one?"

Elliot heard a noise, and as someone touched his shoulder he turned to see that Cyndi had returned. The look on her face said she wasn't happy about the phone call. He'd have to cut it short. "Llewellyn had an appointment the next day with Gary Sullivan, a psychologist. He works out of an office in Tulsa, but he wasn't in. Apparently he only comes in two days a week. But he runs a sideline business out of his home in Donegal. Look, I'm kind of busy right now. I'll call you tomorrow."

"Are you with . . . ?"

"You could say that."

"I hope you know what you're doing, kid."

"That makes two of us," Elliot said. But before he could put the phone away, Cyndi intercepted it. With a smirk, she pressed the OFF button and waited until she was sure the phone was out of commission.

"You need to learn to relax," she said. "Let go of your daytime world and enjoy the evening."

After dinner, Elliot had walked Cyndi home. She lived in the Yorktown condominiums across from the square. He was out of his league all right.

When Elliot pulled into his driveway that night, he noticed someone sitting in a car parked at the curbside in front of the house. He considered approaching the vehicle's occupant, but figured it could be anybody, and decided to wait. He drove into the garage and closed the door.

Once inside, Elliot left the lights off in the living area, then made his way to the bedroom, turning the lights on in that part of the house to attract attention away from the living room. With that done, he went back to the living room, keeping out of the line of sight of the car, and peered through the window. The car was still there. Elliot edged out of the room then went through the kitchen and breakfast nook until he reached the back of the house. When he reached the door leading to the backyard, he slid it open and stepped outside, thankful that Colorado the barking beagle was still at Joey's place.

Elliot walked along the east side of the house and stopped at the gate. Between the boards of the stockade fence, he could see a silhouette in the car, but it was too dark to make out who it was. He closed his hand around the gate handle and slowly depressed the latch, gently pushing the gate open at the same time.

The stranger didn't seem to hear the gate as it scraped lightly against the ground, and Elliot was sure he could get close enough to identify him without being seen. Just as Elliot got the gate open, a weight smacked the backs of his knees, and Colorado, apparently no longer at Joey's house, began to bellow.

Elliot ran toward the car, but the driver had been alerted. He started the car and took off, speeding halfway down the block before turning on his lights. Elliot didn't get the tag number, but he did hear something clank to the asphalt as the car drove away. There would be no use in trying to follow the guy. By the time he got his car out, the lurker would be miles away.

Elliot stepped into the street and walked along the south-side curb until he came upon the object that had fallen from the vehicle. He reached down and picked it up: a parabolic antenna with earphones attached. It was a listening device. They weren't that hard to get. Anyone with an Internet connection could have one in a matter of days.

As Elliot walked back to his house, he wondered who the eavesdropper might have been. A lot of names came to mind— Wistrom, Holsted, Snub the bartender. They all had connections to the case. The question was: Why was he being followed? And why was listening in on Elliot's conversations important enough to risk his tail's being discovered?

Chapter Twenty-Three

Psychologist Gary Sullivan pushed away from his desk, got up, and went into the library, where he poured himself a glass of Merlot. It'd been a long day. Frank McKinley's boy, Danny, had opened up, begun to talk about his involvement with Reverend Coronet. The reverend's handiwork snaked through the town like a disease. But he would undo some of it, if he could. He slid a Dvorak CD into the sound system, then sat down in the leather chair beside the fireplace. The fire was dwindling. He thought about adding another log, but it had burned throughout the day and there was enough residual heat left in the room to be comfortable.

He closed his eyes, hoping the combined effect of wine and music would help him unwind. Drawing deep, diaphragmatic breaths, he guided his thoughts to a place of soothing nothingness.

Somewhere in the background he heard a sound that didn't belong, a doorbell ringing. Setting the wine on the table, he opened his eyes and forced himself out of the chair. He suspected it was McKinley who'd dropped by to ask about Danny. He'd so much as said that he would, in his roundabout way.

Sullivan flipped on the outside light and peeked through the curtain, giving the stranger a once-over. Whoever it was didn't look much like McKinley. He hesitated, but he unlocked the door and pulled it open. Frigid air swirled around his ankles. "Can I help you?" he asked.

The stranger wore a coat with a hood, which he had pulled over his head against the weather. He wasn't a big fellow, but rather slender, Sullivan guessed. It was difficult to tell with all of the clothing he wore. "I was hoping to talk with you," the stranger said. "It's cold. Can I come in?"

The little fellow certainly didn't look threatening. And it was cold. He nodded and stepped aside.

Once the visitor was in, Sullivan closed the door and offered to take his coat, which he promptly removed and handed over. The hood, Sullivan saw now, was attached to a sweatshirt. This the man did not want to surrender. "I've been out for a while," he said. "I'm chilled to the bone."

"Of course," Sullivan said. The visitor had a problem and he sought Sullivan's help. He asked him to follow him into the library.

The library had been an extension of the office at one time, occupying the same large room, until he had the wall and French doors installed.

As Sullivan watched the stranger shiver, he offered him a glass of wine. It wasn't standard practice, nothing of the sort, but his own glass was sitting there, and the man certainly looked as if he might appreciate it.

"Yeah," the stranger said, "that'd be good."

Finding a glass, Sullivan filled it halfway, and handed to the man.

Sullivan sipped the wine for a few seconds, then set it down. "Now," he said, "what do you wish to talk about?"

Before the stranger could answer, the phone in the office began to ring. Sullivan didn't feel as if he could ignore it. He had clients who often called at night. "Excuse me," he said. "Make yourself comfortable. I won't be long."

Sullivan walked out of the room, closing the French doors behind him, and went to his desk where the phone was. He picked up the receiver. "Gary Sullivan speaking. How may I help you?"

The voice on the other end of the line was that of a teenager, looking for someone named Rachael.

When Sullivan got back to the library, the visitor had finished his wine. Sullivan refilled their glasses, and even before he sat back down, the visitor began to speak.

"I shouldn't have come here, Doctor Sullivan. But I can't go into that right now. And I do have a lot on my mind."

Gary Sullivan sat back in his chair and crossed his legs. He wasn't a doctor in the medical sense, but people often called him that. He was a psychologist with a PhD. Even so, he wasn't sure what to make of the troubled young man that had come into his home. "Did someone recommend me to you?"

The stranger stared at Sullivan for a moment, as if their roles had been reversed and he was trying to determine Sullivan's state of mind. "I guess you could say that."

Sullivan studied the young man. There was something about his speech patterns, and the peculiar way in which he tilted his head while listening that was familiar. "Have we met before?"

"I hoped you wouldn't remember me." He leaned back and crossed his ankles. "Mother was never a warm person, Doctor Sullivan. She had trouble expressing her love for us, though I always suspected it was there. For all I know, her childhood could have been worse than mine, but I doubt that's possible. I don't think she actually intended to reach down into the earth and pull up a living hell for us, but she did. She married a sick person, a deranged lunatic. Of course, she didn't know that at the time. I mean, how could she? And neither did we, because we weren't around yet. We were waiting in our own purgatory to be born into it."

"When you say we, are you referring to yourself?"

The stranger grinned. "No, Doctor Sullivan. I have a sibling."

Sullivan took a drink of wine. The visitor's reaction to his question and the way the word sibling rolled out of his mouth sent a chill up his spine. "Were you abused?" From long practice, he kept his voice even.

"Not in the usual sense of the word. Tormented would be closer to the truth."

"And your father was the cause of this torment?"

"Yes. He allowed us only the clothes we wore. He believed we were born sinners, and that we should live a life of suffering to pay for that."

"So he was extremely religious?"

"You could say that. He made us learn Bible verses, and if we didn't commit them to memory fast enough, he punished us. It wasn't as bad at first. We just joined a church, that's all. But then it started: This is how we want you to act, this is how we want you to dress, these are who your friends can be. Before long, we couldn't even think for ourselves. But that wasn't the worst of it. The good reverend had his desires. What do you make of that, Doctor Sullivan?"

"That depends. Are we talking about the church?"

"Bingo."

"My God," Sullivan said. He was aware of the inappropriateness of the words, that they had slipped out of his mouth in an unprofessional manner, but he wasn't feeling right. He was, in fact, quite drowsy. He set the glass of wine on the table. The visitor's story intrigued him, and he wanted to hear more. He'd known people much like the young man's father. He wanted to help this young man come to terms with the abuse he'd suffered so that he could move past it. "Could you describe your father to me?"

The visitor seemed to be standing now, but Sullivan wasn't sure of that. His eyes didn't want to focus.

"He had red hair," the visitor said, "and he always arched his back to make his chest stand out, and he wore cowboy boots and walked heavier than he was."

Sullivan was tired, but an image of the man the visitor was describing formed in his mind. Sullivan didn't see how that could be, it had been such a long time ago, but even as he tried to dismiss such a ridiculous notion, he began to realize who the visitor was. He was the boy, the one they called Justin. Now the phone call he'd received earlier that day, from a man calling himself Detective Elliot, made more sense. He had asked about the Stone family. The story, the description, it all fit.

The visitor began to whisper. "They're dead, Doctor Sullivan. I've tried for years to get the image out of my mind, but it won't go, and I can see them, hanging in his closet, like sides of beef in old man Johnson's meat cooler."

Sullivan's interest was piqued, but he couldn't snap out of the drowsy state he'd fallen into. Standing in his library was the kind of patient psychologists dream of, and he was still speaking. The patient's words, however, seemed to be coming from a distance, and as Sullivan faded into sleep, he began to wonder if the events had transpired at all, or if they were only in his mind, an illusion brought on by an overworked imagination and the wine. He really shouldn't have had that second glass.

"Old Abe hauled them off into the woods, Doctor Sullivan. Like so much trash that needed discarding. She thinks I don't know." He shook his head. "For my protection, I guess."

Chapter Twenty-Four

Detective Elliot was driving south on Highway 75 on his way to Donegal to meet with Gary Sullivan when Douglass Wistrom's father returned his call.

"We decided it was time," Howard Wistrom said. "I called the police here in Billings. I guess they patched me through to you."

"I've been trying to get in touch with you," Elliot said.

"Yes, I'm sure you have. We're good people, Detective. Maybe we didn't go about it in the right way, but Maud and I still believe we did the right thing. We had a long talk about it, though. We're tired of living with it. We want to get it off our chests."

Elliot watched a red pickup truck speed past. "What are you talking about?"

"We didn't adopt Douglass. We found him at Whiteside Park there in Tulsa."

"You did what?"

"Maud and I didn't have anybody, other than ourselves, and it had been that way too long. I got a job in Tulsa. That's how we got there. We'd only been in town for a few weeks when it happened."

"When what happened?"

"The miscarriage."

Elliot paused for a moment, realizing Wistrom must be talking about the death of his natural son. "Go on."

"We've always kept to ourselves. That's our way. We had a small graveside service. Neither of us was ever the same after that, though. So when it happened, it was easy to convince ourselves that the Lord had finally answered our prayers. He'd brought Douglass back to us."

"So, you're telling me you found some kid in the park, and you took him home with you?"

"He asked for our help, said he was lost and hungry. What were we supposed to do?"

Elliot saw his exit coming up, so he moved to the right-hand lane and slowed the car. "Did it ever occur to you that he could've just wandered off from his family, and that they were probably looking for him?"

"No, he was alone, just like us, and he told us as much, but he didn't have to. Maud and I both could feel it, the loneliness that hung around him like a cloud. Maybe it was because we'd been that way ourselves for so long."

Elliot thought about the car parked in front of his house last night, and the listening device its driver had dropped. "Did he ever tell you...?"

"Who he really was?" Wistrom asked, finishing the question. "Where he came from? No. We asked him several times. But he'd get real sullen and wouldn't talk, wouldn't even eat. After a while, we just quit asking. He was about nine years old when we found him. Maybe he couldn't remember. We did right by him, though, raised him like he was our own."

Elliot pulled into the unusual town of Donegal and brought the car to a stop at the intersection of Third and Main. Most small towns in Oklahoma lived and died with the oil boom, but Donegal was not a part of that. A lady wearing a long dress with long sleeves, and a bonnet that covered her face, walked across the street in front of the car. Elliot's first thought was that she was part of an act, a school play perhaps, but he saw no one else dressed like she was. "Thanks, Mr. Wistrom. I appreciate the information."

"You're welcome," Wistrom said. "Now, could I ask a favor of you?"

"Sure."

"Find Douglass, Mr. Elliot, and send him home to us. He can seem a little odd at times. I know that. But there's a lot of good in that boy, too. And he's exceptionally bright, in his own way. We love that boy, Detective, just like he was our own."

The pain in Howard Wistrom's voice went right to Elliot's heart, but at the same time an image of Brighid McAlister, splayed across the parking lot with blood puddling around her midsection, formed in his mind. "I'll do my best."

Elliot didn't think it was going to play out like the Wistroms wanted. "But if you see him," he said, "or hear from him first, it's important that we talk with him."

Wistrom agreed. Elliot disconnected and stuck the phone in his pocket.

The lady in the long dress disappeared into one of the old redbrick buildings along Main Street.

Traffic was next to nothing. A peculiar dead calm seemed to define the atmosphere of Donegal, and as it settled over Elliot, he was taken back to the streets of his hometown of Porter. It'd been equally lifeless that day, in Porter, when Rebecca Yoder, the Amish wife of Benjamin Yoder, and mother to their three children, walked five miles from her home to come into town and put a rifle bullet through the heart of schoolteacher Shannon Fitzgerald, a single woman with an eye for young men. One of them had been Rebecca's son, Mathew.

Elliot had seen a lot of wrong by that time, and he respected Chief Charlie Johnson, the way he kept order in the town when things like murder came around. He'd wanted to be like him. He guessed that was how he ended up a cop.

The sound of a bell, ringing from the handlebars of a bicycle ridden by a boy wearing a Boston Red Sox baseball cap, brought Elliot back to the town of Donegal. He slowed the car. As soon as the boy reached the opposite side of the road and was safely out of the way, Elliot continued east until he found the street he was looking for.

He turned north on Sycamore Drive, but even before he arrived at the address, a mixture of sorrow and frustration raged through him. He wasn't sure what he'd expected to find here, but it wasn't the smoldering remains of the bungalow where he was supposed to meet Gary L. Sullivan.

Elliot climbed out of the car and stared at a set of concrete steps, which led to the yard where the house had been. The bottom step showed, with black letters contrasting against a white background, that he'd found the address Sullivan had given him. He briefly wondered if there could be more than one street that carried the name Sycamore, one with a different designation such as avenue or lane, but he doubted someone who'd grown up in the town would make such an error.

The sound of an approaching vehicle broke Elliot's concentration, and he turned to see a four-door sedan, with the words CHIEF OF POLICE emblazed across the door, pull to a stop behind his car. The patrol car seesawed under the big cop's weight as he maneuvered out of his vehicle, stretching to a height of well over six feet as he closed the door. He looked unreal, unnatural, as he ambled toward Elliot, as if he, too, were an actor who'd just stepped off the stage of a local production. He stopped about four feet away, his feet slightly apart, and put his hands on his hips. "Morning, sir. Something I can help you with?"

Elliot nodded. "This wouldn't happen to be Gary Sullivan's place, would it?"

"Yes, sir, it would."

"What happened?"

"Looks like a fire to me."

"I can see that," Elliot said. "I just spoke with the man last night. We were supposed to meet today, a nine o'clock appointment."

The big man glanced at Elliot's car, then turned back. "Are you a patient?"

Elliot showed his badge. "The name's Elliot. I'm with the Tulsa Police Department."

Keeping his position, the police officer took Elliot's identification, examined it, then shoved it back at him. "Jed Washington. What would the Tulsa Police be wanting with a psychologist from time-bypassed Donegal?"

Elliot looked at the man's name tag. "I'm a homicide detective, Chief Washington. Four days ago a man was found dead in Tulsa. He had in his possession a notepad, which contained the name and address of your Mr. Sullivan."

Jed rubbed his chin. "Now that is a mite curious. Anything I can do to help?"

"I appreciate your cooperation," Elliot said. "Was Mr. Sullivan . . . ?"

The chief nodded. "Along with all of his records. The body was nearly unrecognizable."

Again Elliot asked, "Do you know what happened?"

"It started in the room next to his office. Looks like the fireplace got out of control."

"Do you suspect arson?"

"We're looking into it."

Elliot paused for a moment then asked, "Does the name Jim Llewellyn mean anything to you?"

He shook his head. "Can't say that it does."

Elliot surveyed the wreckage. The smell of smoke stung his nose. "Do you know of anyone who might stand to gain from the destruction of his records?"

The big cop was silent for a moment, his eyes intensely studying Elliot. "How much do you know about Donegal, Detective?"

"Nothing really."

He nodded. "It's not as bad as it used to be, or so I'm told, but it's pretty much a town of factions."

"What exactly does that mean?"

"Either you belong to the Church of the Divine Revelation or you don't."

Elliot thought about the lady in the long dress. "What about you, Chief Washington, what side are you on?"

"I was hired to keep the peace. Folks aren't eager to give me trouble."

"Does the term Stone Family Project mean anything to you?"

"People around here don't talk much, especially about the past. From what I've gathered, there was a family in town that went by that name. They weren't well thought of. I figure they had a run-in with the church. I don't know what happened, but they don't live around here anymore."

"Do you think the church had something to do with the fire?"

"Now, I didn't say that."

"Was Sullivan a member?"

Jed Washington hooked his thumbs into his gun belt. "I've heard that he used to be. But it sounds like you've abandoned your investigation in favor of taking over mine."

Elliot shook his head. "I just don't have much to go on. I'm trying to find the trail anywhere I can."

"I can appreciate that. Just don't go poking around where you don't belong."

"What's that supposed to mean?"

"You figure it out."

"Did you grow up around here?" Elliot asked.

The chief shook his head. "Like I said, they hired me for a reason. I answered an ad in the Fort Worth *Star-Telegram*. That was five years ago."

"How does a small Oklahoma town compete with Dallas and Fort Worth wages?"

The big man shrugged. "I guess Texas just didn't know a good thing when they saw it. So I don't need you sticking your big-city nose in my case."

"That's fine," Elliot said, "but understand this. Wherever my investigation leads, I fully intend to follow, even if it's smack-dab in the middle of your living room."

"Is that a threat?"

"No, just good police work."

"Well, something tells me you're kind of new to this, so let me give you some advice. The next time you go into a jurisdiction other than your own, you might try checking with the local law enforcement before you go snooping around. Things tend to go a lot smoother that way."

Even before the chief finished his spiel, Elliot understood where he was coming from. In his haste to speak with Gary Sullivan, he'd forgotten to check with the chief first. "You're right. I apologize for the oversight."

The chief nodded.

Elliot gestured toward the smoldering remains of Sullivan's house. "I suspect this is related somehow, your Mr. Sullivan and the murders in Tulsa. We need to work together."

"A name written on a notepad is pretty thin evidence, son."

"I realize that, but I have a gut feeling about it."

Chief Washington shook his head. "I don't put much stock in feelings. I only trust what I can see and touch."

"You sound like my captain."

"Then your captain is probably a smart man."

"Maybe so," Elliot said, "but I'm the one working the case. I'd like to know more about this church you mentioned."

"Let's just back up a minute. Now, I didn't intend to give you the wrong impression about the church. I just wanted you to be aware of its strong presence in the community. If it turns out we need to run an investigation, it's something we'll have to deal with. But don't go reading anything other than that in to it."

"Fair enough. Where do we start?"

Chief Washington shook his head. "If it gets down to an investigation, then sooner or later we're going to run into the leader of the church, that being the Reverend Marshall Coronet. He's a shrewd and influential man, Detective Elliot. You get me some solid, tangible evidence and we'll talk. 'Cause I'm not walking into the lion's den with nothing more than a gut feeling backing me up."

Elliot surveyed the damage again, then looked up and down the tree-lined street where Sullivan had lived. "Do you know anything about Sullivan's patients, who he was seeing on a regular basis?"

Chief Washington shook his head. "They were real secretive about it, both Sullivan and his patients."

"When I talked with him on the phone yesterday, he mentioned having someone there, a patient. It's why he cut the call short. But that was earlier in the day. What time did the fire start?"

"I got the call around ten thirty."

"We both know where this is going."

"Well, no we don't. And my offer still stands. Get me something to go on. And I'd prefer you didn't poke around on your own."

Elliot could appreciate the warning but he wasn't sure he wanted to compromise his investigation just so he could kowtow to a small-town cop who'd outgrown his considerable britches. "I need some coffee before I leave. Could I buy you a cup?"

The chief shook his head. "Thanks for the offer, but I've got business to attend to. And don't go getting any ideas. I've got eyes all over town."

Elliot slid into a booth at the diner he'd located and grabbed a menu that'd been stashed between a bottle of ketchup and a napkin dispenser. He needed answers, and he couldn't see how a little friendly questioning could hurt.

A few minutes later, a waitress appeared. She looked like she didn't want to be there but had no choice. From a pocket of her pink smock, she retrieved a notepad and a pencil. "What'll it be, sir?"

Elliot glanced at the waitress. He couldn't recall being called *sir* in a diner before. "Any suggestions?"

Without looking up, she spoke, her face as blank and unreadable as an empty chalkboard. "I'd stay away from the meatloaf."

Elliot studied the menu. Even the waitress's attempt at humor, if that's what it was, came forth with no emotion, as if it'd been rehearsed and repeated each time the question was asked. He glanced behind the counter where deserts were stored in a glass-fronted refrigerated area. "I'll have the apple pie," he said, "and throw a scoop of ice cream on it."

The waitress scribbled on her pad, then stowed the pencil and walked away.

"And some coffee, please?" Elliot added, hoping she chose to hear him.

Moments later, the waitress set Elliot's order in front of him. "Thanks," he said. "Are you from this area?"

With her face still expressionless, she nodded, then turned and left again.

Elliot grabbed a fork and started on the pie, eating it down to the crust where the fruit ended. After that he sat back and sipped his coffee. When he could stand it no longer, he caught the waitress's attention and waved her over. "I was wondering if I might get some information from you."

She glanced sideways, then almost met his gaze. "What kind of information?"

"What do you know about the Church of the Divine Revelation?"

For the first time, Elliot caught a hint of emotion in her eyes. She shook her head. "My job is to work here, sir, not fraternize with the customers."

"Are you a member?"

"Yes," she said, "are you?"

Elliot shook his head. "I've been thinking about joining. But I wanted to talk with some members first."

Her eyes widened. She glanced around, then added, "If I stay here at your table for too long . . ." She cut herself off and quickly walked away, but it was too late. A man had come from the kitchen area and was standing behind the counter. When the waitress drew near, he grabbed her arm and said something to her. She shook her head and said something back, then nodded and came back to the table. "Listen to me," she said. "I'm supposed to tell you something, so in a few seconds nod and say thank you. When I walk away, throw some money on the table and leave."

"What are you supposed to tell me?"

"Directions to Reverend Coronet's house."

Elliot took a napkin and raked loose pie crumbs into a tiny pile on the table. "But you're not going to do that?"

She glanced around. It was taking too long again. "You seem like a nice guy, so just do as I say. Get the hell out of here. And if you know what's good for you, you won't come back."

Elliot took that as his cue to nod and say thank you. He still needed more information, but he wasn't going to get it here. When the waitress left, he pulled his wallet and tossed a ten-dollar bill on the table. Then, hoping the waitress might find a way to use it, he slid one of his business cards beneath the bill.

Elliot started to leave, but an old black man walking by stopped in front of him, blocking him from getting up. He stank of wine and body odor. He looked out of place in the diner. He feigned a cough and dropped a wadded napkin into Elliot's lap. Instinctively Elliot palmed it, and the man shuffled toward the door.

Through the window, Elliot saw Jed Washington coming up the sidewalk. As soon as the old man stepped outside, the chief began quizzing him.

When Chief Washington allowed the old man to continue on his way, Elliot got up from the booth and walked out. Washington was waiting for him as well. "What are you doing here, Detective?"

"Having a cup of coffee, just like I told you."

"What did old Tom say to you?"

"Who?"

"The old man that stopped by your table."

"He didn't say anything. Was he supposed to?"

"Don't get cute with me."

Elliot shook his head. "I don't do cute, Chief Washington. And I'll tell you something else. Your town and its eccentricities might ordinarily be none of my concern, but when it intersects my murder investigation, that changes things. I will cooperate with you and your department, but don't try to stonewall me." He sidestepped the big cop and strode back to his car.

Elliot sat in the car for a few minutes, then grabbed his phone and punched in the number for Judge Broussard. Gary Sullivan kept an office in Tulsa, and it would need to be searched. He wanted to get there first. As he disconnected, he glanced in his rearview mirror to see Jed Washington's broad, toothy grin. He pulled away from the curb, then drove out of town. He wasn't finished in Donegal, but he couldn't operate with Chief Washington following him around. He needed a plan B.

About five miles up the highway, Elliot retrieved the napkin the old man had given him. Unfolding it revealed words written in blue ink. The old guy had given him a message. Seeing a convenience store ahead, Elliot exited the highway and pulled in, stopping on the concrete lot between the gas pumps and the bar ditch.

Placing the napkin on the car seat, Elliot smoothed it flat and stared at the words, which had been hastily inscribed upon the delicate paper. It read: THE FIRE WAS NO ACCIDENT.

Elliot dialed information and got the number for the diner where he'd talked with the waitress. The phone rang twice before she picked up, and when she spoke, Elliot felt a sense of relief. He wasn't sure if she would be allowed the luxury of answering the phone.

"Did you get the tip I left you?" Elliot asked.

Her voice was low, almost a whisper. "What do you want?"

"The old man who stopped in front of my table, how do I find him?"

"He's just an old drunk."

"This is important. People have been killed. There may be more."

She didn't answer.

"Why are you afraid to talk to me?"

The phone was silent. She'd disconnected.

Elliot tapped the steering wheel with his fingers. Through the windshield of the car, he could see the traffic moving up and down Highway 75. The waitress was a prisoner of her own world, afraid to engage in simple acts most of us take for granted. He couldn't help but wonder why she would do such a thing to herself, but as soon as the thought occurred, he realized she probably didn't have any choice, or at least it must seem that way to her. When the phone, which he still held in his hand, began to ring, it startled him. He brought it to his ear. "Elliot."

"I don't have much time, so listen."

Elliot breathed a sigh of relief. It was the waitress. "All right."

"Follow Main north out of town. When you see the old barn, turn east and go until the road ends. There're a couple of empty houses sitting off to the right. You can usually find him there, or close by."

"Could you tell me his name?" Elliot asked. But she was gone again. Elliot stuck the phone in his pocket. His knowledge of the law told him he should leave it alone until he could get Chief Washington on his side, but his sense of doing what needed to be done was telling him otherwise. He needed to check it out. But he couldn't go driving back into town in the same vehicle. He needed a new ride. He put the car in gear and pulled back onto the highway.

Half an hour later, Elliot pulled into his driveway in Broken Arrow. He parked the city car in the garage, then fired up his pickup and backed it out. He was just about to leave when he saw Kelly Anderson coming across the lawn. She walked across the drive and stopped beside the truck. Elliot rolled the window down.

"You're a hard man to catch," she said.

"Sometimes. By the way, Colorado was out last night. He surprised me in the yard."

"Joey left the gate open. Anyway, that's what I came to talk about. I just wanted to thank you."

"For what?" Elliot asked, still expecting some sort of scathing admonishment.

"For giving Joey the dog. I was against it at first. And I suspect most of the neighbors would love to torture you right now. He's a noisy little thing. But I haven't seen Joey this happy in years. He loves that dog, Mr. Elliot. Thank you."

Elliot gripped the steering wheel. In this world of bad, it was nice to see and hear a little bit of good. "You're welcome."

A moment of awkward silence ensued, while Kelly lingered. Elliot suspected she had something else on her mind.

"Maybe, sometime when you're not so busy, I could make dinner for you, a sort of combination appreciation and peace offering kind of thing."

"That would be great," Elliot said, "but it's not necessary."

He paused. He didn't want it to sound like he was saying no. "You haven't done anything to warrant a peace offering," he said. "And you and Joey are doing me a favor, taking care of Colorado."

Kelly pushed a loose strand of hair from her face. "You're a nice man, Mr. Elliot. A rare commodity these days."

After that she walked away, going in front of the truck. Halfway across the lawn, she turned back and smiled, then continued on.

He backed out of the driveway, heart a little lighter despite the gloom that pervades a murder investigation.

Chapter Twenty-Five

Elliot avoided town and entered Donegal using the back roads, not knowing the area, but figuring he'd seen enough on his first visit to muddle his way through. The caper cost him half an hour, cruising up and down gravel roads that were all too similar, but eventually he found what he was looking for: the empty houses the waitress had told him about.

They were the kind constructed in the late 1940s to accommodate young families after the war, and sat deep on their lots, at least fifty feet back from the road, beneath a thick canopy of trees and surrounded by brush.

He pulled off the road and parked in an area that had once been a driveway, and when he climbed out, the sound of the truck door closing behind him spooked a couple of crows out of the treetops. When the birds were far enough away that Elliot could no longer hear them, he listened for any other sound. There was none. It amazed him that small towns like Donegal, less than thirty miles from the city, could be so quiet.

As Elliot walked toward the houses, tiny clouds of dust from the gravel road puffed around his footsteps. Dust coated the mailboxes, the fence posts, the leaves of trees, every available surface area, as though the cluster of houses lay in the path of a crop duster.

A slab of corrugated steel the size of a refrigerator covered the doorway of the southernmost house, and it was this one that Elliot chose to search first. He climbed onto the small concrete porch and paused, again listening for anything out of the ordinary. Hearing nothing of interest, he grabbed the edges of the steel and pulled the makeshift door to one side, then peered into a chasm of darkness. An earthy smell, like that of rotted wood, drifted out of the darkness.

The windows had been boarded over, and the only light—which wasn't much, due to the trees and brush—came through the opening where he stood. Nothing about this felt right, but he'd come too far to turn back now. He stuck his head through the doorway and called out. "Anybody home? The waitress at the diner said I might find you here. I mean you no harm. I just want to talk to you."

The lack of a response did not sit well with Elliot, but he stepped into the house anyway and started across the floor. The wooden planks bowed under his weight, but they held, and when a sensation of being watched waved over Elliot, he pulled a small flashlight from his coat pocket and directed its beam about the room, going from corner to corner. He saw only a collection of spent wine bottles and a few empty soup cans.

Boards creaked behind him.

Before he could react, he felt the impact of something hard smashing against the back of his skull. Then he heard a thump, the clatter of footsteps, and the bang of metal against wood.

Elliot's knees buckled, and his consciousness wavered, but he fought to regain control, refusing to go down like that, not knowing who or why. Still standing, he twisted around, dragging a right hook complete with flashlight as he turned, hoping to connect with something, or someone, but all he saw was the metal rod that'd hit him lying on the floor. He wondered if it had been the old man, frightened into attacking him, only to flee through the front door as soon as he'd delivered the blow, but another sound, coming from the kitchen, quickly dispelled that notion.

Instinctively, Elliot stepped to his left as a steel bar came down, missing his head, but catching his shoulder. The flashlight dropped from his hand and thudded uselessly to the floor. Elliot tucked and rolled as the attacker whipped the weapon through the air, barely missing him each time as he rolled across the wooden planks. Suddenly, Elliot heard the bar clang to the floor, and again he seemed to be alone in the room. It was like trying to fight a ghost.

Panting, Elliot scrambled to his feet and backed into a corner. His eyes had adjusted to the darkness, and though he could not see well, he could detect movement. In this position, with walls preventing an attack from behind him, whoever came at him would have to do it head-on. He hadn't been there long when a form erupted from the kitchen and barged straight for him.

Elliot slid his hand around the handle of the Glock and pulled it free of the holster, then held it in front of him and aimed just above the attacker's head. He squeezed off a warning shot. Amplified by the enclosure of walls, the weapon sounded like a cannon. It did the trick. The attacker changed course and ran out of the house through the front door.

Elliot took off after the assailant, though he harbored little hope of catching him. He was still winded from the gymnastics of avoiding a beating with the metal bar, and the guy had too much of a head start. But as soon as Elliot burst outside, he caught sight of the man disappearing into the wooded area behind the houses.

He wasn't alone.

There were at least four of them, all male and all dressed the same: long-sleeved khaki shirts with matching pants.

Elliot holstered his weapon, then cautiously checked the back of his head. It hurt, but there wasn't much blood. He decided he was okay to search the other houses.

A few minutes later, having found the other houses empty, he went back to the first house and left his business card beside the empty wine bottles. He had a pretty good idea who the men were, or at least who had sent them. Thugs of that nature wouldn't ordinarily attack a police officer, or anyone in a position of authority who could bring heat down on them, which in Elliot's mind meant only one thing.

Someone knew he was going to be there and had ordered the ambush. Had it been the waitress? He didn't think so. She'd been frightened herself. And in the diner, she'd been closely observed. No, she had not betrayed him. She'd been overheard, probably by the same man that'd had words with her after he saw her talking to Elliot.

This, of course, brought up another problem. If the waitress had been overheard telling Elliot where to find the old man, and the idea of that disturbed someone enough to send in a mini-army, they would probably be pretty angry at her as well.

Pulling his phone, Elliot punched in the number for the diner. It didn't surprise him when the waitress answered. He figured whoever had listened in the first time would be hoping to gain more information. "Don't say anything," he said. "When I get through talking, cough once for yes, and twice for no. Do you understand?"

One cough.

"Is the line bugged?"

Two coughs.

"Good. Here's what I want you to do. In about five minutes, an old green pickup truck will stop in front of the diner. You come out and get in the truck, and I'll get you out of there. If that's what you want."

One cough.

"Good enough. Watch for me."

A few minutes later, Elliot saw the diner ahead on the right. Scenarios of Chief Washington driving up at the wrong time kept going through his head. He'd hoped that the waitress would be standing outside waiting for him to come along, but the sidewalk was empty.

When he came to the diner, he slowed to a stop, but neither the waitress nor anyone else came out of the place. Luckily he didn't see Chief Washington either. He considered his options, and he was leaning toward the decision to leave when he saw the front door of the diner open partway to reveal a flash of pink fabric, then close again. Through the glass, he saw someone forcing the waitress back into the restaurant.

Elliot got out of the truck. He figured he'd live to regret his actions, but he couldn't just leave her like that, knowing she was in trouble. He walked quickly to the door. Pushing it open, he stepped inside.

The same man who'd argued with the waitress earlier stood behind the counter. The waitress was there, too. The man held her in front of him, his hands clamped around her arms.

The restaurant was not empty. Customers sat at some of the tables, but none of them looked up as Elliot walked by, nor did they seem to be paying attention to what was going on behind the counter. As if it were just another day, the customers looked though the windows or at their food or at each other, but they refused to acknowledge that something not-right was happening in their presence.

As Elliot drew near, the man tightened his grip on his hostage and said, "This ain't your concern, mister. So why don't you just get out of here."

Elliot's high school football coach had once told him that there was a time for talking and a time for walking. At the time, he wasn't sure what the coach meant by that, but he couldn't imagine that anything he might say right now would do any good. He stepped behind the counter and started toward the couple.

The man's eyes widened and he backed away, heading for the door leading to the kitchen, dragging the waitress with him. Elliot figured he'd better stop him. There would be pots, pans, and knives in there, lots of weapons the man could use. He stepped around the man and blocked the kitchen entrance, but each time he reached for his adversary, the man swung the waitress around, using her as a shield. At the same time, he began backing toward the other end of the counter. Presumably trying to reach the phone to call for help.

Elliot heard the front door opening, and when he turned in that direction he fully expected to see Chief Washington ambling toward him, but it was just another customer who bowed his head like the others.

It was only a matter of time until the big cop showed up. Elliot had to do something. He stepped toward his adversary, but when the man maneuvered his shield, Elliot raised his right hand to get his attention then drove his left beneath the arm of the waitress and grabbed a handful of the man's T-shirt.

Surprised by the action, the man released his grip on the waitress. He shoved her aside, and she stumbled.

Elliot stepped in front of her. "Get in the truck," he said, but he'd no more than gotten the words out when the man lunged at him. Elliot's initial reaction was to sidestep, but the lady was still on the floor behind him. He snapped his left arm forward, as if to jab, but instead of making a fist, he clamped his hand around the man's throat. The unexpected move gave him a half-second window, and Elliot used the delayed reaction time to grab the man's hair with his other hand. Using both hands, he drove the man's head into the counter with a satisfying crunch of bone and cartilage.

The man dropped to the floor, but he wasn't through. He grabbed the counter to pull himself up.

Elliot didn't have time to finish the job. He grabbed the waitress by the arm, the irony of her being dragged around by yet another man not escaping him as he pulled her along.

Outside, Elliot opened the passenger door and loaded the waitress into the truck. With that done, he started for the other side, but again he found himself facing the man from the diner.

He grabbed the lapels of Elliot's jacket and shoved him toward the truck.

Elliot whirled around, using his attacker's momentum, and threw the man to the sidewalk.

Again he staggered to his feet.

Elliot popped a couple of jabs to the man's face, then bashed a right hook into his temple.

He didn't wait around to see what happened after that. He climbed into the truck and sped out of town.

As soon as they reached Highway 75, he opened the throttle, pushing the old truck for all it was worth, keeping the pedal to the floor until the front wheels started to shake and the waitress gripped the dash with both hands. The speedometer showed a hundred and ten.

"Sorry." Elliot backed off until the wheels stabilized, then continued for a few miles. Seeing a promising exit, he left the highway and made his way to Tulsa using the back roads.

Chapter Twenty-Six

A few miles from Tulsa, with the heat off, Elliot turned to the waitress. "Sorry it turned out so rough."

She remained silent.

"I know you're frightened right now, but could you tell me your name?"

Still nothing.

Elliot nodded. "It's all right if you don't want to talk. I understand. If you could help me out with a few things, though, I'd appreciate it. Do you know anything about Gary Sullivan, the psychologist?"

Nothing.

"How did Franklin Taylor know the fire was no accident?"

Her eyes widened, but still no words came out.

Elliot stared through the window. It was as if he'd picked up a shell, an animated corpse, infused with a life force, but possessing no awareness of the outside world. He'd done the right thing. Even so, the captain would take his head off, if he found out. He didn't think that would be a problem, though. The church was a cult that kept its members in line through force and intimidation. Groups like that tend to keep to themselves, iron out their problems in their own way with no help or intrusion from the outside world. They wouldn't go to Jed Washington just yet. Not until they'd exhausted all other avenues, which meant they would be looking for the waitress. He needed a safe place for her.

Elliot made a few calls. A few minutes later, he pulled into a local shelter for women. After getting out of the truck, he went to the passenger side and opened the door. The waitress didn't move, but continued to stare straight ahead. "This is just temporary," Elliot said. "But right now we need a place where you'll be safe."

She sat in the truck and stared through the window.

Elliot closed the door and walked to the shelter, a one-story building that resembled a school more than it did a place of refuge. Once inside, he went to the counter and showed his badge. "Detective Elliot. I have someone in the car, a woman who's been abused. She's terrified."

There were two women behind the counter. One of them identified herself as Leslie Combs. "What would you like us to do, Detective?"

Elliot stretched the truth a little. "The man who abused her is on the loose. We're looking for him, but if he finds her first, and you can bet he's trying, she's in big trouble. I need a place where she'll be safe. Of course we could lock her up, but that wouldn't be right. She's done nothing wrong. Can we count on your help?"

Elliot turned into the parking lot of a clinic on Utica Avenue and stopped. He had taken the truck back home and was once again in the city car. Before he'd left the shelter, the waitress broke her vow of silence, grabbing his arm and saying, "Will Doctor Sullivan be helping me?"

Inside Sullivan's Tulsa clinic, Elliot handed the receptionist a warrant to search the psychologist's office. She gave him a sad smile and said they had been expecting him, then she paged one of the other psychologists, who came out and took Elliot to the office Sullivan had used. Before she could leave, Elliot asked, "Could I have a word with you, please?"

She checked her watch. "I have a few minutes. What's on your mind?"

"How well did you know Gary Sullivan?"

"Our relationship was mostly professional, but we talked now and then. We were friends."

"Are you aware that he also conducted business out of his home?"

"Yes, I am."

"Do you know anything about the nature of his work there?"

She shrugged. "He was a therapist. I imagine he counseled patients."

"What kind of work did he do here?"

"Most of our patients deal with some form of depression. Mr. Sullivan was good at helping people get over addictions. He excelled in that area." She paused and shook her head. "He was a good man."

"Do you know of anyone who might have wanted to harm him?"

"As psychologists, we deal with unstable individuals, Detective. It's all part of the job. But if you're asking me if I know of anyone who specifically had it in for Gary Sullivan, the answer is no." She gestured to the desk. "The key's in the top drawer."

With that, she walked out of the office, leaving Elliot to search the files of Gary L. Sullivan.

About an hour later, most of the office staff had left, and Elliot had found nothing in the files that referred to Donegal or the work Sullivan was doing there or anything remotely related to the case. He was preparing to leave when the psychologist came back into the room.

Elliot sat at Sullivan's desk, and the psychologist stared at him for a moment with a curious look on her face, as if she expected Elliot might change, become the person she'd known, the one who belonged to the high-backed chair, if she closed her eyes and wished it.

She handed Elliot a file made of brown fiberboard. "Gary—Mr. Sullivan—asked me to look this over several years ago. He said it was what got him started, in Donegal, the type of work he did there. I glanced at it a couple times, but couldn't make much sense of it." She paused, then continued. "I expect it might be what you're looking for."

Elliot placed the file on the desk. "People don't ordinarily do things like that unless they believe it's important. Did you and Mr. Sullivan ever discuss the file?"

"Just briefly."

"Would anyone else in the office be more familiar with it?"

"I doubt it. I never mentioned it to anyone. He asked me not to. I'd forgotten about it until . . ."

"It's okay," Elliot said. "I appreciate your giving it to me."

The label on the file read: THE STONE FAMILY.

The name Stone kept showing up. Llewellyn had referred to it in his notes, and Chief Washington confirmed a family by that name had lived in Donegal. And now this. Elliot opened the file and began to read.

Justin, the youngest child of the Stone family, had been a member of the church. Elliot could only infer that the other family members had followed suit. No other names were mentioned. Part of the file seemed to be missing.

Gary Sullivan had been a member of the church as well. But that wasn't all. His capacity within the institution had been that of family counselor. His observations concerning the children, however, overshadowed all of that. Again with no name, another part missing, the file indicated that a nine-year old child, extremely antisocial, bordered on being a full-blown sociopath. He was, according to Sullivan—and in the therapist's own words, contrary to popular belief within the psychiatric and therapeutic communities due to his young age—a disturbed and dangerous individual.

The file also indicated that Sullivan had disassociated himself from the church. No reason was given, but the fact that it was noted in the file caused Elliot to believe that it had something to do with the Stone family.

Elliot looked up and gave the psychologist a brief summary of the file's contents. "Are you sure Sullivan never consulted further with you on this?"

She nodded.

"Do you know anything about Donegal?" Elliot asked.

She looked at the floor briefly, then back to Elliot. "I did a little checking around on the Internet. The church that Gary mentioned in the file. It's . . . unusual."

Elliot thought about the waitress, and the thugs who'd jumped him at the old house. "The Church of the Divine Revelation?"

She nodded. "I believe it's some kind of cult. And I think Gary was . . . I want to say deprogramming, but that wouldn't be very professional. Let me put it like this. Occasionally members of churches such as the one in Donegal will become disillusioned and decide the wrongs they see happening around them are substantial enough in nature that they feel a need to get away from the group. This is not an easy thing for them to do. Groups of this type exercise a tremendous amount of control over their members, and those who choose to leave suffer a certain amount of emotional and psychological damage as a result of their departure. They call them walkaways, Detective. I believe Gary was counseling people who'd decided to disassociate themselves from the church."

Elliot closed the file. He'd already suspected the fire at Sullivan's house was no accident. Now he was nearly certain. "It appears Mr. Sullivan was counseling an entire family of walkaways, a family that went by the name of Stone."

"I think that about sums it up."

Elliot stood and shook the therapist's hand. He needed to have a talk with Reverend Marshall Coronet of the Church of the Divine Revelation, but after his escapades there, unless he could enlist the aid of Chief Jed Washington, he was through in Donegal. "Thanks," he said. "You've been a great help."

Elliot leaned back in his chair and rubbed the back of his head. After leaving Sullivan's clinic, he'd stopped by the office. Chief Washington had told him that Donegal was a town of factions, but his explanation of what he meant by that had fallen a little short of the truth. Elliot plugged another word into the search engine. Reverend Marshall Coronet had been under investigation due to his involvement with a subversive church in Mississippi back in the early eighties. After that, he'd purchased ten acres of land east of Donegal. A couple of years later, the Church of the Divine Revelation came into being.

But that was only half of the story. The town of Donegal was founded by Brian McKenna, an Irish immigrant with strong ties to the old religion, a self-proclaimed dark spiritualist.

Elliot wasn't so lucky finding information on the Stone family. It was as if they never existed.

He glanced at his watch, ever aware of the time constraints the captain had placed him under. He logged off the computer to hit the streets. He needed some information, and he had a pretty good idea of where to get it.

Charles Miller, his old buddy Snub the bartender, wasn't at the bar, but Elliot convinced his partner to give him his address. He found Snub working on a 1954 Mercury convertible, restored, yellow with a brown top. Nice car. "Not bad," Elliot said.

Snub looked faintly annoyed. "What did you expect, to find me wearing a black robe with an amulet draped around my neck?"

Elliot grinned. "Something like that, I guess."

"What are you doing here, Detective?"

Elliot walked over to the Mercury and ran his hand along the polished surface of the fender. "Nice ride."

"Something tells me you didn't come here to talk about cars," Snub said. He took a rag from his pocket and wiped Elliot's prints from the fender. "What do you want?"

"I thought you might be able to help me with something."

"Like what?"

"Like, what can you tell me about the town of Donegal, Oklahoma?"

A look of uncertainty flashed through Snub's eyes. "What do you want to know?"

"Does the Church of the Divine Revelation have connections to paganism?"

Snub stared at Elliot for a moment, as if he was unsure about the sanity of this whole line of questioning. "They claim to be a Christian institution, though I hesitate to dignify it even with that term."

"What do you mean?"

Snub made a gesture like that of a roller coaster going over its highest point. "An extreme group of people, Detective. Completely over the top."

Elliot nodded. "I hear the pagan influence is pretty strong there."

"Who told you that?"

"I've done a little research."

Snub shook his head. "You'd do well to stay away from that town. The atmosphere there is less than healthy."

"I can't do that. My investigation won't let me."

This time the look that crossed Snub's face was burdened with pain. "I met some members of the church once, at a Samhain ritual. They're bad, Detective. The word *dark* isn't strong enough for that bunch."

Elliot nodded. He was beginning to feel sorry for Jed Washington, Donegal's Chief of Police. "How is it," he asked, "that an extreme faction such as the church can coexist with the non-members?"

Snub shook his head. "I don't know. But if I were you, I'd give up my badge before I'd step into the middle of it."

An image of Cyndi Bannister blossomed in Elliot's mind, and he thought of the smoothness of her skin and the sweet smell of her hair and what kind of life they could possibly have together; wives of homicide detectives didn't see their husbands much. He began to wonder if Snub was right. "Thanks," he said. "I'll keep that in mind."

"There's something I've been meaning to talk to you about," Snub said. "I knew Brighid pretty well." He paused, as if admiring the car, and when he looked up again he said, "I'm pretty sure that wasn't her at the bar that night."

Snub's sudden change of course jarred Elliot. "What are you trying to say?"

"She looked the part all right, but the way she moved and the sound of her voice"—he shook his head—"I don't know who that was who left with the guy you were looking for, but it wasn't Brighid McAlister."

"Thanks for the information," Elliot said. As he made his way back to the car, a feeling of despair began to churn in his gut. Every new lead sent him in a different direction, and he was running out of time.

On top of that, his phone was ringing.

The caller identified himself as Franklin Taylor, the old man who'd dropped the note in Elliot's lap at the diner.

Franklin Taylor handed Elliot a cup of coffee, then sat the pot back on the grill, which had come from an old refrigerator and now sat atop a circle of rocks that surrounded a fire pit the old man had constructed. Elliot had found Franklin's place, a small cabin constructed of plywood and two-by-fours, just like the old man had said, about three miles out of town on a hill overlooking the cemetery, a forlorn-looking area surrounded by a rock and wrought iron fence.

He pulled the plastic chair Taylor had provided closer to the fire. It was starting to get dark, which intensified the chill in the air, but the old man had not invited him inside. Elliot figured it was just as well.

The odor of smoke from the fire filtered through Elliot's senses as he sipped the strong coffee. "What can you tell me about Gary Sullivan?"

Franklin Taylor sat on a stump next to Elliot. "I seen somebody messing around his house last night."

"Do you know who it was?"

He shook his head. "Too dark. And I wasn't what you'd call real close, but I seen them all right, peeking in the windows and looking around, like they was worried somebody might see what they's up to."

"Do you remember what time that was?"

"I don't pay much attention to time." Orange sparks snapped and crackled in the air as the old man stirred the fire. "I just know what I saw."

"So you're telling me that you think someone deliberately set fire to Sullivan's house?"

"Yes, sir. That's what happened all right."

"Why would anyone want to do that?"

"'Cause Mr. Sullivan was getting people out of that church, helping them get their heads straight, and make their own decision. That didn't set well with Reverend Coronet."

"But why now? Hadn't Sullivan been doing that for a while?"

The sound of a car coming up the gravel road preceded a beam of light that stabbed through the trees, but the road was above Franklin's camp, and the light missed it. Elliot knew now why the old guy had chosen that spot.

"It's kind of like politics around here," Franklin Taylor said. "You get dirt on somebody, but you afraid to use it 'cause you don't know who got dirt on you. Reverend Coronet knew Mr. Sullivan had dangerous stuff in his files. He just didn't know how much or what kind. It all runs smooth, see, until somebody fools around and tips the scales too much." He paused and shook his head. "I knew it was going to come to a boil one of these days. You can't hide stuff like that forever, no, sir. Sooner or later, somebody going to say something they shouldn't, and there you go. I kind of figured that's why you was here."

"I appreciate your help with this," Elliot said, "but I'm not quite sure what you're trying to tell me."

The old man pointed to his shack. "I try to find shelter where I can. If it gets to raining too hard, or the wind kicks up too much, sometimes I go down to them old houses, you know, where you was looking for me earlier."

Elliot nodded, but he still wasn't following.

"I used to live there. That was my home."

"I'm sorry to hear that, but I still don't understand."

The old man took a swig of whatever was in his cup. Elliot didn't think it was coffee. "There used to be another house a mile or so down the road from there. I never could stay there, though, and nobody else could neither, not even the vagrants who stumble through town now and then. They steered clear of that place 'cause all you had to do was get close to feel something wasn't right about it. Finally the city just tore it down, bulldozed what was left right into the ground."

"What does all of that have to do with Gary Sullivan?"

Franklin Taylor took off his cap and rubbed his hand across his short gray hair. "Mr. Sullivan knew who lived there in that old place. He knew what happened to them, too. That's what got him killed."

"What did happen to them?"

"Well, I don't exactly know. Nobody around here do, else they ain't saying so. But there was a family lived there, went by the name of Stone."

Elliot sat forward. The old man had finally said something that made sense to him. "Did you know them?"

"Not really. They was members of the church. Them people tend to keep to themselves."

"Were you ever a member, Mr. Franklin?"

"Oh, no sir. They don't allow no black folk in that congregation. Don't bother me none, though. Don't want no part of it anyway."

"Can you tell me more about the Stone family?"

"Yes, sir. The man was called Solomon, and the lady, now I believe her name was Kathryn. I don't recall the names of the children, but they had two of them, a boy and a girl."

"I heard they weren't really popular around here. Do you know anything about that?"

"Rumor among the church folk is, they was worshiping the devil, if you can believe that."

"So what happened?"

"Don't know. One day they was here, and the next thing you know, they was gone, the whole family, no signs of a break-in, no blood, no nothing. Far as I know, nobody's ever heard from them since."

"Have you ever considered that maybe they owed money, for back rent or something, and simply pulled up stakes and left during the night?"

"Sure I did. Everybody comes around to that sooner or later. I guess you could say it's the general consensus around here. I don't buy it, though."

"Why not?"

Franklin Taylor pulled a flask from inside his jacket and poured himself another drink, his hands beginning to shake. "'Cause I seen something nobody else did."

Elliot poured himself another cup of coffee. "Go on."

"There's a man lives in the valley, goes by the name of Abraham Saucier, ran a funeral parlor in town. Don't no more, though. I used to see him at night over at the Stones' house, hiding in the bushes next to one of the back windows."

"Do you think he had something to do with the family's disappearance?"

"Yes, sir, I do. I think he killed them and buried them out there in the woods behind the house."

"Did you see any of this?"

"No, sir. I just pieced it together."

"Maybe he's just a Peeping Tom."

"Could be. Ain't nobody around here pays me no mind, think I'm crazy. That's all right. I come and go as I please. You'd be surprised what I see, what I hear."

He got up and poured what was left in the coffeepot over the fire, dousing it. "That's all I got to say. Do what you want with it."

Chapter Twenty-Seven

After leaving Franklin Taylor's cabin, Elliot had called Chief Washington, but he wasn't in his office. Knowing there was little more he could do on the case that evening, Elliot called Cyndi and invited her over for dinner.

While Elliot stirred the spaghetti, Cyndi removed her jewelry and washed her hands, then found the cutting board that hung from a hook fixed to the side of the old cupboard that Elliot used as a pantry. He'd run across it in an antique shop. Cyndi took the cutting board to the center island and began chopping lettuce and carrots for the salad. She looked at home in Elliot's kitchen, and he found himself fantasizing that they were married and it would always be this way.

"You really don't have to do that," he said. "I'd planned on preparing the meal for you."

Cyndi continued working. "Honestly, I'm having a hard time visualizing you as being good in the kitchen."

Elliot checked the pasta, snatching one of the noodles with a fork. "My menu may be limited, but I make a mean pot of spaghetti."

Elliot tasted the noodle for consistency. "I think it's ready." He stirred the sauce that had been simmering beside the pasta, then brought the wooden spoon to his lips, savoring the sweet taste of tomatoes stewed in oregano and basil. "Perfect. You're in for a treat, my love."

Cyndi glanced at Elliot, her face unreadable, but he suspected she was a bit stunned that he would use that word. He bowed before her, a medieval knight honoring his queen. "I assure you, my lady, that my intentions are purely honorable."

She rolled her eyes, then, seeming to know right where everything was, she grabbed a couple of plates and some silverware and set the table.

Elliot drained the pasta, wincing as the steam came toward his face, then dumped it into a bowl and took it to the table. He poured the sauce into another bowl without splattering the countertop and set it beside the spaghetti. With that done, he lit the candles he'd placed on the table and doused the lights.

Cyndi poured the wine, and Elliot took the liberty of dishing up the meal.

Once seated, she rolled a generous portion of pasta onto her fork and stuck it into her mouth, her eyes widening. Moments later, after a few sips of wine, she said, "It's good, Kenny. It really is."

"I tried to warn you."

She raised her glass. "To a long and lasting . . ."

As if she was unsure of how to finish the toast, she paused, and before he knew what he was doing, Elliot spoke up, filling the void as their glasses touched. "Relationship."

And as they stared at each other, frozen in their own capsules of time, Elliot lowered his defenses and allowed himself to realize what the moment meant. He was in love, or at least well on his way to finding it.

The doorbell clanged, accentuated by a pounding on the door, as if the grating sound of the bell alone would not be sufficient to gain his attention.

Elliot glanced at Cyndi, broadcasting through his expression both his annoyance and his apologies.

Her nod said she understood.

He pushed away from the table and strode into the living room, where he opened the front door to find Kelly Anderson, standing on the porch, holding a plate in her hands. She stepped inside and marched toward the kitchen.

Elliot closed the door and followed her. When she entered the kitchen she stopped suddenly, and Elliot could tell by the tense angle of her shoulders that she'd seen Cyndi.

Kelly glanced back at Elliot, then set the plate on the counter.

He shrugged awkwardly. "Cyndi, this is my neighbor Kelly Anderson. Kelly, this is Cyndi Bannister." Elliot paused, then added, "My fiancée." The boldness of this unexpected statement caused a pleasant swell of emotion in his chest.

Kelly spun around and started back toward the front door. "'I'm sorry. I didn't mean to intrude." She gestured toward the plate she'd set on the counter. "I baked a cake. It was too much for Joey and me. I thought you might like some of it."

"Thanks," Elliot said. "Would you care to join us?"

But Kelly Anderson had already opened the door and stepped outside. "I left Joey alone. I need to get back."

Elliot lingered at the door for a moment in a wholly unsuccessful attempt to grasp the enormity of his stunning announcement. Giving up, he locked it, hoping Cyndi hadn't bolted out the back door. When he turned around, she was sitting on the sofa, sipping her wine.

Elliot came around the sofa and lowered himself onto the cushion next to her, sliding his arm across the cool leather back of the furniture before allowing his arm to drop around her shoulder. His pulse was like a jackhammer in his ears.

Cyndi put her hand on Elliot's leg and squeezed it, but it was more of an attention getter than a gesture of closeness. "She was hurt by that."

Elliot was aware that Kelly Anderson had been uncomfortable, seeing Cyndi there, knew that was what she was referring to, but the words tumbled out anyway. "What do you mean?"

"You should have told me you had a girlfriend."

"I don't," Elliot said. "We just met. I had this dog, and . . . well, it's not like that between us."

"You might want to tell her that."

"Why?" He couldn't seem to stop asking questions to which they both already knew the answers. She was sure to take this as an indication of a subnormal IQ.

Cyndi rolled her eyes for the second time that evening. "You really don't see it, do you? That woman likes you, Kenny. She likes you a lot."

A lot? Perhaps on some level he'd recognized a subtle flirtation, but if he had, it'd certainly been below the surface. Cyndi clearly seemed to think otherwise. "I'll try to make it up to her."

Cyndi raised her eyebrows.

"All right. I'll explain it to her, the way it is."

Not only had Cyndi carried her glass from the dining room table, but she'd brought the bottle as well, along with Elliot's glass, which she now slid into his hand. She leaned closer, resting her head on his shoulder. They stayed that way, neither of them speaking for what seemed a long time. At some point, she took the wine from Elliot's hand and set the glasses on the side table. Elliot pulled her close, brushing her hair from her eyes, then pulled her still closer, and their lips touched.

Fragmented thoughts of Elliot's past and visions of his future swirled inside his head, in and out of sequence, like a kaleidoscope gone wild. And he didn't know whether he actually spoke the words or if the feelings they represented merely danced inside his head; but if he had lost control in the warmth of her touch and whispered in her ear, had he told her that he loved her? Her answer came as a gentle rain of warm tears that fell upon his chest.

Silently, he held her while she cried. Gradually, she quieted, and the relaxed rhythm of her breathing told Elliot she'd fallen asleep.

As the emotion of the moment ran through Elliot, he let himself realize that he had not been this happy since . . . Carmen. The thought of her sent shards of guilt racing though him. He wasn't sure why. They'd been teenagers, caught up in some kind of powerful love that defied their age and time, only to have it ripped away from them before its peak. Carmen. Her name ran though Elliot's senses like a lost prayer.

As if fate were against them, a sound as unwanted as an early morning alarm dragged both of them back into the reality.

It was the phone, and on the third ring the machine picked it up. The deep voice of Donegal's chief of police blasted through the house. "This is Jed Washington. Be in my office first thing in the morning. We'll talk about old Abraham Saucier."

Cyndi, blinking as she came out of her dream world, said, "No."

Elliot pulled her close again. "It's all right. It's just the phone."

She was silent for a moment, her face reflecting the puzzlement of one who has yet to shake off the cobwebs and fully realize the situation. Seconds later, she grinned. "You're learning. You didn't answer it."

Chapter Twenty-Eight

At 7:00 a.m. the next day, Elliot walked into Jed Washington's office. Washington sat at his desk, leaning back in his chair with his arms folded across this chest. "You said you had something to show me."

The chief's tone fell somewhere between sarcasm and irritation. Elliot placed Sullivan's file on Washington's desk and opened it, pointing to a name there.

The chief glanced at the page. "Abraham Saucier?"

He pronounced it *Saucy Air*.

"So Shay," Elliot corrected. "It's French. I had a little chat with Franklin Taylor. He told me to ask you about old Saucier."

Washington's stare hardened. "Franklin Taylor's seen too many empty wine bottles, son. You should be careful, talking with people like that."

Elliot shook his head. He'd encountered enough crazies in his time to know one when he saw one, and he considered telling Washington that, but then it occurred to him that feigned incoherence was probably Franklin Taylor's primary defense mechanism. "What is it with you, Chief Washington? Do we have a personality conflict or are you just generally hard to get along with?"

Washington's jaw twitched. "Nothing personal. I just don't need no big-city cop telling me how to run my town."

"That's not my intention," Elliot said. "And maybe if you'd start acting like it was your town, I wouldn't have to."

"What's your interest in this Saucier?" He said it wrong again.

"I'd like to question him, find out what he knows about the Stone family."

"What makes you think he knows anything?"

Elliot tapped the file he'd placed in front of Washington. "Sullivan indicates here that Saucier had some connection with the family."

"Where did you get this file, anyway?"

Elliot smiled. "I found it in Gary Sullivan's Tulsa office."

The chief sat forward. Elliot finally had his attention.

"Bible-based cults, disappearing families, and Satan worshipers. Jim Llewellyn had a fascination with that kind of stuff, Chief Washington. And your little town here would have been right up his alley. Too bad he never got the chance to pay it a visit."

The big cop swiveled his chair a fraction of an inch. "Who's Llewellyn?"

"The one who started all of this," Elliot said, "for me anyway."

"What did he have to do with the town of Donegal?"

"Nothing, I suspect. He was a writer, following an interesting story he'd stumbled upon."

"What kind of story?"

"It had to do with the Stone family. That's why he wanted to talk to Sullivan. Now they're both dead. Kind of strange, don't you think?"

Chief Washington nodded. The expression on his face was that of someone who'd swallowed bitter medicine. "Tell me something, Detective Elliot. Have you ever had a pet?"

The question jolted him back to the small town of Porter, Oklahoma, and the house there where the walls were too close together and an inordinate amount of adolescent time had been spent, completely alone.

"No, sir."

Elliot's reply seemed to him conditioned, like that of a child answering a parent, and he wondered if the words had rolled off his tongue as an extension of his own humility. As Franklin Taylor's had done.

"I got close once, but a neighbor rescued me. Are you going somewhere with this?"

"People get attached to pets," Chief Washington continued, "start treating them like family, get a little upset when they don't show up for dinner." He paused and shook his head. "If they miss breakfast the next day, I've got a real problem on my hands."

"You take pets rather seriously in Donegal."

"Something happens around here, rumors get started. It's good business to act quickly."

"I wonder what kind of rumors got started over the Stone family."

Washington rubbed his jaw. "Don't go jumping to conclusions."

A trapped look came over Chief Washington's face. "What do you know about alternative religions, Detective Elliot?" Thankfully, he seemed to have lost interest in Donegal's missing pets.

"Funny you should ask. The concept keeps popping up in my investigation."

"Just south of town," Washington said, "the elevation drops and goes on like that for several miles. The area is populated by an enclave of people who claim to be descendants of Irish immigrants who settled there about a hundred years ago. They're all members of the church, but they still practice the old religion. We call it pagan." He paused and then added, "Before we go any further, though, let me say this. I've watched those people, studied them for years, and I've never seen them do anything wrong, and that includes sacrificing animals."

Ah. "Good to know. How about people?"

"That's not funny."

"I didn't intend it to be."

The big cop looked at his watch. "There's other talk about town concerning the fate of that family. Some folks claim it was the boy, that he went crazy one night and . . . well, you get the picture."

"When did this happen?" Elliot asked.

"About fifteen years ago."

Elliot thought about the file Gary Sullivan had kept and the words he'd used to describe one of the children, Justin he presumed—sociopath, dangerous—and a sick realization crawled over him. The Stone family had disappeared about the same time as Howard and Maud Wistrom found the answer to their prayers in the form of a boy who was wandering alone in a Tulsa park. They had taken him in and raised them as if he were their own. They called him Douglass.

"I've been planning on paying a visit to the valley." Washington heaved himself up and retrieved his coat from a rack beside the door. "You can ride along if you want."

Washington kept his patrol car, a white Chevrolet Caprice with tan upholstery, in a small lot behind the municipal building that housed his office. Elliot climbed into the passenger side, and as soon as he fastened his seat belt, Washington pulled into a narrow alley that ran behind the building then turned onto Main Street.

A few miles later, they began winding the car down a hill. Elliot realized that, had he followed the waitress's directions when he'd come looking for the abandoned houses and gone through town instead of following the back route, he would have driven past the area known by the locals as the valley, but not through it. This section of Donegal was fenced off. An uneasy feeling churned in Elliot's stomach as Washington pulled up to the entrance. The chief stuck a white card into the reader, and when the gate swung open, he guided the patrol car onto a shiny blacktopped road.

Elliot had imagined an area of cottages like those he'd seen in pictures of Ireland, with thick thatched roofs and smoke curling from the chimneys, and wrinkled old ladies stirring boiling cauldrons. But what he saw was a modern subdivision, a gated community of brick houses with two- and three-car garages.

Washington brought the car to a stop on the street in front of an imposing house with colonial-style columns. He shut the car off and climbed out. Elliot followed him. He suspected they were destined for a meeting inside the house, but Washington did not go toward it. He simply stood beside the car. When a black Mercedes pulled up behind them, Elliot began to understand. Seconds later, several men dressed in business suits got out of the Mercedes—Elliot counted five—and formed a semicircle around Elliot and the chief.

A big man who knows how to effectively use his size is a dangerous opponent. Elliot suspected Jed Washington fell into that category. He towered above the welcoming committee, his big fist resting on the handle of the .38 strapped to his side. "Morning, gentlemen."

One of the men, a slender fellow dressed in what looked like an Armani suit, spoke. "What's this all about, Jed?"

Washington shifted his weight forward. "You remember Ms. Thompson, runs the Laundromat over on Third? She can't find her Shih Tzu. Same kind of thing's happening all over town."

The man straightened his lapels. "I'm surprised at you, Jed. We've been through this before. We don't sacrifice pets in the valley. That's not what this group is about."

Washington stepped forward, breaking through the line, disrupting the rank and file of the micro-army.

Elliot remained where he was, leaning against the squad car with his arms folded across his chest.

"There's more than a few dead pigs out there who might disagree with that," Washington said. "What do you call it, feast of the boar flesh, sacrifice to the winter solstice?" He shook his head. "I don't know, Brian. Laying your hands on a pig and asking it to forgive you of your sins just before you slaughter it sounds a little weird to me."

Elliot didn't move from the car, but kept his position, telling himself to get ready. If Washington was trying to provoke the man, that should have done the trick.

But if the man was shaken by Washington's statement, he didn't show it. He simply shook his head. "Have you ever eaten ham for Christmas, Chief Washington? The Yule feast, which you clearly don't understand, is where that tradition comes from. And it's been going on for a long time, years before Christianity made its debut." He paused and nodded in Elliot's direction. "Who's your friend here? Did you decide you needed reinforcement?"

"Name's Elliot," Elliot said. "Tulsa Police Department."

That got the man's attention. He turned toward Elliot. After a brief moment of contemplation he said, "I've heard about your investigation.

And if you think the pagan community had anything to do with those murders in your city, you're barking up the wrong tree."

"Sorry," Elliot said, "but I didn't catch your name."

The man glanced around, as if he couldn't believe someone would address him in such a manner. "McKenna," he said. "Brian McKenna."

"Thank you," Elliot said. "And if I decide to bark up your tree, Mr. McKenna, you will definitely know about it."

McKenna stared at Elliot briefly, then turned to Chief Washington. "Feisty one, isn't he?"

Chief Washington shrugged.

"The Tulsa Police Department," McKenna said. "Something tells me there's a little more to this visit than missing animals. So why don't we just cut to the chase? What is it, gentlemen? Why are you here?"

"We're looking for someone," Washington said. "Heard he lived around here. Thought you might be able to help us out."

"Did you now? Well that depends on who it is, doesn't it?"

"His name is Abraham Saucier."

Brian McKenna wore sunglasses, but Elliot could almost see his eyes widening behind them. McKenna knew Saucier. "What do you want with him?"

"My investigation has led me in his direction," Elliot said.

McKenna took a while to reply. His demeanor had changed, not quite as cocky as before. "Well I hate to dampen your enthusiasm, gentlemen, but Mr. Saucier doesn't live in this community."

"Well, where does he live?" Washington asked.

"What makes you think I know?"

"Small town like Donegal, someone who grew up here, someone like you, ought to know just about everybody."

"You've got me there, Chief. But I doubt the old relic could have anything to do with murder, especially in Tulsa."

"Why do you say that?" Elliot asked.

"Saucier is an old man, Detective. He doesn't get around very well." He paused, then said, "Go back through the gate and turn right. About a mile up the road, you'll see a white house that sits deep on the lot, up near the tree line. That's Saucier's place. But don't be surprised if he doesn't talk to you. The way I understand it, the old fellow hasn't spoken to anyone in years."

"Thanks," Elliot said. "We appreciate the information."

Elliot and Washington got back in the squad car and left the uncomfortable atmosphere of the gated community, heading for Saucier's place. It was right where McKenna said it would be.

In a sort of valley of its own, the old house existed at an elevation much lower than that of the road, and as Washington guided the patrol car onto a drive that was nothing more than a winding path of beaten earth, a trickle of sweat ran from Elliot's armpit and down his side. As soon as the wheels of the car rolled onto the property, a wave of heat came over him, as if he'd suddenly contracted an infection that left him riddled with fever.

He'd experienced the feeling before. He knew what it meant, could almost see the presence of the black cloud shrouding Saucier's place. A shudder racked him. Something here was profoundly not-right.

Washington stopped the car and turned off the ignition, and when he got out, the driver's side of the vehicle rose a good six inches and all but sighed with relief.

Elliot unfastened the seat belt and swung the passenger-side door open, then climbed out as well.

Chief Washington pulled a cowboy hat from the backseat of the car and positioned it on his head. It was the first time Elliot had seen him wear the hat, and as he watched Washington visually survey the area, he began to suspect that the chief was a little on edge too.

"Certainly is quiet," Elliot said.

"Yeah. Maybe nobody's home."

"I don't see any cars."

"Maybe Saucier doesn't drive."

"Maybe."

Washington put his hands on his hips, still standing beside the patrol car, as Elliot was. Neither of them seemed eager to approach the house. Its beige paint made it seem like a thing crouching, ready to spring from its hiding place in the dust.

Elliot knew from experience that it wasn't always a good idea to verbalize his feelings, especially when they leaned toward premonitory, but he felt obligated to say something. "Do you think we should honk the horn a couple of times, let the guy know we're here?"

Elliot studied the house, paying particular attention to the door and the windows, wondering if Saucier was inside, pinning them down in the sights of a high-powered rifle. "I wouldn't want the man to start shooting at us or anything."

Washington opened the car door and leaned on the horn a few times.

No response, not even the twitch of a curtain.

Washington closed the car door and started toward the house.

Elliot fell in behind him. Seconds later, they stood on the front porch, where Chief Washington searched for a bell. When he didn't find one, he opened the screen and rapped his knuckles against the front door.

The door swung open under the pressure of the knock. Elliot stepped back, instinctively sliding his hand around the handle of the Glock holstered beneath his jacket.

Washington glanced at him. "A little jumpy, aren't you?"

"My nerves have been screaming at me since we drove onto the property. Something's wrong here, Chief."

The chief poked his head inside the door and shouted, "Mr. Saucier. You in there? This is Police Chief Jed Washington. I need to talk to you."

There was no response. Elliot wasn't surprised.

Washington tried again, then he turned to Elliot and shook his head.

They started back toward the car, but about halfway there Elliot stopped and looked back. Beyond the house, the doors to the barn were open. "Wait a minute." He gestured toward the outbuilding. "Maybe he's back there."

Washington paused and rubbed his chin. "He should have heard the horn blaring. I guess we ought to check it out, though."

The barn, not the typical faded red variety but one that'd been painted beige to match the house, sat about two hundred feet behind the living quarters, and as Elliot closed in on the structure a fetid odor, one that reminded him of an unattended campground toilet, invaded his senses. At the apex of the roof, an iron pole, which perhaps a weather vane had been attached to at one time, jutted into the air. Above the front entrance, a utility light glowed, though there was no darkness for it to dispel.

At some point, Elliot wondered why no stray dogs roamed the area, attracted by the malevolent odor, but then he remembered the missing pets, and he fancied that the animals stayed away, having been warned to avoid the area where so many of their brethren had vanished.

A set of sagging double doors led into the barn. There were no windows, and the inside lights had been doused, which left the interior dark except for a swatch of sunlight that spilled through the front entrance.

Glancing at Washington, Elliot continued forward, unable to rid his thoughts of the image of someone waiting inside, brandishing a wheat scythe with which to slice their throats.

When they reached the area just before the entrance, Washington stuck out his arm, but Elliot had already ascertained the need for caution. And then, as if to substantiate his fears, he saw that someone was waiting for them. In the shadows, a pair of legs protruded from the edges of the darkness.

Washington had seen it too. He cleared his throat. "That you, Saucier?"

No response.

Chief Washington frowned, his right hand clutching the handle of his .38. "Are you in there?"

Elliot's eyes had adjusted to the light, and what he saw dictated a different course of action. He turned to Washington and shook his head. Though logic argued against it, the feet attached to those legs in the shadows did not touch the ground, but hovered instead just inches above it.

The look that crawled across Washington's face as he squinted to understand what had caught Elliot's attention said that he now saw it, too. Without looking away, Washington took a step forward. Warrant or not, they headed into the interior of the barn, stopping again when they'd advanced to a point where they could see well enough to quell any doubts they might have had.

A block and tackle hung from the rafters, suspended by a chain, and below that, on the iron hook of the device, a rope had been attached. The end of the rope was wrapped around the neck of a ragged man who dangled like a broken marionette above the ground. Marks on the floor indicated that someone had dragged the body across the dirt and hoisted it with the block and tackle into its present position.

At the feet of the executed man, two immobile, leathery corpses seemed to rear from the dirt floor as though they had clawed free of the ground, digging themselves out of their graves to once again walk the earth and exact their final revenge on the one who had put them there. And encompassing all of this was a huge circle drawn around an inverted star. An upside-down pentacle. Many other pagan symbols decorated the walls of the barn.

Washington stumbled backward, his face turning the lifeless gray of a cadaver. "Ah, hell."

Elliot grabbed the chief's arm to steady him, but he twisted away and heaved, the contents of his stomach spilling onto the barn floor in a sickening splash.

Washington eventually straightened, perspiration standing in beads on his blanched face. "Sweet mother of Jesus."

"My thoughts exactly." Elliot took the shallowest breath possible. "But I think we just solved the mystery of the Stone family, part of it anyway."

"You think that's them?"

"That'd be my guess." He backed out of the barn into the harsh glare of the sunshine, and Washington followed him with a grateful expression.

"You suppose Brian McKenna had anything to do with this?"

"That's a good question. I don't think he would've sent us here if he'd known we'd find something like this. But it appears that Saucier had pagan connections, and McKenna reacted strongly when you questioned him about the old man. If I had to guess, I'd say McKenna knows something about Saucier's involvement with the old murders."

Washington gestured toward the hanging corpse, the one that had yet to wrinkle into a state of decomposition. "Do you suppose this is Saucier?"

"Most likely."

Washington nodded. "Don't touch anything. I need to call the County Sheriff."

"That'd be a good idea."

"Let me ask you something," Washington said. "If Saucier killed Kathryn and Solomon Stone, then who killed him?"

"Another good question." Three bodies, and who was to say there weren't more? "I'd have the area searched for more graves."

"And who the hell dug them up?"

Elliot pulled his phone and called the department. "Give me Captain Lundsford."

Moments later, the captain spoke. "What is it, Elliot?"

"I'm with Police Chief Jed Washington, in Donegal. We just found something. Thought you should know."

"Go on."

"Jim Llewellyn, the John Doe, was working a story about the disappearance of a family here. I believe it's what got him killed. We just found the bodies. They disappeared all right, but not in a mystical sense. Looks like they were murdered."

After a pause, the captain said, "Good work. And, by the way, some lady who said her name was Combs called for you. Said you left someone at her shelter."

Elliot's pulse quickened. Did the captain know about the waitress? "Did she say what she wanted?"

"Whoever you left there is being uncooperative. She wants you to come pick her up." He paused, then added, "Is there something I should know about this?"

"No. I was just trying to help out a friend."

Elliot couldn't see the captain's face, but he could feel his stare nonetheless. "All right," the captain said. "A word of advice, though.

Be careful doing stuff like that. Getting involved in domestic problems can be a bad idea."

"I'll keep that in mind."

Elliot disconnected and stuck the phone in his pocket.

Chapter Twenty-Nine

Elliot tapped on the open door of the shelter administrator's office.

Leslie Combs, the substantial woman who ran the women's shelter, stood when Elliot came in. "Thank you for coming, Detective Elliot."

"You said the lady I dropped off yesterday was asking for me. I don't mind."

She frowned and sat back down behind her desk. "Have a seat, please."

Elliot sat in one of the chairs in front of the desk. Ms. Combs's office was austere, with white walls and subtle earth-tone carpeting. "What can I do for you?"

Ms. Combs sat forward, her arms resting on the desk, her hands folded together. "I was hoping you could tell me a little more about"— she paused and glanced at a file on her desk—"Beverly Mandel, the client you brought to us yesterday afternoon."

Elliot leaned back in his chair. "I don't know much more than what I told you yesterday. But I did some research on the Internet. If you'll do the same, when you get a chance, using *Bible-based cults* as parameters for the search engine, I believe you will gain a better understanding of what we're dealing with."

"But she won't talk to us. She insists on seeing you. Tell me, Detective, what exactly is the nature of your relationship with the client?"

"There is no relationship. I'd never met her before yesterday. I simply offered her a way to escape her circumstances, and she took the opportunity."

The look on Ms. Combs's face was skeptical. "I see. Well, she treats us like we're the enemy. I'm not used to dealing with such behavior."

"I brought her here because I believe she needs protection." Elliot sat forward. "She's really not all that different from your other clients, Ms. Combs. She's spent her life in an abusive environment that she's probably wanted out of for years. She just didn't know how to go about it. The difference is, the source of her pain is more complex. Her enemy is not so readily identifiable. She doesn't know who to trust."

Ms. Combs studied the file briefly. "She certainly sounds like an ideal candidate for our shelter, when you explain it like that, but in reality I'm not sure we're equipped to handle her particular needs. Would it be possible for you to take her elsewhere?"

Elliot nodded. Ms. Combs had thought about this, and she'd already made her decision. "I'll see what I can do. But it'll take time. Could I rely on your generosity for a few more days?"

Ms. Combs closed the file. "Of course, Detective. We don't turn clients out onto the streets. A few days, though, and no more."

"Thanks," Elliot said. "May I speak with her now?"

Ms. Combs pushed back from her desk. "Of course." She stood and walked to the door.

Elliot followed Ms. Combs out of her office and down a hallway with gray-painted brick walls, and floors of shiny green tile. Moments later, they stopped at a room. The door was closed. Ms. Combs unlocked it, then tapped on the facing. "You have a visitor," she said.

Elliot found Beverly Mandel, the waitress, sitting in a corner of the room with her legs drawn to her chest, rocking back and forth in a rhythmic, disturbing pattern. "Leave us alone," she said.

"I don't recommend that," Ms. Combs said. "It's against policy."

"I don't care." The waitress' voice was stern, convincing. "I don't want you here."

Ms. Combs bristled. "Do you see the problem, Detective?" She turned and walked a few feet up the hallway. "Call me when you're ready."

The floor of the room, though highly polished, was of concrete, and the walls were cinder blocks. It reminded Elliot of a sterile bunker; overly clean, but still a bunker. "How are you feeling?" He didn't know what else to say.

She didn't answer right away, and for a moment Elliot thought the conversation would be one sided, as it had been in the truck. She continued rocking. "Why did you bring me here?"

Elliot sat on the floor a few feet away from her. "So you would be safe."

After a moment, when it appeared the waitress would say nothing more, Elliot added, "I've done some research. I know what . . . Well, I don't know what you're going through, but I do know that many other people have gone through it as well. It won't be easy to get out, but it can be done. You've spent a large portion of your life as a member of the church, and now you're second-guessing your decision to leave it."

She stopped rocking, but she didn't look up, and she didn't speak.

"Don't give in to it," Elliot said. "Concentrate on the things that drove you away, whatever was happening within the church that caused you to consider separation."

For the first time since Elliot had come into the room, the waitress rolled her eyes up to meet his. "Thank you. You risked a lot for someone you don't know."

Elliot shook his head. "You make it sound much more heroic than it actually was. I'm glad I could help you."

"I wanted out." Beverly Mandel's face showed that she wanted to cry, but no tears came out. "Since I was ten."

Something in her eyes pleaded with him. He clasped his hands around his knees and waited. Several minutes passed. Then Beverly sat up a little straighter. She smoothed her hair and squared her shoulders.

"I was raised in the church. It's my life. And yet I've known for a long time that it isn't right. When I was ten years old, when my parents joyfully facilitated the gift of my—" She clamped her lips in a hard line for a moment, an internal struggle twisting her features. "They said it was for the good of the church," she continued bitterly. "When I close my eyes, I can still See Reverend Coronet's face above mine. I can still count the beads of sweat on his forehead."

"There are people who can help. I'll make some calls. You're a strong person. You'll get through this."

She nodded dully.

"What they did to you was wrong, Beverly. No one has the right to treat you that way, not even the church."

Once again, the waitress began to rock back and forth.

Sensing she needed time to herself, Elliot quietly got to his feet.

She raised her head. "Why were you in Donegal, Detective?"

Elliot shrugged. "Just police business."

"Does it have something to do with Justin and Elizabeth Stone?"

Elliot sat in the only chair in the room, an orange plastic model with shiny metal legs. "Yes, it does. Did you know them?"

"I went to school with them. Those kids were scared to death. They told anyone who would listen. But nobody did. They said their parents were in league with Satan. And they were the sacrificial lambs."

"Was there any truth to that?"

"I don't know. Reverend Coronet didn't like Mr. Stone. He gave a sermon once, telling us that the evils of Satan were everywhere, his followers walking among us, even within our own congregation. During the whole sermon, he was looking right at Solomon Stone. A few days later, they were gone, the whole family."

"Do you think Coronet had anything to do with that?"

Her rocking had continued, and now she picked up the pace. "There are people within the church who will do his bidding. Nothing would be beyond their reasoning."

"Do you know anything about Abraham Saucier?"

"He was a member of the church."

Elliot stood and handed Beverly Mandel another business card in case she'd misplaced the other one. "I have to go now, but I want you to do something for me. I need you to stay here a few more days. Ms. Combs is a good person. She's on your side. Let her help you, and I'll make other arrangements as soon as I can."

"Am I a prisoner?"

"No. It's completely voluntary, for your protection."

"I don't like it here."

Elliot looked at the featureless cement floor and the cinderblock walls. "I don't either. Give me two days. Then, if you're ready, if you feel strong enough, I'll help you get a job and a place to live. Fair enough?"

The waitress rocked back and forth for what seemed a long time, but finally she said, "You're a most unusual man, Detective."

A lightness he hadn't felt in a long while buoyed him. "I've been called worse. Do we have a deal?"

She sat perfectly still. For the first time since he'd met Beverly Mandel, she smiled. "Two days, Detective. I'll be ready."

Elliot needed more information, and fast. After leaving the shelter, he drove to the nearest library. Seeing the waitress in her present condition caused him to reexamine his own life . . . again. Beverly Mandel reminded him of his mother, a victim of her own world. He couldn't save his mother. But maybe it wasn't too late for Beverly Mandel. His being a cop just might have saved her. He wouldn't have been in Donegal otherwise.

At the library, he pulled into a parking spot, and called Cyndi. When she didn't answer, disconcerting thoughts went through his head, all of which were worrisome beyond reason.

Elliot left a message on her machine, then got out of the car and jogged toward the library. Inside, he hurried across a colorful room, which reminded him of grade school, to a row of computers along one of the walls. Before he reached the computers, though, he heard footsteps, and he turned to see that he was being pursued by the librarian. "Is there something I can help you with, sir?"

Elliot shook his head. "I just need to borrow one of the computers."

"Do you have a library card?"

A child stopped and pointed. "Mommy, Mommy, that man has a gun."

The mother pulled the little boy behind her, fear widening her eyes.

Elliot glanced down to find that his coat had fallen open, leaving his shoulder holster and weapon visible. He pulled his badge, showed it to the kid and his mom, then held it out for the librarian. "Is that good enough?"

The room began to clear of visitors, but Conan the librarian was undaunted. "Could I see that, please?"

Elliot handed her his ID. "I'm in bit of a hurry."

She examined the credentials at length, then handed it back. "You just never know these days."

"It's good to be careful."

Assured he wasn't a threat, she returned to her desk.

Elliot chose the computer next to the window and sat down. After logging on, he typed *Marshall Coronet Church of the Divine Revelation* into the search engine. It didn't take long to find what he suspected was there. Whenever a group, whether it's a church or some other organization, begins to lean in a direction that might be considered contrary to the interests of society, or exhibits behavior that could be subversive or even destructive in nature, that institution runs the risk of being scrutinized by those who monitor such things. The Church of the Divine Revelation and Marshall Coronet had reached such a point about fifteen years ago, right around the time the Stone family disappeared.

Elliot printed the information, then called Chief Washington. Washington, having changed his attitude remarkably since their encounter with the human remains in the barn earlier that day, agreed to arrange a meeting with Reverend Coronet. Until then, he couldn't move forward with the case. But he had something of equal importance to do.

Outside, in the car, Elliot again called Cyndi. This time she answered. "Been thinking about you," he said. After a pause, when Cyndi didn't say anything, Elliot asked, "Is everything okay?"

"Sorry. I just woke up."

Elliot glanced at his watch. It showed 12:05. "I was thinking we might grab some lunch."

"What time is it?"

Elliot told her.

"You've got to be kidding."

"No. But I guess I did keep you out rather late last night. Are we on?"

"Could we make it some other time?"

Elliot wondered what was happening. She seemed distant. "I need to talk to you about something."

There was a pause. "What's up?"

"You're not getting off that easy," Elliot said. "Besides, it's not something we can discuss over the phone."

When Cyndi answered, her voice reflected apprehension. "That sounds serious."

"It is. But in a good way."

"All right, Kenny. But this had better be good."

"It will be."

"Give me an hour, okay?"

"You got it."

"Meet me at Polo's," Elliot said, then disconnected.

Each block closer to his destination, his heart beat faster and his palms grew slick with sweat. By the time he'd reached the jewelry store, he thought he might pass out. He had to sit in the car for a minute, his physical reaction massively out of proportion to what he would expect of a man about to propose marriage.

When he convinced himself to walk through the entrance of the store, it felt as though he'd passed through some kind of portal to another time and place, similar to the old one yet slightly out of kilter in a disconcerting way.

The man behind the counter, who was busy with another customer, wore a tailored suit that made him look like a displaced business executive. Glass cases arranged in a large square acted to both separate the customers from the sales staff and to hold jewelry. Elliot browsed the cases until he found what he was after, then leaned over and studied the selection there.

"Could I help you with something?" The smooth, exotically accented voice made him look up.

A slender woman of African descent stood before Elliot on the opposite side of the display case. Elliot wondered if she'd come from a back room. "I hope so," he said. "I came in rather decidedly, and yet now I find myself a little overwhelmed."

The elegant lady unlocked the case and pulled out a tray of rings, which she had undoubtedly decided had Elliot's attention. Placing the tray on the glass countertop, she said, "Perhaps if you could tell me what caused your sudden interest in diamonds, I could be in a better position to offer my advice."

Elliot nodded, appreciating her grasp of the situation. "The possibility of engagement. I'm actually contemplating marriage."

The lady smiled. "Who's the lucky girl?"

"Her name's Cyndi. Could I see some others?"

The lady removed the tray she'd placed on the counter and quickly replaced it with another. "Do you know her style preferences?"

Elliot felt a blank look slide over his face as if the thought had just occurred to him, though he knew that wasn't true. He was well aware he knew very little about Cyndi. "No. I'm afraid I don't."

The lady winked. "One of those grab-the-moment decisions?"

"Something like that."

Selecting one of the rings, the lady handed it to Elliot, then held her hand, fingers splayed open, beneath his chin. She wiggled her fingers. "Go ahead, hon. You're going to need the practice."

Elliot slid the ring onto her finger.

Afterward, the lady placed her hand on her cheek and turned her head slightly to one side. "What do you think?"

Elliot nodded. This was going to be more difficult than he'd thought. "Nice," he said, and pointed at the next ring. "Could I see that one?"

She tilted her hand under the light, displaying the fiery sparkle of the stone. "Sure thing."

Many demonstrations later, Elliot walked out of the store with a velvet-covered box in his hand.

The aroma of fine food greeted Elliot when he stepped inside Polo's, and as his eyes adjusted to the judicious use of light, a hostess appeared before him.

"Will you be dining alone today?"

Elliot shook his head. "My fiancée will be joining me shortly." Each use of the word gave a delicious thrill.

The hostess led Elliot to a secluded high-backed booth, then put place settings for two on the small rounded table. Elliot had wanted a nice setting for the occasion, and one that would make it easy for Cyndi. He'd chosen the Polo Grill in Utica Square. She wouldn't even have to drive.

Elliot slid into the booth, positioning himself where he could see Cyndi when she came in, and leaned back against the gray and burgundy cushion. A few minutes later, a conservatively dressed waiter stopped by the table. "Would you like to order now, sir, or do you prefer to take a little more time?"

"Give me a few minutes," Elliot said. "Someone's joining me."

The waiter performed a practiced half bow, then disappeared.

Elliot sank back into the cushion again, and let his mind wander through the events of the past few days. His list of suspects kept growing, and yet it seemed that he was no closer to solving the case than he'd been in the beginning. The case itself kept growing. He hoped it would not become unmanageable.

Some time later, after Elliot had checked his watch a few times, the waiter appeared beside the table again. Cyndi had asked for an hour, and Elliot had spent more than that at the jewelry store. It'd been nearly two since they'd talked on the phone, agreeing on Polo's as the destination. "A few more minutes," Elliot said.

As soon as the waiter left the area, Elliot grabbed his phone and dialed Cyndi's number. She didn't answer. Once again, unwarranted but bothersome thoughts began to run through Elliot's mind, scenarios of what-if, all of them crawling along the edges of fear, leveraged by a large amount of self-doubt. Who was he trying to fool? Cyndi was out of his league. He'd known that from the start. He opened the ring box and studied the diamonds, wondering as the cut of the stones expertly caught the available light, if he'd made a mistake. He closed his hand around the box, sliding it back into the inside pocket of his jacket as it snapped shut, then signaled for the waiter.

"I guess I won't be ordering after all," Elliot said.

The waiter shook his head. "Not a problem, sir. And don't let this get you down. It happens to the best of us."

Chapter Thirty

The case, difficult as it was proving to solve, was still progressing better than Elliot's aborted attempt to ask for Cyndi's hand in marriage. With his pride left on the table at Polo's, he joined Jed Washington in Donegal.

Elliot knew Washington had neglected to inform Reverend Marshall Coronet that Elliot would be at the meeting the Donegal police chief had arranged. It made for an awkward situation, but it was the only way they'd get in without resorting to legal tactics. And Elliot needed to question the good reverend about his association with the Stone family.

They were not alone in the office. Elliot counted ten men who stood silently around the perimeter of the room, all of them dressed in khaki pants with matching shirts. He forced himself not to rub the back of his head.

Reverend Marshall Coronet strolled into the room with a grin stuck to his face, a devious curvature of the lips brought on by his imagined superiority. "Chief Washington," he said, "how good of you to stop by. Let me take your coat, all right."

The look on the reverend's face soured when he saw Elliot, and he turned his attention to Washington.

Elliot removed his own coat and folded it across his arm while Chief Washington and Reverend Coronet shook hands. Elliot didn't offer his. He had no desire to feign friendliness with this creep.

Coronet's office, a large rectangular room with polished oak floors, had no furniture other than Coronet's desk and chair, and it was quiet except for the haunting sound of an old song that played in the background, the hollow and tinny quality of the broadcast perhaps coming from a radio set that had transcended time, connecting to some 1940s DJ as he faithfully spun another song across the airways.

"Sorry," Coronet said, pushing a button or something inside his desk, which caused the music to stop. "I love old records, all right. It's a passion of mine." He paused and looked at Elliot. "Who's your friend?"

Reverend Coronet was not what Elliot had expected. His stocky build and close-cropped hair rendered his appearance that of a drill sergeant masquerading in civilian clothes, and his habit of repeating *all right*, saying the phrase as if it were one word so it came out sounding like *ahh-ight*, only enhanced the effect.

"This is Detective Elliot," Washington said, "with the Tulsa Police Department."

"Tulsa?" The word rolled off Coronet's tongue as if it were dirty. "What brings him to our little town?"

"Murder," Elliot said. He didn't appreciate being talked about in the third person, as if he wasn't in the room. "There seems to be an epidemic lately."

The reverend grinned and stuck out his hand. "Let me formally introduce myself, all right. Reverend Marshall Coronet, at your service."

"I know who you are," Elliot said.

"Do you now?"

Elliot indicated the sentries. "I ran into your welcoming committee yesterday."

Reverend Coronet sat in his chair, taking pleasure, Elliot suspected, in their having to stand. "So that was you? Those old houses are on church property, Detective Elliot, part of the compound here, all right. Might I ask what you were doing out there?"

"Looking for someone," Elliot said, catching a glimpse of Washington as the chief glared at him.

"And who might that be?"

"He prefers to remain anonymous."

"Anonymous? I like that word. Did you happen to find this anonymous person?"

"No. I had a little tussle with your boys in brown instead."

"Well, Detective Elliot, seeing as you're a police officer, I'm sure you're aware that kidnapping is against the law."

What about child molestation? Elliot thought, but said, "Kidnapping? What are you getting at?"

"I'll tell you what I'm getting at, all right, the whereabouts of Beverly Mandel."

"Who?"

"Don't act stupid, Detective. You talked with her at the diner. She sure had your attention then."

Elliot decided to go along with the innocent act. Coronet had no way of proving it. "I assume you're referring to the waitress? I didn't talk to anybody else."

"That's right, the waitress. She seems to be missing. And since you were the only stranger in town, well I'm sure you can see how that must look to us."

"What's this all about?" Chief Washington asked. "Didn't I warn you not to go poking around Donegal behind my back?"

"I apologize for the infraction," Elliot said, "but someone dropped me a note when I was in the diner, saying the fire at Gary Sullivan's house was no accident. As you might imagine, that piqued my curiosity. But you'd already made it clear that you wouldn't cooperate unless I had more proof. I thought this might be it. The waitress told me where the guy hangs out, some abandoned houses on the outside of town. I wanted to talk to the man. That's the only reason I was there."

"What's all of this about the waitress?"

Elliot shook his head. He figured Washington knew he was talking about Franklin Taylor. "I don't know. She seemed fine when I talked with her."

Elliot addressed his next answer to both Chief Washington and Reverend Coronet. "I'm a police officer, gentlemen. My only interest here is in solving the case. I did not kidnap anyone from your town."

Washington nodded, but Coronet's expression remained skeptical. "Do I detect an element of deception in your answer, Detective?"

"I imagine you're quite the expert in that area."

"Well. I hate to sound like a schoolchild, but you know what they say: Takes one to know one."

"Come on, gentlemen," Washington said, "let's try to remain on a professional level."

Reverend Coronet leaned forward. "Enough with the small talk, all right. It's time to address the nature of your visit. What brings you to my compound, Detective Elliot?"

"Solomon Stone and his wife, Kathryn," Elliot said. "Did you have anything to do with their murders?"

Coronet drummed his fingers against the top of his desk. "News travels fast in a small town, Detective. I know you found some bodies in Abraham Saucier's barn, but I don't know who they are, or who put them there."

Elliot shook his head. "Do I detect an element of deception in your answer?"

A hint of a frown flashed across the reverend's face.

"Isn't it true," Elliot continued, "that the Federal Bureau of Investigation was looking into your affairs, and your association with the Church of the Divine Revelation, and wasn't this happening right around the time that the Stone family supposedly disappeared?"

"I suspect you already know the answer to that question, otherwise you wouldn't have asked it."

"I'll take that as a yes."

"Take it however you want, all right. I didn't kill Solomon Stone, and I didn't kill his wife."

"What about the kids?"

"What do you mean?"

"Kathryn and Solomon had two children, a boy and a girl. Do you know what happened to them?"

"No, sir, I do not."

Elliot nodded, but he knew better. The Reverend was quite fond of children. "I gather from what I've seen, with the living quarters on the compound and all, that your congregation, your church, is a rather close-knit community?"

"What are you getting at?"

"Isn't it true that Solomon, his wife Kathryn, and their children were all members of the church?"

"Again, I think you know the answer to that."

"I also know that Solomon Stone was feeding information to the FBI," Elliot said, pushing the envelope of truth. "He was trying to bring you down, Reverend, so he could take over your church. That's a pretty strong motive for murder in my book."

"That may be, but I didn't do it."

"Do you know who did?"

"No, sir."

"Isn't it true that Gary Sullivan was once a youth counselor in your church?"

"You've done your homework, Detective. Yes, at one time he served in that capacity."

"He also kept a file on Solomon's son, Justin, part of which he took with him when he left. Do you know where the rest of that file is, and why he kept it in the first place?"

"No, to the first question. As for why he kept it, Justin Stone was a willful and unruly child. Sullivan was good with children. He was trying to help the boy."

"Why did Gary Sullivan, a longtime member, suddenly decide to leave the church?"

"We had a difference of opinion. This is not a prison, Detective. People come and go as they please."

"Did it have something to do with the Stone family, Justin in particular?"

Reverend Coronet pushed back from his desk and stood. "If you're going to arrest me, Detective, then do it. Otherwise, I'd like to ask you and the good chief to leave my compound, immediately."

With that, the men dressed in brown who had lined the perimeter of the room stepped forward, surrounding Elliot and Chief Washington. "Of course," Elliot said. His bluff had already worked better than he'd expected it to. "Just one more question. Does the name Jim Llewellyn mean anything to you?"

Marshall Coronet didn't answer, but Elliot saw that the name did indeed register with the reverend. Elliot unfolded his coat and pulled it on. "Thank you for your time, Reverend Coronet. You've been most helpful."

Several of the men escorted Elliot and Chief Washington to Washington's car. As they drove out of the compound, Chief Washington whistled. "That was pretty impressive, Elliot. You really grilled the guy. I was taking notes."

The church buildings and the rows of small houses where the members lived were all painted a stark white, giving the impression the men were passing through a military base. "Thanks," Elliot said.

"You're a natural. Do you think Coronet did it?"

"Reverend Coronet's not the type to do his own dirty work, but I'd bet a year's salary that he had a hand in it. The trick is in proving it." As Elliot said the words, a morbid thought occurred to him. "Tell me something, Chief. Did you find any more graves out at Saucier's place?"

"Nope. We're still looking, though."

As the unsettling line of reasoning that'd struck Elliot began to evolve, a sick feeling ran through him, and he began to suspect that if Washington's crew did find another grave, it would be a child-sized one.

Jed Washington grinned. "But I do have something for you. We managed to lift some prints from Saucier's barn. The only ones we found that weren't Saucier's, belonged to a Tulsa man. Does the name Douglass Wistrom mean anything to you?"

Chapter Thirty-One

At the office once more, Elliot swallowed the rest of his coffee then crushed the cup and tossed it. The Llewellyn case file sat on his desk, an unorganized mess, from which he needed to make some sense, highlight the major points, and create a workable summary. Captain Lundsford wouldn't stand for anything else. Lundsford wasn't your garden-variety captain, but he wasn't a bad guy really. Elliot logged on to his computer and saw the e-mail icon flashing. He loaded the program, his pulse quickening.

I guess you didn't believe me. I told you to drop the case, but you didn't listen. Now you've gone too far.

Elliot thought of Cyndi. She hadn't answered her phone since they'd talked before lunch. He grabbed the phone and tried again. Still nothing, not even an answering machine. His stomach churned as he grabbed his coat and headed for the door.

Before he reached the exit, Captain Lundsford appeared in front of him. "Are you all right, son?"

Elliot had to concentrate. "Something's come up."

"It can wait."

Before Elliot could respond, Lundsford had his arm around him and suddenly they were in his office. Elliot took a seat without being asked. He didn't know if his legs would continue to hold him.

"I've got a case for you," the captain said. "A south-side couple, just built a two-million-dollar house on one of those lots off Sheridan."

Lundsford's eyes began to narrow, closing a little more with each word. "Three days after they moved in, the wife finds the husband floating facedown in the pool. High profile. Should be good for you."

"What about the case I'm working?"

"Put it on hold."

"I'm close. I can wrap it up in a few days."

"Really? Sounds to me like you solved a fifteen-year-old murder in Donegal, but not the one you were supposed to be working on."

"But it's connected. The notes in Llewellyn's file prove that."

"That's a pretty weak connection. He was working a story there, but the hooker probably gave him the drugs. Maybe she didn't mean to kill him, but I think she did."

Elliot started to tell Lundsford about the prostitute not really being the prostitute, but he didn't. How could he explain something like that?

181

The captain would dismiss it as another of his gut feelings. "There have been some new developments."

"Yeah? What have you got since we last talked?"

Elliot gave the captain a complete rundown, including the disturbing e-mail he'd just received.

Captain Lundsford listened intently, jotting down notes now and then, and when Elliot had finished he nodded and said, "Do you have any idea where Wistrom could be?"

"No, sir. Not at this time."

Lundsford stared blankly at the wall momentarily then said, "We'll put out an APB."

He picked up the new case file from his desk and handed it to Elliot. "In the meantime, get started on this."

Elliot considered pressing the issue, but he knew Lundsford was right. And since he needed to check on Cyndi, the quickest way out of Lundsford's office would be to agree. "Yes, sir. I'll get right on it."

Lundsford lowered his head and began to scribble on a notepad, which meant the meeting was over. Elliot stood and headed for the exit, but just as he cleared the doorway, the captain said, "You've done good, Elliot."

Elliot paused. That was completely unexpected. "Thanks," he said. "I appreciate that."

Elliot left the office and headed straight for the parking garage. When he found his car, he drove to the Yorktown, where Cyndi lived.

When he arrived, he parked at Utica Square, then crossed the street and stopped at the guard shack. As soon as the guard came out, a neat young man with an athletic build, Elliot identified himself and asked if he could go up to Cyndi's apartment.

The guard rubbed his forehead while he examined Elliot's badge. "I don't think I can let you do that, Detective, not without Ms. Bannister's okay."

"I understand what you're saying, but she might be in trouble."

"What kind of trouble?"

Elliot did his best to explain the situation.

"Who sent the e-mails?"

"I wish I knew," Elliot said. He paused, then added, "Why don't you try calling her? Maybe she's in now."

The guard hesitated, then ducked inside the small building where he worked. A few seconds later, he came out shaking his head.

"What if something's happened to her?" Elliot said. "Surely you can understand my concern?"

"Yes, sir. But our protocol addressing the protection of our residents is strict and straightforward."

Elliot watched a black Mercedes exit the parking lot. "Could you have someone check on her, go to her door and knock, ring the bell or whatever?"

The guard pulled the collar of his jacket up. "Just a minute," he said. Again he went inside the shack. A few long minutes later he returned. "I talked with my supervisor. She's going to send someone up to check on Ms. Bannister, but that's the best we can do."

Elliot buried his hands in his coat pockets. In the silence that ensued, he heard a car door slam shut, a sound that had come from the lot across the street where he'd parked, but he saw no one.

A few seconds later, the guard said, "I applied for the Police Academy once."

Elliot turned away from the lot to answer. "Is that right?"

"Yeah, I didn't get it, though. I guess they weren't hiring then. They told me to try again later."

"You should," Elliot said. "You'd make a good cop."

"Thanks. Maybe I'll do that."

"You from around here?"

"Not originally. We moved down from Pennsylvania when I was twelve. My dad got laid off from the mill. He'd met some guy at the airport in Dallas a few months earlier. He managed a couple of hotels here in Tulsa. The plane was late and Dad had stopped off at the bar for a drink." He paused and shook his head. "So dad calls the guy up. He gave him a job, and we've been here ever since."

The phone inside the shack rang. "Hang on," the guard said, "that's probably her."

The guard's face said it all when he came back out. "Sorry," he said. "Ms. Bannister's not at home."

Elliot's stomach churned. "Did they go inside?"

"Yes, sir. The guard used his key. No one was there. The apartment's empty." He paused then added, "There were no signs of a disturbance, though. Everything looked okay, in its place I mean. I'm sure everything's all right. She's just not at home right now, that's all."

The guard's words did little to settle Elliot's nerves. "Thanks," he said. He handed the young man one of his cards. "If she shows up, will you give me a call?"

He took the card. "Sure thing. No problem."

Elliot crossed the street to the parking lot where he'd left his car, with self-admonition running through his head. He should have paid more attention to his intuition, which kept telling him something wasn't right when he'd talked with Cyndi. She'd seemed distracted, even confused. He dug his keys from his pocket and punched the remote, but just as he reached for the door, he saw movement from the corner of his eye, and he spun around to find himself staring into the anger-contorted face of Michael Cunningham.

"Where's Cyndi?" he asked.

Elliot shook his head. "I haven't seen her since last night." He didn't mention that he'd talked with her on the phone earlier. "You know you really shouldn't sneak up on people like that."

Cunningham jerked his thumb toward the building where Cyndi lived. "She's not home, and she doesn't answer her phone. I checked with her parents. They haven't seen her either."

Elliot realized, and not for the first time, that he actually knew very little about Cyndi. He hadn't even thought to ask about her parents.

Cunningham took a step forward. "I need some answers, Elliot."

Elliot stepped away from the car. It was a strategic move. He didn't want to be pinned against anything if a struggle broke out. "Come on, Michael. You know as well as I do that we're not going to get anywhere this way."

He shook his head. "Everything was fine until you came along. This wouldn't have happened without you."

Elliot took a deep breath, resisting the urge to reflect Cunningham's aggression. He'd known when he was just a kid, even before he joined the football team and Coach Sims had confirmed it, that he was the major cause of his own problems. He'd spent a lot of time trying to distance himself from that kind of behavior. But he was beginning to wear down, and Cunningham's irritation acted only to increase the adrenaline that surged through him. He began to assess the situation and his adversary's ability to deal with it.

A car in the parking lot passed by, catching Elliot and Cunningham in its lights, and for a moment Elliot thought the simple act of being exposed, taken from the darkness, might ease the tension, but as soon as the car pulled onto the street, Cunningham stabbed his finger toward Elliot's chest. "Tell me where she is, Elliot. Don't make me ask you again."

Elliot raised his hands, though only for emphasis, to aid in communication as he started to speak, but Cunningham took the gesture as an act of aggression. He made his move.

He came at Elliot wide open, showing his inexperience, his chin hanging there for the taking, his arms flailing in wide arcs with no real muscle behind them. Not that he didn't have any, he did. He just didn't know how to use them.

For Elliot, once a confrontation escalated to the point of physical contact, things decelerated, unfolding in a motion that was both slow and predictable. At times, the advantage this offered seemed unfair, as if he actually knew his opponents' moves a split second before they did. Knowing this was impossible didn't make it less real. He took a half step to his left and launched a straight right at Cunningham's face.

Cunningham stumbled backward, clutching his nose. Blood seeped between his fingers. He launched another attack, charging forward, again swinging wide. One of the punches caught Elliot on the jaw.

Elliot sidestepped, then dug a hook to the body, which found Cunningham's liver, and like an animal sensing the kill Elliot put his weight into it, twisting his body to concentrate the blow.

With that, Michael Cunningham, former all state, offensive lineman for the Tulsa Golden Hurricanes went down. Elliot had to fight the urge to finish him off. Perhaps it was some kind of genetic memory, a survival instinct born of necessity in a time when letting your opponent off the hook went beyond bad judgment, teetering on the brink of foolishness. But he did not. He held back and watched Cunningham fall, not a merciful drop, but a slow, agonizing decent, his face broadcasting his disbelief.

Elliot helped Cunningham to his feet. He had no fight left in him. "Where's your car?" Elliot asked.

He didn't answer.

Elliot scanned the parking lot until he spotted Cunningham's red BMW. Throwing Cunningham's arm over his shoulder, he walked his colleague to his car. Once there, he dug the keys from his pocket, then opened the door and helped him in, which more or less involved letting him fall onto the seat. "You all right?"

Again Cunningham did not answer.

Elliot handed him the keys. He seemed okay, so Elliot left him there and walked back to his own car.

After a short drive, Elliot parked his car and walked into the Hive, a bar where music always played. He pushed through the crowd, making his way from one end of the bar to the other. Along the way, various girls stepped in front of him, trying to dance, but he kept moving, hoping to see what he was looking for: the sensuous face of Cyndi Bannister. It was where he'd run into her before, and he'd hoped it might happen again, but of all the people crammed into the place that night, Cyndi was not among them.

Elliot made his way to the bar, and when the bartender saw him, her mouth began to move, but he could not hear her. The band they had on stage, a bunch of guys wearing baggy jeans and black T-shirts, had their amps cranked up too high. Elliot pointed to the kind of beer he wanted.

Elliot stayed at the club long enough to finish the beer he'd ordered, then walked out. Several minutes later, he pulled into the driveway of his home in Broken Arrow. He didn't know what to do next, so he sat there in the darkness, letting the events of the past few days run through his head, like some kind of late movie that he'd forgotten to shut off. Cyndi had to be somewhere. He couldn't just give up. He had to find her.

There were other places to search, bars and clubs where people gathered to unwind with music, companionship, and booze. He punched the garage door opener, then traded the company car for his truck.

Chapter Thirty-Two

Elliot had stayed out late looking for Cyndi, and he hadn't found her. Morning had arrived too early. But he wasn't walking on firm ground with Lundsford, and he couldn't complicate things by missing the nine o'clock appointment the captain had set up for him.

Just off Sheridan Road, Elliot found a street that led him to the address Captain Lundsford had given him, that of a newly constructed home built for Ashton and Monica Wheeler. Ashton didn't live there anymore. He was dead.

Elliot pulled into the circular drive and parked, but he didn't feel like going through with this. His mind was still on Cyndi. The Llewellyn case still concerned him as well. He couldn't help feeling as if the captain had asked him to abandon an unfinished job.

Chapter Thirty-Three

Elliot left his office and took the elevator to the parking garage. Darkness had set in, and as he walked across the concrete floor toward his car, he checked his watch. It showed 7:00 p.m. He'd spent the entire day following dead-end leads that'd come from his interrogation of Monica Wheeler, and as he climbed into his car and fumbled the keys into the ignition he began to wonder if his fate was to be assigned to one unsolvable case after another.

Elliot wrapped his fingers around the key but hesitated as a sensation of impending danger tiptoed around his senses. He wondered if someone had tampered with the car, but then realized it was a ridiculous notion brought on by fatigue and frustration. He turned the key, but just as he twisted it he heard a noise. It was his phone. He flipped it open and brought it to his ear and the sensation of not-right intensified. "Elliot."

"I suggest you pay attention this time."

The voice that came over the phone was deep and riddled with base, like the confidence-robbing sound of Enrique Savage, and while a tingling of nerves buzzed up Elliot's spine, he wondered if Enrique was in the car with him, if he'd somehow busted out of his cell and was in the backseat, hunkering down with a satisfied grin on his pasty white face, and a gun pointed at Elliot's head.

Elliot twisted around, looked in the backseat. It was empty. He scanned the garage but saw no one. "Who is this?"

The caller did not answer right away. Elliot could hear him breathing in the background.

"If you want to see your girlfriend again," he continued, "do exactly what I tell you. The slightest deviation will not be tolerated."

The phone went dead.

Elliot hit MENU then CALLS, but the phone number had been blocked. The phone dropped from his hand and fell to the seat. The car was running but he hadn't put it in gear. A current of fear ran through him "My God. What have I done to you, Cyndi?"

In a near involuntary action, Elliot slid the car into gear and backed out of the parking space. He dropped it into drive and pressed the accelerator, driving into the night. He had no idea where he was going. *Do exactly as I tell you*, the voice had said. But how could he when the caller hadn't told him anything? He'd left him hanging, like he was supposed to figure it out on his own by utilizing the kind of hoodoo magic Captain Lundsford was so fond of ridiculing.

Elliot drove until a particular brand of sign, glowing through a window, caught his attention, and he had to confess to not knowing exactly where he was, but he'd found a bar and right now that's exactly where he wanted to be. He parked and went inside. He couldn't remember having been there before, and several of the rough-looking patrons turned their heads as he walked by, which told him it was one of those places you didn't go unless you belonged there. He didn't really care right now. He went to the bar and ordered a beer, then sat a table in the corner.

Elliot's present state of mind didn't lend itself to the accumulation of details, but what he'd seen behind the bar didn't require a heightened state of awareness to get his attention. Pinned to the wall alongside an array of required permits, was a sign of hate, a swastika. These people had no use for him, but he had news for them. It was right back at them two fold. He reached inside his coat and readied the Glock.

Elliot finished the first beer and was halfway through the second when a couple of guys with shaved heads decided it was time he left their little hideaway. They got up from their tables and walked over to his.

One of them leaned forward, placing his hands on the table. "You look a little out of place, mister. Are you lost, or just stupid?"

That's when Elliot's phone rang. He knew who it had to be, which meant he had to take the call, and he didn't have time for small talk with his new friends. He wasn't sure what came over him at that instant, a sort of craziness to be sure, but his next actions were those kind that exist only within the confines of our imaginations, that secret world of fantasy where we play out ridiculous scenarios, knowing full well that we would never actually do such things. Elliot flipped open the phone and brought it to his ear, and at the same time he ripped the Glock from its holster and planted the barrel firmly against the forehead of the man who had spoken to him. As a silence fell over the bar, Elliot spoke into the phone. "Elliot."

The other party didn't answer, but Elliot knew he was there. He could feel his presence. Keeping both the Glock and the phone in place, Elliot pushed away from the table and stood. He forced his opponent to sit in a chair at the same table, then he slowly backed out of the bar. Luckily, his welcoming committee didn't try to follow.

Once he was outside, alone on the sidewalk, Elliot pressed the phone closer to his ear. "Who the hell are you," he asked, "and what do you want from me?"

"Don't be ridiculous, Detective Elliot. Your lack of good judgment got us in this little jam. Now it's up to you to get us out of it."

"What the hell's that supposed to mean?"

The voice that came over the phone was just as intimidating as before, but this time Elliot detected something that he hadn't picked up on earlier, a trace of apprehension and a mechanical quality, as if the caller was speaking into some kind of voice-scrambling device. Elliot thought about the listening equipment the individual who'd parked outside his house had dropped as he'd sped away. The equipment could have been purchased at the same outlet. He made a mental note to do some checking around, find out who'd recently acquired such things in the Tulsa area.

Once again Elliot's phone relayed the distorted voice. "Are you listening?" Without waiting for an answer, the caller instructed, "This is what I want you to do."

Chapter Thirty-Four

Douglass Wistrom pressed his face against the cold steel of the gate and peered into the black expanse ahead of him. The compound was supposed to be a self-sufficient community, like a town unto itself where the followers of the Church could live in harmony with church and community being one and the same, but it didn't work out that way, becoming instead just another eccentric neighborhood in a town where normalcy was the exception and not the rule. Most of the cottages were empty now, and the smattering of small white houses that were still occupied needed fresh paint and a host of other repairs.

Just outside the gates of the dwindling community, Douglass stood quietly in the darkness, which he'd been waiting for, contemplating what he might do once he reached the reverend's house. As he started to climb the fence, however, his phone went off. He wanted to believe that he'd simply forgotten to turn it off, but to be honest he hadn't even considered it, and he cursed quietly as its ring tone reverberated through the night, breaking the silence like an alarm tripped by a careless burglar. He wrestled it from his pocket, its light shining like a beacon as he flipped it open and brought it to his ear. But the familiar voice that came over the phone eased his anxiety, and he had to admit to being both surprised and relieved that she had called him. Hearing her voice brought a touch of sanity to an otherwise desperate situation.

Being in Donegal had unraveled his nerves, affecting him on levels of consciousness that he'd buried, and for good reason, but he'd be all right as soon as he got out of this place, and back to never-never land. He paused as he realized he'd never said that before. Those were her words, and she had been just as shocked as he was that he'd used them. But a lot had happened in the last few days. He wasn't himself, or was he? Was he the man behind door number one or the imposter inside box number three?

Nothing made sense anymore. He'd dreamed of this, going home and experiencing things left behind. In a moment of grandeur, he'd entertained the idea there would be an article, even a Pulitzer in it. At the very least he'd thought it might be, if not nice, then enlightening, but now that he was here, he couldn't wait to get back to the comfort of their covenant, their make-believe world where they never spoke of what had come before. He was unnerved over the location she'd chosen, but his feelings at this point were of little consequence. To put it bluntly, he had no choice in the matter. And it wasn't that far from his present location. The houses she'd spoken of were just on the other side of the wooded area east of the compound.

Douglass Wistrom turned away from the gate to the compound and started toward the trees. Going through the woods at night would not be easy. Clouds covered the sky, restricting the available light to nearly nothing, but there had been a pathway that'd run from the old house where he'd lived to the church grounds, and if he could find that, the trip would be manageable. He searched the edge of the forest, using the light from his cell phone occasionally when a particular area looked familiar, and a few minutes later he found what he was looking for. The pathway had not disappeared or even faded, but was even more obvious than he'd remembered. It was still being used.

He stepped onto the path, which led him into the trees, and about twenty minutes later he stood on the other side of the wooded area just above a clearing where several houses sat in the distance, barely visible in the darkness. The scene played with the eye, leaving what he saw hovering somewhere between imagination and reality like the faded ghosts that they were.

He made his way to the largest structure, the only two-story in the bunch, and as he drew near, the appearance of the place sent a shiver up his spine. It looked just like the house he'd lived in as a child. Over time, he'd driven that which had been from his mind, the troublesome memories being replaced by a peaceful existence of love, his own bedroom, and a closet full of clothes for school. But as he stared at the house, trying to convince himself that it wasn't the same place, was in fact some specter arising from deep beneath a buried house of his nightmares, he began to suspect that in some sort of hellish purgatory it all still existed. That he needed only to make a wrong move, take a step in the wrong direction, and he would fall through time to be caught in the midst of some lost dimension where all that he had run away from still lived.

Stumbling across the weed-tangled lawn, worrying perhaps too much about being watched by someone lurking in the black wilderness that surrounded the area, Douglass reached the house and climbed onto the porch. Living in make-believe, it seemed, had inspired paranoia rather than the confidence of someone in control of his own destiny. Once again, he chanced using his cell phone for light, and when he flipped it open, he saw that there was no door blocking the entrance, but just a hole full of darkness where it had been. He did not step readily through the portal, but slowly pushed his head into the void and called out. "Hello, anybody here?"

The lack of a reply only served to deepen his anxiety. He wondered, and not for the first time, why she had chosen such a place. To safeguard their anonymity, they kept no physical ties and met only when the situation called for it, and even then only in predetermined locations. In the past few days, the need for such get-togethers and the frequency of their occurrences had increased dramatically, which could mean only one thing: their lives, make-believe or not, were in jeopardy.

Disregarding his internal alarm, which was telling him to get the hell out of there, Douglass Wistrom stepped inside the house and took a few steps across the wooden floor of the living room. He called out again. "Anybody here?"

As he'd feared, again he received no answer, and he began to worry that he'd gotten the location wrong. But she'd been quite specific in her instructions, and he'd followed them to the letter. He flipped open his phone and shone the faint light around the room, half expecting to see old man Saucier, back from the dead and crouched in a corner, a sly grin spreading across his ghoulish face, or perhaps Reverend Coronet, his arm outstretched and his hand readied to clamp on Douglass's shoulder, adding a personal touch as he buried a knife in his back. But he saw no one. The room was empty. He shook his head. She'd been quite unhappy about his killing Saucier. He'd tried to explain that he had not intended to. Things just got out of control. He'd panicked.

He made his way into the kitchen and after a quick search, which turned up nothing, he returned to the living room and walked across the floor toward the first bedroom. Before reaching it, however, he saw something, the little half door, which caught the light from his phone with such authenticity that he began to suspect that this was not some incredible doppelganger he'd stumbled into, but a ghostly version of the actual place he'd called home. He could not deny the faded blue paint. When he brought the phone closer, the blood ran from his head, and he braced himself against the wall to keep from falling, for what he saw told him that he had indeed been sent back to the origin of his sin. He stared at the symbol, and he knew that it was the same one that had been carved into the wood of the half door in their house, an inverted crucifix, which she told him was proof of Mom and Dad's unholy affiliation.

Much had happened in that closet, the slanted one beneath the stairs where nothing was stored except the lingering memories of their torture, which was the punishment favored by Father, the taking away of their freedom. At some point, though, it'd become not punishment but reward, where she would share with him her knowledge and her friendship, such that he would never experience again, for he was to find no equal in the world that they, at her insistence, had created for themselves. She also told him of the carnal pleasures, which Reverend Coronet had tried to extract from her only to be denied by Father, though not for her benefit or rescue, but to save her purity and virginity as an appeasement, an offering to gain favor with the lord of darkness.

With no one else to turn to, he believed in her. He lived in the palm of her hand, hoping not to be squeezed too tightly lest the air be driven from his lungs. He could not stop himself, and he watched as his hand closed around the latch of the half door that hid the closet where they'd spent too many hours of their lives. Cool against his fingers, the latch released, and the small door swung effortlessly away from the wall.

He bent his knees and leaned forward, and in the faint odor of old musty books coming out of the hole in the wall, he shone the faint bluish light into the void, and there he saw her clothes, the same ones she'd worn during their last meeting, folded in a neat pile, and beside them on the floor of the closet was a handgun and a folded piece of paper.

He opened the paper and saw, written in a hand he did not recognize, two words: YOU'RE NEXT.

As the paper fell from his hand, he reached for the gun then flashed the cell phone around the room, its blue light falling on nothing but empty space, and while what-if scenarios played through his head, he thought of her, and though he'd vowed never to again speak her name, *Elizabeth* slipped like an old habit from his tongue.

His hands shook so that he could barely use the keypad, but he managed to punch in the number, using what power the phone had left to call her. He cursed as voice mail picked it up. He closed the phone, but then a distinctive sound, one that came from outside filtered into his ears. Someone was coming. He could hear them thrashing through the brush.

Chapter Thirty-Five

Leaving downtown Tulsa, Elliot pulled onto Highway 75 and headed south to Donegal. The caller's insistence that he go immediately wasn't enough to ensure Elliot's cooperation, but the threat of harm to Cyndi was.

When Elliot reached the outskirts of the small town, the fuel gauge caught his attention, and he pulled off the highway and onto the lot of a station, stopping next to a pump.

Elliot slid his card into the reader but nothing happened. He thumbed the intercom, and the clerk came on, telling him to go ahead and fill up, then bring the card in.

After filling the tank, Elliot went inside the store.

The clerk shook his head. "Seems like that thing never works."

"Maybe you should get it fixed," Elliot said. When he turned back to look at the pump, he thought he saw someone walk behind his car.

The clerk said something, which caused Elliot to turn back around, and when he looked outside again, the person was gone.

"Do you want a receipt?"

"Yeah," Elliot said. "Sure."

Maybe it was his overstimulated imagination, playing mind games, but Elliot thought the person he'd seen wore brown pants with a matching shirt, much like the uniforms of Reverend Coronet's men.

Outside, Elliot walked around the car but saw nothing out of the ordinary. He climbed in and started the car, then pulled back onto the highway.

Neither the moon nor the stars penetrated the cloud cover. The darkness seemed to squeeze the effectiveness from the beams thrown out by the car's lights, and perhaps it was for that reason that Elliot did not immediately see the van in front of him. Its red taillights appeared from nowhere, as if the vehicle had just materialized, back from being lost somewhere in the Bermuda Triangle only to be deposited onto the tarmac of Highway 75 less than thirty feet ahead of him.

Elliot hit the brakes. The pedal fell uselessly to the floor. He turned hard to the right.

Something dripped in Elliot's face. He tried to wipe it away, but a strap held his hand above his head, while his own weight pinned his other arm behind his back. Seconds later, he realized what had happened. The car had rolled over, and he was lying on the inside of the roof, his right arm tangled in the seatbelt above his head. He twisted then pulled and freed his right arm. He felt for the door handle, found it and pulled. Nothing happened. The door was jammed.

He fumbled around and found the window switch, then toggled it back and forth, trying to figure out which way to go with it, then rolled the window down—up, in the car's present position.

Freeing his other arm, Elliot wiggled through the window. Pain arced through his arm. He grabbed for it, finding it wet and sticky, and at that moment he realized what had dripped into his face. Blood. He was cut and bleeding.

Once out of the vehicle, he stood and reached for his shoulder holster. The Glock was gone. He checked his pocket for the small flashlight. Gone too. Both must have fallen out during the crash.

He kept another flashlight in the glove box, but getting to it would be a problem. The passenger side of the vehicle rested against the wall of the bar ditch.

Elliot glanced at his watch. He still had time. He stumbled back to the driver's side, then lay on his stomach and wiggled back inside the car. The way he figured it, he had no choice. The caller had told him to be at the rendezvous point at 7:45. He didn't want to be late. The caller had made it clear that he didn't appreciate him not following his orders.

Elliot fumbled around in the darkness and found the dashboard, then ran his hand along it until he came to the glove box. Inside, he found the flashlight. Switching it on, he directed the beam to his injury. A nasty gash ran about four inches up his forearm.

He scooted back out of the vehicle and stood. Propping the flashlight on the vehicle's upturned bottom, he took off his jacket, unbuttoned his dress shirt, then tore off his T-shirt and wrapped it around the wound. He re-buttoned his shirt and worked his way back into the jacket. With that done, he lay down again and shone the light inside the car, moving the beam around until he found what he was looking for: the Glock. Grabbing the weapon, he tucked it into his shoulder holster, then got to his feet again.

Directing the light ahead of him, Elliot saw the van that'd caused the accident. The vehicle had pulled off the highway and parked on the shoulder. He decided to check it out, see if everyone was all right. Perhaps they could give him a ride.

Without pausing to think it through, he proceeded toward the van, setting a pace that was too fast, intimidating, but a sense of urgency had begun to form in his gut, and the closer he got to the vehicle, the stronger the feeling became. As he neared the rear of the van, he wondered if the actions of its driver had truly been random, or if instead they had been executed by careful design. He imagined Cyndi inside with a hulking maniac behind her, a knife drawn to her throat.

The concept that the driver of the van and the caller, who'd just minutes earlier laid down instructions for Elliot, were actually one and the same was not farfetched. Elliot drew his weapon and edged along the side of the vehicle.

Against his expectations, Elliot found the van seemingly unoccupied, its windows rolled up, the doors locked tight. He pressed his face against the glass of the driver's side window and peered inside. The cab was empty. He pounded on the glass.

After that, he went to the rear of the vehicle and knocked on the doors and windows there. When he got no response, he shone the light down to view the vehicle's license plate. It had none. Where the tag should have been, there was a symbol, which had been crudely painted onto the metal of the van. It was a five-pointed star with two circles around it, one point purposely facing the earth and the head of goat imposed onto it. The back of his neck prickled.

Elliot fell against the van, his thoughts scattered like a madman's, but the sound of the passenger side door slamming shut wrenched him back to sanity. Someone had just exited the vehicle.

With the Glock readied, Elliot edged around to the driver's side. He got there just in time to hear someone thrashing through the brush. He shone the light toward the noise and saw movement, a figure cutting through the trees.

Elliot ran after the driver, the caller, or whoever it was. He'd intended to go that direction anyway. He had fifteen minutes to make his rendezvous point, which the caller had given him, and he'd never make it following the road on foot, but cutting through the woods, he just might. And if he caught up with his fleeing friend, he just might get some answers.

Elliot pushed through the brush. He couldn't see or hear the person who'd run from the van, but he knew he was out there. He plunged ahead, making too much noise, unable to hear his nemesis if he decided to turn the tables and come after him. He wondered if his haste might be counterproductive, but then he remembered the caller's threats and the possibility that he might have Cyndi. Seconds counted.

Elliot increased his pace, well aware that whoever he was chasing might have stopped running, and could be waiting for him behind the next tree, ready to put a bullet in him as he came into view. But he couldn't block the image of Cyndi being held hostage by this lunatic, and if he turned out to be who Elliot suspected he was, the deranged son of Kathryn and Solomon Stone, there was no telling what he might do.

When Elliot took another step, his foot caught on the underbrush, and as he plunged forward, dancing to keep his balance, the flashlight beam skipped around the foliage, momentarily revealing a portion of a man's face.

Elliot steadied himself then jerked the light back in the direction where he'd seen the person. No one was there, though in the cold humid air, the scent of the man's body odor lingered. Turning in a slow circle, Elliot shone the light around his immediate area. The beam illuminated parts of shrubs and pieces of trees but nothing else. The darkness seemed to close around him. Even though he'd seen the man run away and disappear into the black thicket, Elliot suspected he was near, perhaps behind him, turning as he turned.

Resuming his journey, Elliot pushed forward, hoping his irregular trajectory would lead him near his destination. He wondered why the caller would so adamantly demand that he follow his instructions, only to pull in front of him on the road, causing the crash, and then lure him into a romp through the woods. It made no sense. There were easier ways to kill a person, if that's what he was trying to do.

As that thought wafted through Elliot's head, he heard the crack of a rifle. The projectile buzzed past his ear, splintering the bark of a tree just inches from his head. He switched off the light and crouched in the brush. He'd seen the blast from the barrel. Whoever had fired the shot was about fifty yards west of his position. He was either circling around or he'd changed course. Elliot also considered the possibility that he'd become disoriented, which meant that he was the one heading in the wrong direction.

He had a decision to make: Follow the shooter and hope for the best, or keep to his present course. Working purely on instinct he chose the latter. He got up from his squatting position but just enough to walk. He left the light off.

A few minutes later, the tress and brush gave way to grass. He'd reached a clearing. When he rose to his feet, he saw a small bluish light, bouncing around in the darkness about a hundred yards away in the valley below.

Elliot heard a noise, the sound of leaves crunching behind him, and he reached for his shoulder holster, but as his hand closed around the handle of the weapon, something heavy slammed into the back of his neck and everything went black.

Chapter Thirty-Six

Elliot awoke in darkness. He raised his head, then ran his hand across his face, feeling a series of indentations that'd been caused by his lying on something rough. He had no idea where he was. He remembered dreaming.

Perhaps the answer was as simple as that; he was in fact still asleep and at any moment he might fall back into another nightmare, where Brian McKenna and Reverend Coronet would come out of the darkness, laughing while they watched McKenna's clan set fire to a stack of wood beneath an alter, atop of which lay a bound and screaming sacrifice.

As Elliot's senses came back, he began to determine where he was. The worn texture of the wooden floor, and the unsettling yet familiar scents of liquor and body odor left little doubt in his mind. He was once again lying on the floor of the abandoned house, the one where the waitress had sent him and where Reverend Coronet's men had ambushed him.

When he sat up, a pain like an ice pick being shoved through his head shot through him. As far as he could determine, he was alone. He ran his hand across the floor, searching for the flashlight. No such luck. He patted his jacket, feeling the shoulder holster, then ran his hand inside the coat and wrapped his fingers around the handle of the weapon, pulling it free. Intimately familiar with the firearm, he determined even in the darkness that it was still loaded. It seemed senseless that his captor would leave him armed, and though it went against logic, he suspected it'd been done for a reason.

He got to his feet and readied the weapon. With that done, he began to inch forward, and when he bumped into a wall, he ran his free hand along it until he came to a doorway. He'd found the kitchen. The entryway's arched design and his memories of being there before told him this. Now that he had his bearings, he knew that the front door was located behind him and a few feet to the left.

Elliot turned around, and at that point he saw, due to the varying shades of darkness, exactly where the exit was. He started toward it, moving in slow, even steps, not wanting to trip over anything, or make enough noise to alert his captor, if he was still around.

When Elliot reached the doorway and stepped out onto the porch, he saw someone down in the valley that fronted the old houses. He appeared to be tending a campfire. Elliot glanced around the area but saw no one else. He failed to see the rationality of the situation. His captor, if that's who stood beside the fire, had left him armed, and he was clearly not trying to hide at this point. Something wasn't right.

Nevertheless, Elliot crept across the weathered wood of the porch, carefully choosing his footsteps. When he reached the edge, he lowered himself to the ground. After crouching in the tall grass, he rose to a semi-standing position then started toward the man, cautiously descending the small hill leading to the valley.

When Elliot reached a point about fifty yards away from the man near the fire, he paused. The man had his back to him. To his right, the forest he'd emerged from loomed like a dark metropolis. To his left was the road, which led back to town. He suspected he could sneak past, going either way, and leave without alerting his mysterious friend, but then he would never know what the man's game was, or if he had Cyndi held captive nearby. He checked his watch. The appointed time was long past.

With a heaviness in his chest, Elliot considered calling Chief Washington. He felt his pocket. The phone was still there. He pulled it out and flipped it open. Pressing the power button yielded no result. Somehow, calling Jed Washington didn't seem like a good idea anyway. The possibility existed, even though remote, that the man tending the campfire was not the same man that'd lured him into the woods and bashed his head. That might explain why he sensed something wasn't right about this. And if the chief came out to find Elliot lurking in the darkness of Donegal's outskirts, trying to arrest one of his old fishing buddies, that wouldn't go down very well.

The man stood and turned toward the forest, his movement leaving the side of his face exposed.

Elliot thought he recognized the profile, but in the dim light he couldn't be sure. He appeared to be carrying on a conversation with someone, speaking and gesturing with his hands, but if anyone else was there, Elliot certainly couldn't see them, and at this distance he couldn't make out what the man was saying.

Again he turned, which left him facing Elliot. Like an overzealous scoutmaster, terrifying his young troops with ghost stories, the man appeared ugly, his features distorted by the flickering orange glow of the firelight, but the realization of who he was shot through Elliot like a current through wire.

Elliot squeezed the handle of the Glock and stared at the distinctive face of Douglass Wistrom. He now wished his phone had worked. Washington needed to be here to make the arrest. But he wasn't here, and Elliot couldn't just let the suspect go.

A twig snapped behind him, and the sudden sound, coupled with his already frazzled nerves, caused him to leap upright.

Whatever it was caught Wistrom's attention as well. He spun around, facing Elliot head on.

Elliot started toward the suspect. "Detective Elliot of the Tulsa Police Department. Don't move."

Wistrom stood firm for a moment, frozen in shock perhaps, but it didn't last. From his pocket he pulled a handgun, which he aimed at Elliot, and with a crazed look invading his face, he began to charge, screaming like a man who had lost everything.

Elliot readied the Glock. "Drop the weapon."

Wistrom kept coming.

Elliot fired a warning shot.

Wistrom screamed and fired a shot of his own.

Elliot had no choice. He squeezed off two rounds. One of them caught Wistrom. He fell to the ground, a wail like that of a wounded animal gurgling from his throat.

Elliot knelt beside the man. "Try not to move. I'll get help."

Wistrom shook his head.

"Where's Cyndi?" Elliot asked.

The question seemed to drive fear through Wistrom. His eyes widened and again he shook his head.

"You told me to meet you here. Why?"

A look somewhere between astonishment and disbelief crossed Wistrom's face, as if the mysteries of the universe had just been revealed to him. "Not me," he said, the words barely escaping his lips.

"Your fingerprints are all over Saucier's barn. If you didn't kill him, why were you there?"

"Parents," he said. "Looking for answers."

Wistrom struggled to get the words out. Elliot wanted to stop him, tell him to rest, but he could not. He wanted to hear, to know. So he asked the question that burned in his mind. "Are you Justin Stone?"

The man's eyes widened, but he said nothing.

"Did you kill Abraham Saucier?"

"Lost my head. Accident."

"Were Kathryn and Solomon Stone accidents, too? Did you kill them? Did you murder your family?"

A tremble started in the man's hand, the one that Elliot held, then coursed through his arm and soon his whole body vibrated. When the shaking stopped, he began to cry, and he motioned with his free hand for Elliot to come closer. Perhaps he wanted to lighten his load, share his burden by confessing his sins to the only person available.

Leaning over, Elliot put his ear close to the man's lips, hearing what sounded like the faint whispers of a frightened child, which came out as, "Brighid."

"The prostitute? Did you kill her?"

He shook his head.

"What then?"

The man struggled to hang on. His breathing was short, ragged. He tried to speak but nothing came out. He ran his tongue across his lips and tried again. "You got the wrong one."

After that, the man closed his eyes, and while Elliot held his hand the life slipped from Wistrom's body. Elliot wondered about his last statement. Perhaps he was referring to his invisible friend, the one he'd talked with while Elliot watched him from the grass.

Elliot heard the unmistakable sound of footsteps crunching through the leaves. Someone was approaching. He looked up and saw the hulking form of Chief Jed Washington, staring down at him.

Elliot rose to his feet. He'd always heard that the dead don't wear masks of fear, or surprise, or anything else for that matter, but as he stared down at the body of Douglass Wistrom he did not believe that, for his face continued to plead with Elliot, trying to explain his actions, even after Elliot had put a bullet in his chest.

Chapter Thirty-Seven

Chief Washington had not miraculously appeared at the scene that night. Someone had heard the rifle shot that was fired at Elliot and called it in. Washington got the news a few minutes later. As a result, he drove through the area and saw the campfire. There had been nothing supernatural about it, yet his timing had been impeccable. He'd seen enough to know that Elliot had acted in self-defense.

Elliot walked across the dining area of Goldie's on 21st Street and chose a booth along the wall. A few minutes later, Sergeant Conley came over and sat across from him. It'd been two weeks since Elliot had killed Douglass Wistrom, or Justin Stone in the lonely valley outside Donegal. He was still on administrative leave, a forced sabbatical that Elliot had needed more than he cared to admit.

Elliot unfolded his napkin and placed it across his lap. Conley's seemingly frivolous jocularity was deceptive. With a caring for others that stretched the boundaries of human kindness, he could have been a priest, a psychologist, even a good bartender. He wound up a cop instead. He took a bite out of the cinnamon roll he'd picked up, then grinned as if he was about to crack another of his dry jokes. "What's the matter, Elliot? You look like the only kid on the block without an ice cream cone."

Elliot couldn't help but smile. "I have a lot on my mind."

Conley nodded. "Don't we all. Feel like talking about it?"

Scenarios of the crazy events that'd all started with an unidentified dead man at Windhall went through Elliot's head. "I killed someone, David. I can't get it out of my head. I'm not sure I ever will."

Conley took a sip of coffee, then set the cup on the table. "If it helps, you're not the first cop to feel that way. I wish I could say it'll get better, but I'd be lying." He paused then added, "You did good, kid. You solved a tough case first time out. That's no small feat."

"I guess that's what's bothering me."

"What the hell's that supposed to mean?"

"I'm not so sure I have solved it."

"What kind of talk is that? You nailed it. Captain Lundsford's beside himself."

A vision of Justin Stone's pleading face unfolded in Elliot's mind. "He told me he didn't do it."

"They all say that."

"When they're dying?"

203

Conley held an unfinished piece of cinnamon roll and he shook it for emphasis as he talked. "I know what you're doing here. You're beating yourself up because you put a bullet in a man."

"Maybe, but you might change your mind about that after you hear the rest. I stated in the report that the suspect was alone, nobody else around."

"Ain't that the way it was?"

"That's what I thought at the time. Maybe I was confused by the concussion. But later, when it all started playing through my head, I remembered things more clearly."

Conley stuffed the last bite of cinnamon roll into his mouth, then shook his head. "No, you got it all backward. It's later when things get fuzzy, not the other way around."

"When I first saw the suspect, he was in the valley about a hundred yards away."

Conley shrugged.

"If I was watching Justin Stone in the valley, then who snuck up behind me and knocked the wits out of me?"

The cheerful look drained from Conley's face. "What are you saying?"

"He wasn't alone. Somebody else was out there in the woods that night."

Elliot didn't say anything else. He'd seen Conley keep his spirits up in some pretty dire situations, but the information he'd just given his friend seemed to place a weight on his shoulders.

"What are you going to do?" Conley asked.

"I'm not sure yet."

Conley stared at Elliot for a moment then said, "There's more to it, isn't there, something you're not telling me?"

Elliot thought about his answer. He wasn't sure he had the right to lay all of this on the good sergeant. But he had to tell someone. He nodded.

Conley swallowed the last of his coffee, then scooted the cup to the edge of the table, signaling the waitress to refill it. "All right, kid. Let's have it."

"Graves," Elliot said.

"Come again?"

"I've been in touch with Jed Washington, chief of police in Donegal. They've searched Saucier's property from corner to corner, the woods behind it and the area around where the old house stood, where the Stone family lived, before it was bulldozed into the ground. They didn't find any more graves."

"Were they supposed to?"

When the waitress appeared to refill Conley's cup, Elliot turned his right side up and took some as well. After doctoring it with cream and sugar, he said, "Kathryn and Solomon Stone had two children."

Conley set his cup down, half dropping it, slopping coffee over the rim. "I don't know, kid. Maybe you're trying to read too much into it. You got some time left. Enjoy it. Go fishing or something, get your mind off work for a while."

"Yeah," Elliot said, "maybe I'll do that."

"There is something I don't understand," Conley said.

"What's that?"

"Why did Wistrom leave those religious symbols behind. It's almost like he was trying to draw attention to himself?"

"He was trying to throw us off. You see the sigil of Baphomet is a satanic symbol, or at least it's been adopted by them. Since pagans don't believe in God, they don't believe in Satan either. Wistrom was trying to take the heat off the pagans by implicating Satanists."

Elliot left Conley at Goldies, and after climbing into his truck he began to drive. He had no particular destination in mind, though his route to Woodward Park wasn't what you would call circuitous.

When Elliot parked and got out of the truck, the typically crowded park hosted only a few wandering couples, and the expanse of grass and plants boasted a more severe deprivation of color than he remembered from previous visits, a level of dormancy from which recovery seemed, at the moment, hopeless.

Beneath the protective canopy of a park shelter, a squirrel held an acorn between its paws, chattering at a nearby crow, though the large black bird seemed to take it as an invitation rather than a warning and edged closer.

Elliot studied the area where the azalea bushes grew. No one walked the pathway that wound through the rocks and bushes there. Stepping onto the grass, he descended the small hill until he reached the area. Traffic sounds from 21st Street filtered through the quietness, encroaching on the solitude of the park.

When Elliot came to a suitable location, a park bench beside the trail, he sat and watched the guilty cars go up and down the street. When his mind drifted to the case, as it often did since the ordeal in Donegal, he wondered if he should heed Sergeant Conley's advice and consider the case closed, a job well done. It didn't feel that way. On the contrary, it seemed rather than being laid to rest that the surface had only been scratched. He feared that no matter what he or anyone else thought, closed or not, it would eventually come back to haunt them.

And of all the loose ends, which dangled around the case like unfinished business, the one that bothered him the most was the role Reverend Marshall Coronet had played in setting off a series of events that eventually led to the convenient solving of one of his problems.

On the other end of the spectrum, another unsettling notion lay in the facts, and though this didn't feel right, unlike his gut instincts, the possibility supported logic. He'd felt the presence of someone other than Justin Stone in the woods and in the valley by the old houses that night. And the only other person he'd actually seen, one who'd seemed to appear from nowhere, was Donegal's own chief of police, Jed Washington.

At the apex of Elliot's confusion, he heard something other than the noise of traffic, a familiar voice, one which he surely did not expect, and he wondered briefly if he truly had taken the first steps down the path to insanity, though when he turned toward the voice, she was there and as real as ever. She wore a gray wool coat with a red scarf thrown around her neck, the color of the accoutrement complementing quite seductively the pink of her cheeks. It was Cyndi Bannister.

Elliot stood, and while no thoughts came to mind that he could verbalize, he suspected his expression told her how he felt, because she came to him, falling against him and laying her head on his chest. Tears came to Elliot's eyes as he drew her near and kissed the top of her head, for she looked not at him but at the ground, and when she did give in and allow herself to face Elliot, he saw that she, too, was crying.

"I'm sorry, Kenny."

Elliot shook his head. "When you didn't show up at Polo's, I thought you'd changed your mind. And I thought you wouldn't want to see me again."

"No, it's nothing like that. It's just . . . Well, I knew what you meant when you said you had something important to talk about. Because I'd been thinking about it, too. I was scared, didn't trust my feelings, wasn't sure of what I might say or do. So I left for a few days to think things over. It was wrong of me. I shouldn't have put you through that."

"Do you trust your feelings now?"

Cyndi looked away for a moment, staring across the barren plants that would bloom into lush azaleas in the spring. When she turned back, she said, "I've never met anyone quite like you, Kenny. I'm still not sure what that really means, but I'm willing to take it one step at a time, if you are."

"Absolutely."

The word came out of Elliot's mouth without hesitation, almost without thought, an involuntary reaction of speech, though his feelings for Cyndi were anything but involuntary.

"Good," Cyndi said. A smile brightened her face. "I talked to my parents. They want to meet you."

Elliot thought about that for a moment. In a few seconds, he'd gone from one step at a time to meeting the parents. Then again, nobody ever said that expression came with a speed limit. "Sure," he said. "I'd like that."

She pulled away and straightened her coat. "Come on, let's go."

"Right now?"

A curious look crossed her face. "Why not?"

"Do they know we're coming?"

She shrugged.

The air lacked movement, but that did little to dull the edge of the cold. Elliot pulled his coat together and buttoned it. "All right."

With that, Cyndi turned and started up the hill, toward her car.

Elliot followed. About halfway to the parking lot, he asked, "How did you know I'd be here, at the park I mean?"

Cyndi shook her head. "I was about to ask you the same question."

They walked in silence, and when they reached the parking lot, Cyndi pulled her keys from her coat pocket and unlocked her car.

"I've been thinking," Elliot said, "about my occupation, whether or not I should give it up, you know try something else."

Cyndi said nothing, but Elliot saw a glimmer of hope in her eyes.

"You know how I feel about it," she said, breaking the silence. "But I won't ask you to do that. I love you, Kenny. Cop or not, that'll never change."

"Did you just tell me that you loved me?"

Cyndi hesitated, as if to ponder the thought herself. She took the lapels of Elliot's coat and pulled him toward her, her face seeming to reflect a profound epiphany. "I've never said that to a man before."

Elliot searched her eyes for sincerity. He found it difficult to believe that someone as attractive and seductive as Cyndi would never have cause to utter such words, even if only in the heat of passion. "I'm flattered, perhaps even amazed."

"That's what I like about you, Kenny. You're so honest. It's almost scary sometimes."

"I've never thought of honesty as being frightening."

"You wouldn't, would you? You're a most unusual man. But you belong to me now, and that's forever."

Elliot could resist no longer. He pulled her close and brought his lips to hers, lingering in the pleasure. Afterward he said, "I love you, too. And that's forever."

Chapter Thirty-Eight

The Bannisters lived near 3rd and Lewis, close to the university where Doctor Bannister had worked. The red brick cottage, an eighty-year-old bungalow preserved by hard work and diligent maintenance, looked in good enough shape to have been constructed yesterday. The driveway, which consisted of parallel strips of concrete separated by grass, ran beside the house, ending at a one-car garage, also immaculately maintained. The nice but modest home of a college professor.

Having rung the bell and been invited in by her parents, Cyndi and Elliot now stood inside while Mr. and Mrs. Bannister hovered close by, staring at Elliot, sizing him up. He felt like a teenager that'd brought his date home past curfew. The Bannisters seemed kind and gracious, though Elliot detected a hint of sadness behind their smiles, as if they privately lamented the loss of a loved one. He wondered if they'd had other children.

Seeming to sense his discomfort, Cyndi placed her hand on his shoulder. "Mom, Dad, this is Kenny, the guy I've been telling you about."

Doctor Bannister, a lean man with graying hair, stepped forward and shook Elliot's hand. His dark eyes shone as he introduced himself, telling Elliot in a not-so-convincing tone to call him George.

Elliot wondered if the one-car garage at the end of the drive housed an old British sports car, the kind associated with college professors. "Nice to meet you," he said.

Then, like members of a bluegrass band taking turns at the microphone, Doctor Bannister stepped aside and back, allowing the missus to come forward and take her turn in the spotlight. Elliot wondered if she might display her hand for a kiss, but instead she extended it, taking only his fingers, squeezing them gently. "Why, you're a fine-looking man, Mr. Elliot. I'm Evelyn."

She sounded Scottish, her accent, perhaps due to years of American influence, having faded to the point of being only slightly detectable. "Come sit with us."

Still holding Elliot's hand, she spun around and led him into the living room.

Elliot glanced back to see Cyndi, covering her mouth to stifle a giggle.

In the room where they sat, two couches faced each other in front of a fireplace, and a Navaho-pattern rug with red overtones covered part of the hardwood floor. Evelyn Bannister seated Elliot on the west end of the first couch with his back to the front door, while, to his surprise, Cyndi sat across from him with her mother, a wiry little woman who'd kept her figure through the years. She reminded Elliot of a retired athlete, perhaps spending years on the ice with a pair of skates.

The dining room table, its chairs and the china cabinet, which Elliot could see from his position, consisted of polished maple, as did the arms of the couches and the coffee table between them. On the coffee table, which separated the couches, a tray of cookies sat beside an English teapot with matching cups. Evelyn Bannister filled one of the cups and offered it to Elliot. "Thanks," he said. He glanced at the cream and sugar but decided against it, afraid that he might become clumsy and break the fancy dishes.

The room grew quiet. For a moment, the soft tinkle of spoon against china filled the void, but afterward Elliot heard the gentle *thunk, thunk* of a clock sitting on the fireplace mantle. When he bit into a cookie he'd taken from the tray, a crunching sound echoed through his head. Finally, Mrs. Bannister asked, "Are you from Tulsa, Mr. Elliot?"

"No. I grew up in Porter, about thirty miles east of here."

Mrs. Bannister smiled. "We go there every year. George always gets overheated, the festival being in July, you know, but the peaches are worth it. Cyndi could take it or leave it, but I believe George would climb to the moon for a piece of my peach cobbler."

"I would at that. And on to Mars, if the truth be known."

Evelyn Bannister raised her shoulders and smiled over her teacup. "True love is forever, wouldn't you say, Mr. Elliot?"

Elliot rested his cup and saucer on his knee for support, hoping the action would keep the cup from rattling. For reasons he didn't understand, Mrs. Bannister's loaded question, probably intended to let him know he'd better not hurt Cyndi's feelings, caused him to think instead of Carmen Garcia, his high school sweetheart. His leg jiggled the teacup, and he planted his heels on the floor. "Yes, ma'am."

As silence returned, Doctor Bannister set his cup on the table and stood. "If you don't mind, Mr. Elliot, I've something I want to show you."

Elliot gladly rose and followed Doctor Bannister out of the room. When they reached a doorway at the end of a hall, his short-lived relief faded. Like a kid peering across the threshold of the principal's office, he realized the preliminary was over, and the inquisition was at hand. With a slight gesture of his head, George Bannister offered Elliot the privilege of entering first.

Books lined the walls inside the office, neatly arranged on shelves that towered from floor to ceiling. In the center of the room sat a two-sided desk made of mahogany.

Doctor Bannister strolled into the room. Elliot halfway expected him to open a closet and slip into a brown tweed jacket. He didn't have to conceptualize the pipe. As soon as Bannister sat at the desk, he pulled one from a drawer, packed it with tobacco, then struck a match, hovering the flame over the bowl until it lit. Afterward, he threw the match into an ashtray and motioned for Elliot to join him.

Elliot sat in the chair on the other side of the desk.

Bannister blew smoke into the air. "Cyndi was barely sixteen the last time she brought a young man home for our approval. I take that to mean she's rather serious about you." He paused to draw on the pipe. Seconds later, he added, "The question is, how do you feel about her?"

Elliot considered his answer. A few hours ago, he'd thought Cyndi was out of his life. Now he was sitting in her dad's office, hearing what sounded like a premarital speech. He wasn't sure if his hesitancy sprang from confusion over his feelings or fear that they might again be ripped from his heart if he acknowledged their existence. "I'm in love with her, Doctor Bannister."

Bannister continued to smoke, looking past Elliot at something beyond the window. When he returned his attention to Elliot, he held the pipe in his teeth and spoke around the stem. "I'm inclined to believe you. But there's something you need to know. Cyndi is the best thing ever to happen to Evelyn and me. We love her dearly."

"I understand. And you have my word that I will always respect her and treat her well."

He smiled. "I'm glad to hear that. She's a spirited woman. Quite a handful in the beginning, surprise around every corner, pleasant ones for the most part. And of all the rooms in the house, she fancied this one. Always in here. Always reading. I didn't mind. Nothing was ever bothered or left out of place. She's quite intelligent, you know."

Elliot looked around the office, trying to imagine a young Cyndi and what books she might have chosen. "It's one of the things I find attractive about her."

"Indeed. But I wonder if you know the extent of it."

Doctor Bannister opened the top drawer on his side of the desk and pulled something from it. Reaching across, he handed Elliot a silver frame, which held a photograph of a child sitting in the same chair he now sat in. The shot had been well taken, clearly showing the face of a little girl, her eyes cast studiously onto the pages of an American history book. "This must be Cyndi?"

"One of the few childhood shots I have of her. Having her picture taken terrified her, she screamed at the site of a camera." He shook his head. "But she outgrew it." He glanced toward the doorway. "She never knew about this one. I still put it away when I know she's coming. Silly of me, isn't it? And beside the point anyway. Look at what she's reading. That's what I wanted to show you."

Elliot glanced at the photo, but he'd already noticed. "Not exactly Doctor Seuss, is it?"

Bannister relit the pipe. "She never cared for children's books. Of course I wondered about it, but she seemed happy. I never gave it much thought until she came to the breakfast table one morning, when she was ten years old, and struck up a conversation with me concerning the life and times of Thomas Jefferson."

Still holding the smoldering match, Bannister continued, "I could've been talking with a graduate student."

Elliot studied the photo, noticing the undeniable features of the child's face. It was Cyndi all right. He handed the photo back.

Bannister stashed it away. "Evelyn thought we should have her evaluated. At ten years of age, she tested out with an IQ of 130. She's a genius, Mr. Elliot. She tries to hide that from others. I don't know why. But when she decides to know you, she'll know you to the core."

Elliot wasn't sure what to say, so he remained silent. He'd known Cyndi was special, but according to Doctor Bannister it went much further than that. It was something to think about. Would he be able to keep her entertained, not being on her level? He decided it didn't matter.

"You've done quite well for yourself, Mr. Elliot. Cyndi's a rare and beautiful person. Keep her happy, and you keep me happy."

"You have my word," Elliot said. "I work long hours as a detective. Cyndi and I have talked about it. She says she understands, and is willing to cope with it, if it's what I want. It is important to me, more than just a profession, but Cyndi comes first."

Doctor Bannister stood. "Just remember what I said."

Chapter Thirty-Nine

"I saw her, Detective. It was Elizabeth."

Elliot moved a box aside so he could sit down. Beverly Mandel, the waitress from Donegal, had called and said she needed to see him, said it was important. It'd been a little over two weeks since Elliot had found the place for her, but she'd yet to settle in to the apartment. Nothing had been put up.

Cyndi hadn't been thrilled about Elliot's attending to police work outside office hours, but she said she understood. He didn't tell her what it was about. He hadn't been himself lately, but he knew better than to make that kind of tactical error.

Beverly was referring to her childhood acquaintance, Elizabeth Stone. Elliot's inclination was to jump all over it, question the waitress in detail about the possible sighting of an elusive, perhaps even ethereal, suspect. But he held back. If it was fantasy, which it probably was, he didn't want to upset her any further. "Where exactly did this happen?"

"I thought she was dead. But I saw her."

"Have you talked to Doctor Patton about this?"

Her eyes grew angry. "I'm not making it up."

"I didn't say that. You've been under a lot of stress lately. I worry about you."

"You should be worried, but not about me."

The small apartment near 71st and Sheridan was a bit pricey for Beverly's budget, but it was a busy area with plenty of restaurants where she could work. Changing the subject seemed like a good idea. "Any job offers lately?"

She sat beside Elliot on the sofa, leaning forward, her knee touching his. "I know you think I'm crazy. Lord knows I haven't given you reason to think otherwise. But I'm not delusional, Kenny. You have to believe that."

Elliot studied her face. She seemed sincere. "All right. I'm listening."

She glanced away, looking at the floor. "When someone comes along who stands out as unnerving in an unnerving world, you pay attention. We were all afraid of her."

Having said that, Beverly got up and walked out of the room. When she returned, she handed Elliot a package, a rectangular object wrapped in brown paper. She sat beside him again. "Please don't open it. Not here."

Elliot laid the package on the sofa.

"I was there that night."

Elliot glanced up. "Where?"

"My friends dared me, said I would see Satan himself if I snuck up and peeked through the window."

She turned around and raised her blouse, exposing a portion of her back. Several long, thin scars marked the skin there. She'd been beaten, probably with a leather strap. "Reverend Coronet gave a rather poignant sermon that night, telling the congregation that the Stone family was an incarnation of evil. I wanted to see for myself." She let the fabric drop over her back again.

Evidently, the reverend had found out about her excursion. Elliot could hold back no longer. "What did you see, Beverly?"

"She was sitting at the kitchen table, humming a tune, and her parents were laid out on the floor."

"Anything else?"

She shook her head. "I was afraid. I ran into the woods."

"Where were you, exactly, when you recently saw her?"

Beverly Mandel got up from the sofa and went to the window.

Elliot followed.

She pointed through the window. "She was right there, sitting in a car."

"In the parking lot?"

Again, Elliot began to wonder about the waitress's sanity. "Do you know where she is now?"

"She's close, much closer than you think."

A chill ran up Elliot's spine. "Could you take me to her?"

The waitress didn't answer. She just stood there, shaking her head and crying. Then Elliot's phone began to ring. Out of habit, he checked the caller, and when he saw Chief Jed Washington's number displayed on the screen, he stared at it for a moment, then glanced back at Beverly.

"You should answer that," she said. She went to the sofa and got the package she'd given Elliot earlier and again handed it to him as she opened the door. "Call me when you've had a chance to look this over."

Beverly Mandel shoved Elliot out of the apartment. When she closed the door, he heard the deadbolt engage.

Chapter Forty

Later that night, Elliot twisted the key in the lock and pushed open the door of his house, fantasizing that Cyndi would follow him inside. She did, but he sensed that it was more out of concern for his welfare than anything else—seeing that he got safely to bed without hurting himself. The glass of wine at dinner had turned into a night on the town.

Elliot closed the door, relishing their being alone together a little more than he should have, and he pulled her close, uttering the words without hesitation. "Stay with me."

Cyndi allowed him a soft but subtle kiss, then gently pushed him away. She switched on the light. "I'm seeing you to bed, then I'm going home."

When they walked deeper into the house, a familiar raucous baying outside broke the silence. Elliot rolled his eyes. "Joey's dog. Scourge of the neighborhood. Everyone hates me for it. Except Joey."

Cyndi peered through the glass of the patio door, then drew the blinds.

He'd brought in the package Beverly Mandel had given him, but whatever it was could wait until tomorrow. He dropped it into the rack by the couch and went through the bedroom and on into the bath, wishing Cyndi would stay. But who was he trying to kid? She was merely echoing his own values. All the more reason to love her. He brushed his teeth then fumbled into his pajamas. Just the bottoms. He could never tolerate the tops.

When he came out of the bath, Cyndi pulled the covers back and fluffed the pillow. He came to her, but she pushed him onto the bed and gently removed his hand from her arm. "You need to sleep."

For once, Joey's dog seemed to have taken a break from his incessant barking.

Elliot crawled under the covers, trying to flood his head with good intentions, but when Cyndi's smoky gray eyes found his, desire strangled his logic. Her eyes betrayed a secret: she fought a similar battle, wanting him, perhaps as much as he wanted her. The flush in her cheeks and the quickness of her breath gave her away further.

Her throat flexed as she swallowed. "We should wait."

The warmth of her touch radiated through Elliot as she ran her hand across his chest. He summoned what willpower he had left to agree with her. "I know."

She pulled the covers over him and switched off the light. The words *good night* escaped from his lips as he heard her footsteps softly padding across the carpet as she left the room.

Moments later, though, he realized he'd been mistaken. The bed dipped softly, and as Cyndi slipped beneath the covers and pressed what seemed the entirety of her being against him, Elliot's fantasies crumbled and paled in the wake of that which was real. Upon their first meeting, she had awakened something inside of him, an animal hunger that he had managed to control. He no longer could. He pulled her close and brought his lips to hers, and while the heat of her soft breasts shot through him, he gave in and he loved her, loved her like there was no other, no beginning and no end, just the two of them, born of the same fire and now reuniting all of which had come before.

Chapter Forty-One

A shaking sensation dragged Elliot out of his sleep, and when he felt Cyndi's hand upon his shoulder he immediately realized why. Thudding echoed through the house. Someone was at the door. He glanced at the clock. Six a.m.

Cyndi rolled over to get out of bed, but Elliot stopped her. "I have a lot of friends, but I've made some enemies, too."

He jumped out of bed and struggled into the pair of denims he'd left on the floor. Sleepiness and alcohol dulled his senses, but he stumbled to the nightstand and found the .38 he kept there, checked it, then slid the weapon into his back pocket.

He made his way through the living room in darkness, but when he reached the front door he paused, then flipped on the outside light and peered through the peephole. Again it malfunctioned, coming on only for an instant, but in that microburst of time Elliot saw a man, dirt clinging to his clothes, as it would after he'd clawed his way from the grave.

The light flashed on, then off, and even though Elliot knew it was impossible, there was little doubt in his heart that he'd again looked into the pleading eyes of Justin Stone. The man he'd killed was on his doorstep.

Elliot slammed his hand against the wall to jar the faulty light switch, then threw open the door, and when he reached out he touched not a ghost but the substance of reality. When the light made another attempt, he saw that he indeed gripped the shoulder of someone in the flesh, but it was not Justin Stone.

Standing on the porch, his face twisted in pain, his mouth gaping open, from which escaped a sound like the guttural groan of a wounded soldier, was Joey Anderson.

Tears streamed from Joey's eyes, and he cradled an animal that drooped from his hands in a crude arc, its head and legs dangling lifelessly across his arms.

"He's dead, Mr. Elliot. My dog is dead."

As was usually the case, Joey was not alone for long. Like a drowning victim coming up for air, his mother came out of the darkness. "Joey . . ."

"I'm sorry," she said. "I tried to stop him."

218 BobBob Avey

Elliot's eyes were fastened on the dog, but Joey's misfortune dominated his senses. Joey had been dealt a bad enough hand in life. He didn't deserve this.

A buzzing sound filled Elliot's ears, and numbness ran through his limbs, as if he, too, had tasted fate and remained standing only because he'd joined the ranks of the living dead. "What the hell happened?"

"I don't know," Kelly said. "We found him lying near the back door."

The loss in Joey's face spoke of his failure to comprehend why such a thing should happen. Elliot extended his arms and offered to take Colorado's body, to relieve Joey of the burden of touching the carcass.

Joey backed away. "We bury him. You help me."

It was closer to a demand than a request, the alternate, more worldly version of Joey that Elliot had glimpsed earlier when he'd held the gun. He put his hand on Joey's shoulder. "All right. Just give me a minute to get dressed."

Elliot strode into the bedroom and threw on a sweater, then headed for the garage to get the digging tools. When he reached the door leading to the garage, Cyndi came out, holding a long-handled shovel. The one with the good, sharp blade. The one he would have chosen.

She held it out. "Thought you might need this." Moisture shone in her eyes. "Poor Joey."

Elliot took the shovel, feeling wetness on the handle. Cyndi had been crying. "Yeah," he said. "It's got to be tough for him." He started toward the front door. "I won't be long."

Just before Elliot left the house, he heard water running in the sink. Cyndi, washing her face. Their first night together had been stained by an act of cruelty. Young, healthy dogs like Colorado didn't just fall over dead by themselves.

With the shovel in his hand, he stepped outside and closed the door behind him. Kelly Anderson and Joey stood on the lawn next to the garden where dormant rose bushes poked through the soil. When Elliot drew near, Kelly gently urged her son toward the sidewalk, and while Elliot followed she led them along the darkened walkway. They crossed Kelly and Joey's front yard, then went through the gate of a stockade fence to the back of the house.

A floodlight cut a bright swath across the yard. Elliot shook his head then went to the southwest corner of the lot. Placing his foot on the blade, he drove the shovel into the ground.

When he'd dug deep enough, Elliot turned to Joey and nodded.

He seemed to understand. He walked over and lowered his arms, letting Colorado's body slide from his grip and fall into the grave. The carcass hit the soft earth with a dull thud.

Elliot covered the hole, then leaned the shovel against the fence and went to Joey. He hugged him, feeling the boy in a man's body quiver with tears. "I'm sorry, Joey. I'm sorry."

Then Elliot squeezed Joey's shoulder, turned away, and walked back to his house.

Chapter Forty-Two

Elliot went back inside his house and closed the door behind him. After entering the bedroom, he stripped off his clothes, soiled from burying the dog, then wearily stumbled into the shower.

When he climbed back into bed, Cyndi rolled toward him, and he wrapped his arms around her, lying in silence, listening to her rhythmic breathing. The lamp on the side table was on, but it didn't seem to matter. She fell asleep in spite of it.

Elliot held her as she slept, afraid to do the same for fear that she might disappear and not be there when he awoke. Thoughts of their wedding conjured in his head, but the happy thoughts were tainted. He saw Cyndi's dress and it was not white. He was to blame. He shouldn't have drank so much, shouldn't have asked her to sleep with him.

At some point, Elliot drifted off.

Somewhere between consciousness and sleep, the face of a young prostitute invaded his senses.

He glanced at Cyndi, then toward the clock. It was 7:30 a.m. Just a bad dream.

When he again closed his eyes, however, he saw not the lingering image of Cyndi, but the colorless dead face of Brighid McAlister. His eyes flew open, and he ran his gaze, over and over, across the features of the lovely woman sleeping next to him. How could he have missed it? Had the heavy makeup, the bushy black hair, the lifelessness of Brighid's corpse skin blinded him, clouded his senses? Whatever the reason, those barriers no longer existed. With their removal, the likeness jumped out at him. Jim Llewellyn's prostitute bore a strong resemblance to Cyndi Bannister.

The death words of Justin Stone formed in Elliot's mind. "Brighid."

Elliot rolled over and got out of bed. The covers slipped down, and Cyndi's smooth abdomen was revealed. A hint of a shadow stained her skin there, like the remnant of a temporary tattoo. Nausea crawled through him.

As he left the bedroom, he recalled what Snub the bartender had said. "I don't know who it was in the bar that night, but it wasn't Brighid McAlister."

Elliot went to the living room and sat on the couch This couldn't be happening. He wondered if he thought hard enough he could wake up from this nightmare. He closed his eyes as tightly as he could. He even pinched himself. All to no avail. He still sat in the darkness of his living room.

His arm dropped over the side of the couch, and his hand touched the magazine rack. He felt the package Beverly Mandel had given him. He brought the package to his lap, then flipped on the lamp beside the couch. The package was addressed to him. The waitress had planned on mailing it.

He tore away the paper, and his throat tightened as the removal of the wrapping revealed its contents—a large book with a black and red cover that read: DONEGAL, OKLAHOMA, CLASS OF 1988.

Like an enemy flag that refused to go down in defeat, a yellow sticky note marked one of the pages. Elliot placed his thumb along the marker and opened the book, spreading the pages.

Encircled in red, set off from the others by a smearing of lipstick, the likeness of a particular student burned recognition into his mind. The child in the yearbook was the same one featured in Doctor Bannister's prize photo, the one he kept hidden in his desk drawer, his coveted secret snapshot of his daughter when she was ten years old.

A searing pain started in his stomach and spread to his heart.

There was no mistaking it. The photos were nearly identical. But the caption beneath the yearbook likeness did not read Cyndi Bannister. Displayed there instead, as final as words on a death certificate, was the name Elizabeth Stone.

Elliot grabbed the phone and dialed information. When he had the number for Doctor George Bannister, he dialed it. When Bannister answered, Elliot asked, "Cyndi, she's your child, right?"

"What? Who is this?" He was groggy, half asleep.

"It's Elliot, Kenny . . ."

"Yeah, I remember. What did you ask me?"

Elliot took a deep breath, letting it out slowly. Please say yes, he thought, but said, "Is Cyndi your natural-born child?"

"No, she isn't. I thought you already knew."

"She's adopted?"

"That's right. Cyndi always wished we were her real parents. She didn't want us to talk about it. I guess that's why we didn't bring it up."

"When?" Elliot asked.

"The adoption? Cyndi came to us late 1988, around November, I believe."

Elliot let the phone slide from his hand. Cyndi's adoption coincided with Howard and Maud Wistrom's finding their Douglass in the park. It also happened right around the time that the Stone family dropped off the radar screen.

Elliot thought of Joey's dog, Colorado, his sudden silence last night, and knew what had happened. Whether it was intuition or a form of hoodoo didn't really matter. He got to his feet, dropping the yearbook to the floor, then headed for the garage.

Once there, he went to the row of shelves along the west wall and found the jug of antifreeze he'd left there. The bottle was sticky, the surface of the shelf beneath it, stained.

She'd poisoned the dog.

Elliot staggered back inside, wishing he could rip the fabric of reality from its lofty perch and stuff it so deep no one would find it. He started toward the bedroom, desperation choking his sanity, and a dark understanding ran through him, a carnal notion that had begun to form even before he'd fully grasped what was happening: He could let it go, leave the blame where it lay, buried in the ground with Cyndi's unfortunate brother.

As the black thoughts wove through Elliot's senses, Cyndi called out to him, and he thought he heard her say, "Are you coming back to bed, Kenny?"

Whether the words were real or imagined, they came forth as dark, shapeless, writhing spirits, skulking in dark corners and casting up knowing gazes, black eyes in dead, white sockets that possessed an all-too-personal knowledge of that which he kept hidden, secrets he could scarcely bear to realize.

If he loved her, would he turn his back on all he was, all he believed in?

He stumbled into the bedroom and found it void of any presence other than his own. He flipped on the light. The bed was empty. He ran his hand across the sheets, seeking her warmth that lingered there, though at the same time fearing that she might lurk behind him.

Elliot went through the house, turning on lights and calling her name, but she was gone. She'd slipped out, he suspected, while he was in the garage checking the antifreeze.

The answering machine was blinking. He stabbed the button to check it.

This is Jed Washington. We got a positive ID on the corpses in Saucier's barn. It was Kathryn and Solomon Stone all right. Oh, and you can scratch the other grave, bones turned out to be canine.

Another bad thought occurred to Elliot. He hadn't seen the yearbook when he'd searched the house. He ran back to where he'd left it, but it, too, was gone. Then it dawned on him. The return address of the package. Beverly Mandel. Cyndi had seen the name and the address. Elliot put his hand to his forehead. They'd taken Cyndi's car last night. She'd left it parked on the driveway.

Elliot ran to the garage and hit the opener. When the overhead door rose, he saw the driveway was empty. Cyndi's car was gone.

He scrambled back into the house, then threw on some clothes. He yanked open the nightstand. The .38 was missing.

He went to the closet. The Glock was still there. He slid into his shoulder holster, put on a jacket, and raced from the house.

When Elliot pulled into the parking lot of Beverly Mandel's apartment complex, he saw that the door to her apartment was open. He phoned the department, explaining what was happening, then jumped out of the truck and ran up the stairs.

Elliot saw Cyndi, using the waitress as a shield. She'd backed herself and her hostage into the bathroom. She held the .38 she'd taken against the base of Beverly Mandel's skull. The look in her eyes said she meant to use it. There was something different about her as well. Dangling from her neck was an amulet, a five-pointed star with a single point facing the earth.

Elliot slowly stepped into the small, tiled room. He heard a simultaneous annunciation, "Kenny," coming from both Cyndi and the waitress.

"Hello, Cyndi. Wondered where you went." He almost choked on his words. He shrugged, acting as if a complete loss of understanding surrounded him. "What are you doing?"

Beverly Mandel's eyes were like saucers.

Cyndi kept the .38 in place. "Just protecting myself, don't you see? No one else knows." She used the gun for emphasis. "Just our little problem here."

A cry escaped from Beverly Mandel's lips.

"But I can take care of that. Now step back out of here. I don't want to hurt you."

Elliot forced a smile. "I believe that. I don't want to see you get hurt either." Again, as he looked into the face of Cyndi Bannister, he was reminded of Brighid. Maybe it was the anger in her face, or the lack of makeup, but the similarity was undeniable. "Why did you kill Jim Llewellyn?"

Cyndi remained silent for a moment, but then said, "Got it all figured out, haven't you? I let you get too close, let my guard down." She paused, then continued. "Llewellyn poked his nose in it a few years back, but I managed to scare him off with some nasty e-mails. But he decided to come back, stir things up again. I couldn't risk it."

"Where's it going to stop? Jim Llewellyn, Gary Sullivan, Brighid, who's next? Beverly, then me? Would you, Cyndi? Would you kill me?"

Beverly Mandel tried to scream, but Cyndi slapped her hand over the waitress's mouth. "I thought you were different, Kenny, thought you understood. But you're just like the rest. You don't understand me at all."

"I think I'm beginning to. Reverend Coronet controlled his flock through fear of sin and Satan. All you had to do was play along, plant a few rumors in the right ears. You had the people of Donegal so busy looking over their shoulders for the devil that they never saw you coming. You used me, got close and blinded me with your charms. Let it be over now, Cyndi. Put the gun down. Let me help you."

She tightened her grip on the waitress. "You're pretty smart, but you're wrong about one thing. It might have started out that way, but I meant what I said." Again she paused, and when she spoke her voice was low, almost a whisper. "I do love you, Kenny. But it's too late. There's nothing you can do."

"Sure there is. If you'll put the gun down, we can walk out of here, together."

She shook her head. "Then what?"

"I don't know. But I'll bet it beats the alternative."

"In your mind maybe, but not in mine."

Tears threatened to pour from Elliot's eyes, but he stopped them. "We can still have a relationship, by mail, and by phone. Even visitation. And someday, if things work out, we could be together."

She glanced around, considering the offer, then shook her head. "They'll never let me out."

Then, even though Elliot knew it was the wrong time, when he was trying to talk her down, the question came out. "Why did you do it, Cyndi? Why did you kill your parents?"

Her eyes grew wild, her face contorted. "You don't know what it was like, living in fear, like prisoners of war, only the enemy was Mommy and Daddy." She started to cry. "It wasn't always bad, until we joined the church, and everything went to hell." She closed her hand around the amulet that hung from her neck. Then Cyndi loosened her grip on the hostage, though she did not let her go but kept the waitress in front of her as she removed the .38 from Beverly Mandel's neck, and pressed the barrel against the hostage's temple.

"Don't kill me," Beverly said. "Don't let her kill me, Kenny."

Dizziness swept through Elliot, threatened to take his balance. "No."

"It's the only way."

"No, Cyndi. For God's sake. For my sake, please don't do this."

For a moment, that little part of the world inside the apartment stood still as silence, laced with death, permeated the air. Then, to his own surprise, Elliot charged forward, his body pinning both the waitress and Cyndi against the wall.

Cyndi screamed, a guttural howl that ran fear through Elliot. Her strength surprised him. She bucked and pushed like a two-hundred-pound defensive lineman, but still he held her, searching all the time for the .38 she held. When his hand found the weapon, he yanked it from her.

Elliot pulled Beverly Mandel behind him, then placed the barrel of the .38 in the center of Cyndi Bannister's forehead. "It's over," he said. "It's over."

Elliot's feet were like bricks as he turned and walked Cyndi, or Elizabeth, whoever she was out of the bathroom. The action sent an ache through his heart, and his knees grew weak, but someone stepped forward and steadied him.

It was Michael Cunningham. He looked at Elliot for a few seconds, emotion flickering in his eyes. Then he nodded. "Nice work, Detective."

Elliot staggered into the living room and dropped into a chair. Several uniformed officers had come into the room, including Mendez, who, for all his mouthing off, worked alongside the other cops like they were family.

At some point, the officers brought Cyndi out. Elliot half expected her to scream, to curse his name and denounce any feelings she might have had for him, but she did none of those things.

She remained docile and quiet, and as the officers led her away, her soft gaze held his. "I love you."

Elliot could no longer hold back, and tears began to leak from his eyes. And even though he knew that it would not be a good idea, that he should let it go, he pulled himself from the chair and went to the door, and watched as they loaded Cyndi into the patrol car. He could not deny his feelings for her, but a sickness ran through his gut for having been drawn into her deception. And his heart ached as he watched her go, though he could not now bring himself to call it love.

Chapter Forty-Three

Elliot pressed his face against the glass of the patio door and watched a neighbor's cat crawl across the top of the stockade fence. Exactly one month ago today, fate had taken Cyndi from him.

The devastation crumbled the world of George and Evelyn Bannister, causing them to sell their home and become missionaries, living somewhere in Jamaica, last Elliot had heard.

Abraham Saucier's life proved to be heavily involved with McKenna's brand of paganism. He'd enticed young Elizabeth Stone with mysticism and dark spiritualism's condolence of just about anything, their motto of "Do what you will." She'd most likely come in to the world without a conscience, but her brush with the dark side no doubt acted as a catalyst. Reverend Coronet simply recognized Elizabeth's potential and encouraged old Abe to council her.

Elliot wiped the glass where his breath had condensed. The way he saw it, there wasn't much difference between Reverend Coronet and Brian McKenna. They just brainwashed their victims with a different brand of propaganda.

He slid the door open and stepped out onto the patio. Though the frigid air stung his face, he sat in a patio chair and watched one of the remaining leaves let go, relinquishing its hold on the barren oak, and he was reminded not of death but of rebirth, for the leaf would melt into the soil and return in one form or another. But Elliot suspected it wasn't the molecular basics of life that concerns most people, but rather their worry for their own sentience and self-awareness, whether or not these things would continue after death.

Elliot closed his eyes and uttered a prayer, for without faith what was he, but an animal seeking the pleasures of yet another day's existence.

She haunted him still, and he found himself fearful, awakening during the night, teetering on the brink of desperation, and always with a whisper of a kiss moving across his lips, and a feeling of a presence in the darkness.